RICK MOFINA

THEY DISAPPEARED

D0003648

HARLEQUIN®
entertain, enrich, inspire™

Recycling programs
for this product may
not exist in your area.

ISBN-13: 978-0-7783-1381-6

THEY DISAPPEARED

For questions and comments about the quality of this book please contact us at CustomerService@Harlequin.com.

www.Harlequin.com

Printed in U.S.A.

This book is for
Margaret Slavin Dyment

1

New York City

This trip is going to change us forever, Jeff Griffin thought as the jet descended into LaGuardia.

He looked at his son, Cole, age nine, excited to be on his first plane and marveling at Manhattan's skyline poking through the clouds. Then Jeff glanced at his wife, Sarah, at her hand, her wedding ring.

Until a year and a half ago, they had been living a perfect life in Montana, where Jeff was a mechanic and a volunteer firefighter and Sarah was a schoolteacher. They'd come to New York for Cole because he'd always dreamed of seeing Manhattan. It seemed like the best thing to do, given all that they'd been through.

"It's always going to be hard for us, Jeff," Sarah had told him. "But we just can't give up."

While Sarah lived in hope, Jeff couldn't help but think that this vacation to New York was a requiem for the life they once lived.

The landing gear locked into position with a hydraulic thud.

Jeff exhaled slowly and turned to Cole.

"Wow, Dad, this is so great! I can't believe we're really doing this!"

Jeff looked at Sarah. She gave him the promise of a smile and he held on to it, thinking that maybe, just maybe, he should reconsider.

After their plane landed, the Griffins moved through the arrival gate and joined the rush of passengers heading to the baggage claim area.

The air smelled like industrial carpet cleaner and pretzels.

Cole was energized by the bustling terminal as they made their way to the crowds at the carousels. Sarah went to the restroom while Jeff and Cole got their bags.

Jeff shouldered his way to the conveyor, plucked Sarah's red bag from it, then his own. Cole had followed him and hefted his backpack from the carousel. Sarah had bought a new one for him, for the trip.

"Looks like the one." Jeff gave it a quick inspection, black with white trim and mesh side pockets. He glanced quickly at the blue name tag without really reading it; blue was the right color for the tag. Then he helped Cole get his arms through the straps.

As they waited for Sarah, Cole tried counting all the carousels in their area but there were too many. He loved the blurring pace as people jostled to heave their luggage onto trolleys before wheeling them out through the main doors.

"I wish Mom would hurry up, Dad. Can we see the Empire State Building from here?"

"Maybe on the cab ride to the hotel—there's Mom."

"All set." Sarah smiled, joining them.

They left the terminal through the automatic doors.

Jeff spotted a row of news boxes. They reminded him that the travel agent had mentioned that a major event would be taking place when they were to arrive. The headlines shouted about it. UN: Whole World in the City Again! said the *Daily News.* Tighter Security for World Leaders Means Gridlock for All! blared the *New York Post.*

As they queued up for a taxi in the ground transportation pickup zone, they didn't notice that among the throng of arriving passengers, one man had taken an interest in Cole.

He was in his late twenties, a slender build with wild blond hair. His face was void of emotion. He looked European, a youngish student bohemian traveler. As he walked by them, slowly and unseen, his attention locked onto Cole's bag.

The man hesitated.

The Griffins got into their cab. He stopped and watched, his face suddenly darkening with concern as they drove off.

His backpack was black with white trim and mesh side pockets.

It was identical to Cole's backpack.

2

New York City

Their taxi merged onto the Grand Central Parkway and the driver lifted his head to his rearview mirror, which had a rosary hanging from it.

"Welcome to the capital of the world. Where are you coming in from?"

"Montana," Jeff said.

"Cowboys and land spreading out to the mountains," the driver said.

"That's right."

"Is this your first time to the Big Apple?"

"No, I've been here for a few conventions over the years, and—" Jeff glanced at Sarah. "We were here together, a long, long time ago."

"Well, you picked a good time to return."

"Why's that?" Jeff asked.

"We got the president and about one hundred world leaders coming into town over the next few days for the UN meeting. Lots of security, sirens and helicopters. Messes up traffic."

"Yeah, we saw that in the newspapers."

"The president and helicopters, wow," Cole said.

"It's a huge show and a glorious pain."

The road clicked under the taxi's wheels as they moved onto the Brooklyn-Queens Expressway. Sarah looked out her window at the endless flow of apartment buildings, warehouses, factories and billboards. One showed a laughing baby's face next to a smiling young woman in a graduation cap and she thought of their daughter, Lee Ann.

They were moving west toward the Midtown Tunnel when they came to a gently sloping segment. The tip of the Empire State Building emerged in the haze ahead as Manhattan's skyline rose before them.

"Look at that! I gotta take a picture!" Cole said. "Oh, no, Mom, I put my camera in my backpack and it's in the trunk. That was dumb, oh, no!"

"Here, use mine."

Sarah fished her small digital camera from her bag. Cole, a technical master, clenched an eye, took a photo and showed his parents.

"Oh, this is awesome!" Cole said.

Moments later the taxi slowed. An overhead freeway sign guided three lanes to the great stone mouth of the Midtown Tunnel. Lines of traffic moved through the tollgates. The tunnel gleamed in brilliant orange and yellow as it curved under the East River to Manhattan.

Cole took more pictures until they surfaced somewhere near Fortieth Street and Third Avenue. As they looked at the skyscraper-lined canyons and the shining high-rise condos, Jeff's cell phone rang. The call was a 646 area code with a number he didn't recognize.

"Hello?"

He heard nothing and after several seconds of static he hung up.

"Who was that?" Sarah asked.

"Wrong number, I guess." Jeff shrugged.

The sidewalks were a bazaar of action with streams of people hurrying, waving at taxis amid sirens, horns. Steam plumes curled from the hot dog stands. People panhandled and street merchants argued with delivery truck drivers while motorists screamed at jaywalkers who blocked streets.

They were a world away from Laurel, Montana.

Their hotel, the Central Suites Inn, was on West Twenty-ninth Street in the two-hundred block, not far from Madison Square Garden. They checked into their twelfth-floor room. It was large with two double beds.

"I need to freshen up," Sarah said.

"All right, Cole and I will unpack and get changed," Jeff said. "Then we can go out for dinner and maybe walk to the Empire State Building."

Cole claimed the bed nearest to the window. He unzipped his backpack at the foot of it and dumped its contents. T-shirts, shorts, a chocolate bar, a bag of potato chips, maps of New York, a hoodie and socks fell out. All of it was unfamiliar, especially the man's shaving kit.

"Uh, Mom, Dad?" Cole said.

Sarah set her things down and surveyed the heap. "Oh, for goodness' sake, he's got the wrong bag." She inspected the backpack. The luggage claim bar code was torn. The blue name tag was faded and smudged. "I thought you guys checked this?"

"It looks exactly like Cole's bag." Jeff looked it over.

"A little, but the zippers are different."

"What are we going to do, Mom?" Cole said. "I need my stuff."

"We'll call the airline, don't worry, honey." Sarah pulled a printed page from her bag and went to the room's desk. "See, I put this paper inside all our bags. It has our hotel and cell phone numbers, so whoever has your bag can call us."

While Sarah and Jeff searched their airline tickets for a lost luggage number, Cole turned to the strange belongings. One item drew his interest.

A tiny plastic toy jet.

He pushed a small button on top of it, lights flashed and it made a jet engine sound. Cole loved it. He moved behind the curtains, pressed the toy against the window, taking it on a flight over Manhattan's tall buildings.

"I can't find a claim number on my part of the ticket," Sarah said just as Jeff's cell phone rang.

"Hey." Jeff looked at the display before he answered. "It's the same number that tried to call me when we were in the taxi."

"Mr. Griffin? Jeff Griffin of Laurel, Montana?"

"Yes."

"This is Hans Beck, I tried calling you earlier. I got your number from your backpack. I have it, there was a mix-up at the airport and I was hoping you'd have mine? It looks just like yours—it has some clothes, snacks, maps and my razor inside."

"Yes, we have it."

"Good, can we trade them as soon as possible? I am running late for a train. According to your information, you're at the Central Suites that's near Penn Station?"

"Yes, we can exchange the bags now if you like." Jeff nodded to Sarah, who smiled with relief and indicated that she would take a quick shower. After a few more minutes Jeff had worked out the bag trade with the caller.

"Cole! Let's go get your backpack, son!"

Startled by his dad, Cole, who'd been running the

plane up and down the curtain, let the toy slip to the lower end as he pushed the curtain aside.

"Really?" Cole stepped from the window. "Now?"

"Yes, really, yes, now. So put all that stuff back in the bag. Everything and let's go." Jeff had unfolded a map on his bed and studied it. "The guy who's got your backpack is going to meet us now, so move it!"

Overjoyed at getting his possessions back, Cole forgot about the plane and gathered all the items as fast as he could, shoving them hastily into the backpack while his dad glanced at the map.

This Hans Beck had a German-sounding accent. Maybe he was a student, Jeff thought as he and Cole walked toward Madison Square Garden with his backpack.

They were to meet in front of a diner on Thirty-third Street across from Penn Station. Beck said he was twenty-nine, five foot eleven with blond hair. Jeff gave a description of himself and Cole, noting they would also recognize each other by the backpacks.

About twenty minutes after Beck had called, they spotted him on the street at the appointed location. Beck's hair was unkempt, his clothes disheveled. He was dragging anxiously on a cigarette, his face taut.

This guy's either on drugs or under some sort of pressure, Jeff thought.

"Are you Hans Beck?"

Beck blew a stream of smoke skyward and nodded.

"Jeff and Cole Griffin."

They traded handshakes, then backpacks.

Immediately Beck began rummaging through his.

"Everything's in here, right?" Beck said, snapping his head around at the sound of car horns from the traffic.

"Sure. We didn't take anything, if that's what you mean," Jeff said.

"No, no, man." Beck focused on Cole, then winked. "Because you're too young to use my electric razor, right?"

"That's funny," Cole said. "The airplane you have in there is cool."

"What airplane? You looked inside?"

"Sorry." Cole glanced at his dad, then at Beck. "It was when I thought it was my backpack. I saw the little toy plane."

"Everything's in there," Jeff said.

"What? Okay. I'm really late." Beck looked around to the street, closed the bag, then hoisted it onto his back. "Yes, I packed it so fast, I'm not sure what I put in there. Well, I have to split. Thanks."

Beck disappeared into the crowds entering Penn Station. Jeff's attention followed him with a ping of unease before he turned to Cole.

"Let's get back to the hotel, son."

3

New York City

Hans Beck gripped his backpack and pinballed through Penn Station.

For a fleeting moment he considered boarding a train, any train, and getting away.

No use. They're watching, waiting. And I need the money.

Beck had lied to Jeff Griffin about having to catch a train. Instead, he had to meet his contact and complete this delivery.

He'd nearly blown this job.

How could he have been so stupid to have picked up the wrong bag? In his time as a courier he'd never screwed up like this. His customers were enraged. He'd never had contacts so intense. He didn't know who they were, or what they were involved in.

He didn't want to know.

When he'd given them the Griffin backpack in error, they took no comfort in his assurance he would retrieve the misplaced bag.

Well, he did it, just as he said he would.

So everyone should relax, he told himself. *We've got*

the right bag now. Soon this would be over and he'd be on a plane to Aruba awaiting a large deposit in a numbered account.

Beck left Penn Station and hurried by the post office and deep into the heart of the Hudson Yards. He moved quickly beyond the Long Island Rail Road maintenance tracks, where Thirty-third Street dipped into a wasteland near the Hudson River.

He was nearly jogging now as he hurried along a chain-link fence that surrounded a site where a massive foundation, reaching down several stories, was under construction. The sun had set, the entire area was deserted. He heard the hum of a motor, then brakes, and a panel van stopped suddenly beside him.

A side door slid open and he got in. It was crowded inside because several men were in the back working. A couple of them were talking on cell phones. Two others were working quickly on laptops.

The men had already acted on the information sheet they'd found in Cole Griffin's bag and had quickly searched the family. They'd also taken pictures of Jeff and Cole on the street, making the exchange with Beck.

Everything had unfolded with urgency.

The men seized his backpack, dumped its contents, probed them, then tore through the empty backpack.

Whatever they needed was still missing.

For the first and last time in his life, Beck had failed to make a delivery.

His final thought was that a plastic bag had swallowed his head and his struggle against the forces holding him was in vain.

Everything went black.

His corpse was wrapped in a plastic sheet and hefted

into the construction site. It was concealed under a layer of gravel at the base of a footing that would be filled with fifty cubic yards of concrete the next day.

4

New York City

The next morning the Griffins went down to the lobby for breakfast.

The dining area was crammed but Sarah spotted a table for them. Jeff and Cole moved with the crowd along the breakfast bar, loading their trays with sausages, eggs, cereal, fruit, toast, juice and coffee.

Jeff saw Sarah at the table with her phone, reading, then responding to a text message.

Who is she talking to?

It consumed him as they ate and discussed options for the day but he'd have to deal with it later. Cole was wearing a New York Jets T-shirt and ball cap they had bought the night before, along with his new souvenir New York key ring bearing his name. He'd clipped it on the belt loop of his jeans. After flipping through his guidebook, Cole decided he wanted to take a tour bus down to Ground Zero, then a ferry to the Statue of Liberty.

"But can we go to Times Square first?" he asked. "There's a giant screen there that takes your picture and a toy store with a Ferris wheel inside. Can we go there?"

Jeff consulted his map of New York.

"Are you up for the walk?"

"You bet! And every time I see the Empire State Building I'm taking more pictures. Can I go back for another juice, Mom?"

"Sure."

When they were alone, Jeff nodded to Sarah's phone.

"So who were you talking to?"

"Valerie, back home. She was asking if we got in okay."

"Valerie. Anybody else?"

"Jeff, please don't do this."

"Who, Sarah?"

Her face reddened; she was on the verge of losing it with him. Instead, she seized her phone, cued the message, then thrust it at him.

"Valerie. See? Valerie."

"Sorry."

Sarah put a hand to her mouth, blinking back tears. She looked toward the food bar to see Cole waiting his turn to fill his glass at the juice dispenser. She looked at Jeff.

"On our way in from the airport I saw this billboard and—" She halted, shifted her thought. "I don't want a divorce and I don't think this is the time or place to tell Cole that you want one. We can't break his heart, Jeff. We have to hang on and work this out."

He noticed she was twisting her wedding ring.

"I never blamed you for what happened," she said. "I was out of my mind, we both were. I was angry but I never blamed you for what happened. Get this through your head. I love you. We have to fight to hold this family together, not tear what's left of it apart, please."

Upon seeing Cole returning, she dropped her voice to a whisper. "Why in God's name can't you see that?"

Jeff looked at her without speaking, his mind racing with a million thoughts before Cole returned, sensing unease.

"Are you okay, Mom?"

She touched a tissue to her eyes.

"Just a sad memory, sweetie."

"All right." Jeff cleared his throat and stood with his tray to clear the table. "Let's get going."

They walked east to Seventh Avenue, then Broadway bound for Times Square. The city pulsated under a clear sky with the thud of a passing helicopter, the ever-present wail of sirens and traffic, telling him that he had to come to a decision. It weighed on him as they moved north along Broadway. Here, amid the whirlwind, he considered Sarah's words.

We have to fight to hold this family together. We have to hang on and work this out. Was she right?

"Dad? Are you going to get in the picture with Mom now?"

Cole's question pulled Jeff from his thoughts and he took an immediate assessment, estimating that they were somewhere around Forty-fourth and Forty-fifth Streets near Seventh Avenue. The streets were crowded, traffic was heavy. Not far from where they stood, massive neon signs soared in spectacular glory, exuding an air of controlled chaos. News reports flowed nonstop in electronic ribbons of light that wrapped around several buildings.

They were at the edge of Times Square.

Sarah had just taken Cole's picture and returned her camera to him.

"Over there, Dad," Cole said from behind the view-

finder. "Get next to Mom. I want to get that big flashy
sign behind you—then we'll go down to the center of
Times Square, hurry!"

Jeff put his arm around Sarah, then felt her arm sol-
idly around his waist. It felt good, it felt right, and a
bittersweet sensation rolled over him. He couldn't remember the last time they'd touched each other, held
each other. This was not easy. They both made an effort to disguise the emotional turmoil churning under
the smiles they'd manufactured for Cole.

Finally, he took the shot.

"All right," he said. "Can we get one of us all together?"

"Let me ask somebody," Jeff said.

He took the camera from Cole and went a few yards
down the crowded sidewalk to an older man wearing a
Yankees ball cap taking photos of two women, likely
his wife and daughter. Jeff asked him if he would mind
taking a Griffin family photo with Sarah's camera.

"Be happy to."

The man took the picture but when Cole requested he
take one more, nothing happened with the camera. The
man looked at it. "Looks like your batteries are gone."
The man handed it back. Jeff thanked him and turned
to Cole and Sarah.

"I forgot to put in fresh ones," Sarah said.

"It's okay." Jeff glanced around, spotting a suitable
store behind them. "I'll go in there and get fresh batteries. You stay right here, don't go anywhere."

"All right," Sarah said. She and Cole began inspecting the jewelry, statues, artwork and T-shirts on a vendor's cart. Jeff stepped toward the store but was stopped.

"Sir, could you spare any change for a veteran?"

A man with bushy dark hair and a beard flecked

with bits of something white held up a hand in a dirty worn cyclist's glove. He was in a wheelchair and missing his right leg. He wore torn jeans, a filthy John Lennon T-shirt and a tattered raincoat. His chair was reinforced with metal coat hangers and had a U.S. flag affixed to it. Jeff looked into his leathery weatherworn face, his brown eyes, and figured him to be in his early thirties. Guys who'd served deserved better, Jeff thought.

"How'd you lose the leg?"

"IED in Afghanistan. I ain't had a decent meal in days, sir."

Jeff thrust his hand into his pocket and pulled out two crumpled fives.

"Here."

The man stared at the cash.

"Thank you. God bless you and your beautiful family, there, sir."

Jeff went to the store—Metro Manhattan Gifts and Things.

It had a narrow storefront of soot-streaked stone and a large window cluttered with a galaxy of tacky items. Discounts on jewelry, T-shirts and posters were listed on the chalkboard sign outside.

Inside, rock music throbbed from a radio station. The walls were jammed with T-shirts, ball caps, trinkets, posters, knickknacks. A young man was on a ladder, pulling down a cardboard box overflowing with scarves for two women. Racks filled with chips, chocolate bars and snack cakes bordered one side of the store, next to coolers filled with soda, juices and water.

Compact video recorders, cell phones and other electronics covered the wall behind the counter near the cash. A mounted security camera watched from above. Jeff took his place in line behind half a dozen customers.

As he waited, he saw Sarah and Cole through the window, browsing at the cart. They looked happy and the image sent his mind racing back to that last moment of perfection. Back to that time when he'd sat in his truck in their driveway and watched Sarah with Cole and their baby daughter, Lee Ann, through the window.

The last time they were happy.

And now he'd brought his family here, to the brink of disintegration.

Kransky the Shrink had been right; they couldn't just overcome the blow of Lee Ann's death. They had to adapt to it and allow each other to deal with it in their own way.

Throughout their ordeal Cole had been the rock of the family. He'd accepted that God had made his baby sister an angel and took her to heaven first to wait for them. Cole just got on with being a kid and continued obsessing about seeing New York City, the way most kids obsessed about seeing Disney World.

In this way Cole was the calm, healing force, holding them all together against the threat of destruction.

And the threat was not Sarah.

It's me.

After all this time, Jeff realized that he'd failed to accept how Sarah dealt with her own grief and guilt. She blamed herself for being three hundred and forty miles away when their baby died. Jeff blamed himself for being in the next room asleep. He had been so numbed and blinded by his anger, his guilt, that he let it give way to paranoia, thinking wrongly that Sarah had turned to another man for comfort.

He'd let it all reach the point where it was tearing them apart.

What have I done?

Standing in line, waiting to buy batteries, it dawned on him. Maybe it had started when he felt Sarah's arm around him, tight. But when the truth hit, it hit him like a freight train. Sarah was not cheating on him. She did not hate him. What he was doing was wrong. The last thing he wanted was to separate. He agreed with Sarah, when their baby girl died they went out of their minds with grief. They'd both been consumed with guilt and anger over losing her.

He replayed Sarah's plea.

We have to fight to hold this family together. We have to hang on and work this out.

She was right.

They'd been through enough.

Suddenly Jeff felt like a man waking up.

How could I have been so stupid?

It was his turn at the counter and the clerk at the register, a girl in her twenties with a diamond stud in her left nostril, fuchsia streaks in her dyed white hair and tattoos on her arms, smiled as she chewed gum and bobbed her head to an old David Bowie song.

"I need some batteries."

"What size?"

"Double A, I think. Wait, let me check, sorry."

Horn blasts from the street competed with the music inside as Jeff opened the battery compartment. It took him three attempts. The clerk snapped her gum and eyed the other customers while she waited.

Patience in New York came at a premium.

"Yes, double A," he said. "Better give me three of those four packs."

She slapped them on the counter.

"Here you go."

Jeff paid.

He returned to the street ready to tell Sarah that he'd come to his senses. This trip would change everything.

For the better.

He went to the vendor's cart but they weren't there.

He looked up and down the street.

No sign of Sarah and Cole.

What's going on?

They must've gone into a store, he thought, and entered the nearest one, a crowded retail sportswear outlet. Inside he searched the packed aisles, scanning the shoppers for Sarah and Cole. He glimpsed a flash of green—the back of a boy's New York Jets T-shirt as it disappeared behind a display of jackets.

There's Cole.

Jeff hurried after him, ready to scold Sarah for vanishing, but he stopped cold. The boy was not Cole.

Jeff took immediate stock of the surroundings.

No sign of Sarah and Cole.

He hurried out and rushed into the next business, a crowded deli where he again took swift inventory. Again, he found no trace of his wife and son. He moved on, searching in vain. He stood on the sidewalk and scoured the storefronts across the street—but it was futile.

Jeff could not find Sarah and Cole.

Then, above all the crowds, the traffic, the noise and confusion, he heard the first high-pitched ring in the back of his mind. It shot to his gut where disbelief battled his fear that maybe something was wrong.

5

New York City

Jeff scanned the crowds, threading his way a few yards in one direction, then a few yards in another.

"Sarah!"

He looked up and down the street.

They disappeared.

He reached for his cell phone and called Sarah's number. *This is nuts. Where'd they go?* It rang several times before going to her voice mail.

"Hey, you disappeared on me," Jeff said. "Where are you? I'm standing by the souvenir cart."

He studied the nearest storefronts again: a sports store, an electronics store, a ticket seller, a place fronted with plywood that was under renovation. Had they gone into one? Which one would they enter? He wasn't sure. He'd told them not to move.

Did Sarah even hear her phone ring?

He called her number again. Again, he got her voice mail.

He scrutinized the street. Faces blurred as streams of people dissolved into chaotic rivers amid the smells of perfume, sweat and grilled spicy meat. Human features became indistinguishable as people brushed against him, bumped him.

"Are you looking for your wife and son?"

Jeff turned around to the man in the wheelchair—the man to whom he'd given ten bucks.

"Yes, did you see them?"

"I think they got picked up."

"Picked up? What do you mean?"

"Well, I saw it from the corner of my eye. I wasn't focused on it, but it looked like two guys picked them up."

"What two guys?"

"Two guys sorta helped them into a van or an SUV and they drove off."

"What're you talking about?"

"It happened real fast, like everyone was in a hurry."

"Where?"

"Right there." He nodded to the spot where Jeff had left them.

Nothing was making sense. Jeff shook his head.

"I doubt that. My wife wouldn't go with anyone. She doesn't know anyone in New York."

"It looked like they were pulling your boy and your wife was trying to stop them and then they took her, too. It was real fast and smooth."

"What? That's crazy."

"I'm telling you what I saw."

"Hold on."

Jeff went to the ponytailed man selling souvenirs from the cart where Sarah and Cole had browsed moments ago. The man was wearing a tie-dye T-shirt and dark glasses.

"Who?" the man said after Jeff had explained.

"My wife and son. They were just here looking at

your cart a few minutes ago. Did you see them go into a store?"

The ponytailed man scratched his three-day growth, then shrugged.

"Sorry, pal. It's hectic here with people and traffic. People get picked up and dropped off around here every two seconds. I didn't see anything."

Jeff turned back to the wheelchair man.

"I think you saw someone else," Jeff said. "I think they're in a store."

"No, it happened."

"Did they say anything—where they were going, or who they were?"

"Sir, I don't know."

"What about the vehicle? What color was it?"

"Silver, white, I'm not sure…white, yeah, maybe white."

Jeff ran his hand through his hair, unable to dismiss his unease over what this wheelchair guy claimed to have seen.

It just doesn't make any sense.

"I think you're mistaken and that you saw some- one else."

"I know I saw it out of the corner of my eye, but listen to me—it happened. It didn't look right. I'm just tell- ing you what I saw because you seem like a nice fam- ily. If you don't want to believe me, that's your choice."

The man clamped his hands on his wheels and rolled away.

No, Jeff thought. *I don't want to believe you because this can't be real.*

Jeff took a quick breath, reached for his phone and tried Sarah again. But before he pressed her number, he saw something small and shiny in the street, near the curb.

A key ring.

Its clasp was open.

He picked it up. It was looped to a miniature novelty blue-and-white New York license plate with a name on it.

COLE.

Cole's key ring.

It was in the gutter, where it would've fallen if he'd gotten into a vehicle.

Oh, Christ, it's true! Oh, Jesus, no!

My wife! My son! Abducted from the street!

Why? Who would do this? Why?

Jeff trembled at the absurdity, the horror, as he looked in every direction searching for something, anything, to subdue the wave of alarm rising around him. This was the edge of Times Square—*the crossroads of the world...*. The concentration of people, the comings and goings, the enormity of it all, was dizzying.

He pulled his fingers into a fist around Cole's key ring.

6

New York City police officers Jimmy Hodge and Roy Duggan were walking the beat: extended Times Square.

Earlier that morning, at the top of their tour, they'd helped two other cops corner a perp after he'd tried to boost a Mercedes on Seventh Avenue. Duggan happily let those two do the paperwork because he and Jimmy had good numbers this month—no danger of a white shirt breathing down their necks for stats.

Now they were back on patrol and a coffee break was overdue.

Duggan, a third-generation uniform with twenty-three years on the street, was telling young Jimmy, his rookie partner of four months, about a deli on Forty-seventh when a white guy in his thirties rushed up to them.

"I need help!"

Instinctively Hodge and Duggan braced while giving him the instant head-to-toe. Worried demeanor, sweaty. Six foot, medium build, muscular, clean-cut, brown hair, jeans, golf shirt with Laurel Montana Volunteer Fire Department insignia. Nothing in his hands but a cell phone.

"What's the problem?" Hodge asked.

"My wife and son have been abducted."

Hodge traded a quick glance with Duggan.

"Your wife and your son?" Hodge reached for his notebook.

"It happened a few minutes ago!"

"Take it easy, let's start with some ID and names," Hodge said.

The man identified himself as Jeff Griffin and Hodge started notes for a report.

"Okay, Jeff, tell us what happened and where," Hodge asked.

The man walked them to the location, recounting the few details he had. Hodge took notes, asked short questions. Duggan said nothing. As their radios crackled with cross talk Duggan studied Jeff, listening, absorbing and watching through jaded brown eyes that seldom missed a thing. Nearly finished, Jeff turned to the wheelchair man, panhandling some fifteen yards up the street.

"…and that guy there in the wheelchair said he saw two men 'help' them into a van or an SUV before it drove away."

"You got this from Freddie?" Duggan said.

"Is that his name, the soldier who lost his leg in Afghanistan? He said 'it didn't look right' when he saw them being taken away."

"Freddie sees a lot of things," Duggan said.

Jeff nodded, clearly reassured he had a witness that police knew. But then Duggan elaborated.

"Sometimes Freddie sees things that aren't there, depending on whether he's on or off his meds. He didn't lose his leg overseas—he slipped at a subway station platform. Train crushed it. Did you give him money?"

"Ten bucks."

"He always tries to help people who give him money. He's not a bad person," Duggan said.

"What're you saying?" In the tense silence, Jeff looked hard at Duggan, then Hodge, sensing doubt. His face showed an oncoming rush of helplessness. "What? You don't believe me? Christ, what am I supposed to do here?"

"Maybe it's like you said," Hodge offered. "Maybe they went into a store and Freddie got mixed up. Maybe you should wait a bit?"

Suddenly remembering his one piece of evidence, Jeff reached into his pocket, then held up Cole's key ring.

"I found this in the street, right where they were! We got this for Cole yesterday. He'd clipped it to his pants this morning! You've got to help me!"

Duggan's face tightened as he blinked at Cole's key ring. His instinct, forged from two decades of police work, was now telling him that the situation had changed.

"All right, here's what we're going to do," Duggan said. "I'll talk to Freddie. Jeff, give Officer Hodge any recent photos you have. We'll start a canvass with other uniforms and I'll call a car for you, Jeff."

"Why?"

"This needs to go to the detective squad at Manhattan South."

Duggan talked into his walkie-talkie as he started toward Freddie. Jeff cued up the photos on his camera and sent them to Hodge's BlackBerry. He took more notes from Jeff, added more details.

Then Hodge hit Send.

"I've just shot the information and pictures to every cop patrolling this area," Hodge said.

Duggan returned from taking Freddie's information and was on his radio again searching the traffic.

"Jimmy, email your notes for the sixty-one to Sergeant McBain. I'll call him. Jeff—" Duggan nodded to the street "—your ride's here."

A siren yelped and a marked NYPD radio car, lights flashing, pulled over. Duggan leaned into the empty passenger section, had a quick conversation with the officer behind the wheel. Duggan then opened the rear door for Jeff, who saw Hodge huddling with four other uniformed officers who'd arrived.

"Jeff, this is Officer Breedo. He's going to drive you to the station house," Duggan said. "He'll take you in to Sergeant McBain, who'll refer you to the detective squad. They'll take over. Here's my card with my cell and email—we have your information."

"Thank you."

"We're going to circulate and look for Sarah and Cole here while you work with the detectives. The squad at the Fourteenth Precinct has more resources than we do. They'll decide what steps to take next."

"Okay. Thanks."

Jeff got in the back.

The seat—vinyl patched with duct tape—was separated from the front by a plastic divider. There was little legroom. The back windows were up tight and would not open. The rear smelled of lemon-scented cleaner, barely masking the trace of vomit and despair. When Breedo slid the divider open, Jeff welcomed the relief as breezes from the open front windows carried Breedo's cologne to the back of the car.

"It's about ten blocks away. I'll have you there in no time."

The siren yelped again, then wailed nonstop as Breedo maneuvered the Crown Victoria through traffic. Jeff was no stranger to emergency vehicles. He took in the controls for the overhead lights, siren, public address, search lights, the small computer terminal. Breedo's police radio issued a never-ending stream of coded transmissions.

Traffic ahead parted for them.

"See?" Breedo tapped his computer's monitor. Jeff saw Sarah and Cole's picture. "We're getting information out there."

Jeff's gut writhed with relief and fear.

Then he noticed the visor above Breedo, where the faces of a woman and two girls around three or four years old smiled down from a color snapshot.

"That your family in the picture above you?"

"Those are my girls. Duggan says you're a firefighter in Montana."

"Volunteer. I'm a mechanic."

"My brother was a firefighter. We lost him in the Towers."

"Sorry to hear that."

The siren wailed.

Jeff tried Sarah's cell phone once more.

Again, it was futile. *"Hi, this is Sarah. Please leave a message."* Keeping the phone pressed to his ear, he clung to her voice for a moment before another stab of concern hit him and he let go.

Breedo caught it and met him in the rearview mirror.

"Don't worry, Jeff, we're going to find your wife and son. Don't worry."

"Yeah, thanks."

He saw Breedo's profile as he drove. Then Jeff saw himself alone in the rearview mirror, stress lines carved in his face, worry bordering on fear clouding his eyes.

If this is a nightmare, then why can't I wake up? Wake up!

Jeff got out Cole's key ring, then the camera, and looked at the last picture taken of the three of them together.

He turned back to the window.

Manhattan blurred by and the siren rose to a near-scream.

7

New York City

The Fourteenth Precinct was situated on Thirty-fifth Street between Eighth and Ninth Avenues in a three-story cream-and-coffee-colored building.

Breedo escorted Jeff to Sergeant McBain, a burly man on the north side of fifty. He was studying his computer at his desk and paused to gaze at them over his bifocals when Breedo introduced him.

"Sarge, this is Jeff Griffin, Duggan and Hodge's sixty-one."

McBain threw his attention to Jeff.

"Did the officers find my wife and son?" Jeff asked. "Did they call in?"

"No, I'm afraid nothing's come in yet." McBain removed his glasses to get a better read on Jeff. "I've spoken to the patrol officers and looked at their notes. From what I understand, Mr. Griffin, your wife and son left with two men in a vehicle, in an alleged abduction?"

"Nothing's alleged, they were taken—what's going on?"

"Nothing's going on, Mr. Griffin. We're opening an investigation. We'll do all we can to help you locate your wife and son." McBain replaced his glasses and made a few strokes on his computer keyboard. "All right, Detectives Cordelli and Ortiz will talk to you. Officer Breedo will take you up to the squad."

As they headed upstairs, Jeff told Breedo that he could not understand why everyone was skeptical when he needed their help.

"A lot of people mislead us," Breedo said. "Or change their story."

Arriving on the floor, Breedo led him down a hall to the fluorescent-lit squad room and a maze of government-issue metal desks. The walls were lined with file cabinets and clipboards holding crime reports, crime stats, corkboards with maps, wanted posters, shift schedules. One schedule had huge block letters: UN DETAIL SHIFT. A large flat-screen TV, mounted to the ceiling, was tuned to an all-news channel reporting on the UN meeting.

The area was abandoned except for one guy in plain clothes hunched at his desk, talking loud on the phone. The day shift was out. Jeff's mind raced. Minutes ago he was walking down the street with his family. Now here he was, walking through a police squad room. Breedo stopped at two conjoined desks, then rolled over a cushioned swivel chair.

"Have a seat. I'll find Cordelli and Ortiz."

Jeff surveyed the desks. Their sides were pushed against a wall, under a well-used board displaying memos, calendars and personal items.

To the left: a framed degree from Long Island University for Juanita Ortiz, a newsletter photo of a beaming female cop in formal blues receiving her shield under the headline Detective Second Grade. There was a snapshot of a man and woman with a little girl, about five, by a mountain lake. The girl had an orange butterfly on her finger.

On the right side of the board: a framed degree in Criminal Justice for Victor Cordelli from Saint Joseph's College, a framed autographed photo of a man with two members of the New York Yankees on either side. There was some kind of award for Detective Cordelli— First Grade for "Exceptional Duty" in the NYPD Intelligence Division. No photos of a wife or kids. There was a card with an array of vulgar handwritten notes: "Hey, Cordelli, condolences on twenty freakin' years with the NYPD."

Each desk had a computer monitor and keyboard. Here, Jeff saw file folders fanned over desks, and notebooks bound with elastic and neatly stacked. On one of the desks was a splayed copy of the New York *Daily News* with the same headline he'd seen in the boxes a short time ago while walking with Sarah and Cole from the hotel to where— *Oh, Jesus!*

He ran his hand over his face.

They just disappeared! They can't be gone! Who would do this? Why? Why aren't police rushing to search for them?

"Mr. Griffin?"

He turned to a woman in her mid-thirties, tawny hair pulled into a ponytail. She wore a dark blazer, matching pants, white shirt, looked sharp.

"Juanita Ortiz, and this is Vic Cordelli."

Both detectives carried brimming coffee mugs but managed firm grips when they shook his hand. He declined their offer of a drink. They sat down. Juanita turned to a fresh page in a new notebook.

"I'm sorry, we just cleared another case last night,"

Ortiz said. "And we know you told the patrol officers everything but we need you to tell us what happened."

As Jeff recounted the morning, Cordelli leaned back in his chair. He was wearing jeans, a polo shirt, his ID and a shoulder holster holding a gun. He had a goatee, was about Jeff's height, but was wiry and revving in a higher gear. Sipping from his mug like he really needed it, Cordelli eyed him over the rim.

After Jeff finished relating events, Cordelli asked to see Cole's key ring.

"And you found this in the street where you last saw them?"

"Yes."

Cordelli turned it over in his hand a few times before returning it. Then he asked to see all the pictures in Sarah's camera and immediately downloaded them to his computer. From his vantage Jeff could partially see the photos as Cordelli scrutinized them one by one and Ortiz continued the interview.

"Jeff, will you volunteer all information about credit, bank and cell phones you and Sarah use?" she asked.

"Of course." He pulled out his wallet.

"If this is a robbery," she said while recording account numbers, "we'll track charges, withdrawals, maybe get photos from an ATM, that sort of thing. It helps."

"Is that what you think happened?"

"It's one theory," Ortiz said.

"If the men wanted to rob them, wouldn't they've let them go by now? God, they could be doing anything to them."

"Take it easy. At this point," Cordelli said, "we're not sure what it is."

Jeff's breathing quickened.

Was there something he was overlooking, or forgetting?

One by one images from the morning flowed across Cordelli's monitor—the street, Cole, Sarah—haunting Jeff as he turned back to Ortiz, who went over her notes. She asked a spectrum of questions, probing a little deeper about Sarah, her job, her disposition, family medical conditions and family history. Jeff told her everything but withheld mention of Lee Ann and its toll. It was too painful, entangled with his own guilt, and irrelevant as far as he was concerned.

"What about my wife's cell phone?" Jeff asked. "I read somewhere that you guys can track cell phones, that there's technology to pinpoint where people are through their cell phone."

"Sometimes," Cordelli said. "May I see your phone?"

Cordelli turned it on, expertly buttoned and scrolled through its menu and functions. "Is your wife's phone similar?"

"It's the same."

"These are older models. The tracking ability you're talking about is limited on this type." Cordelli returned Jeff's phone and went back to studying the photos, adding, "And as for tracking roaming signals, the phone has to be turned on. Even then, we need warrants to get the phone companies to release that information—but we can expedite them."

"Is there anything else you can do with the phone?"

"We can get a warrant to essentially clone your phone."

"What does that mean?"

"Any calls, texts, downloads—received or sent—will also come to us, to a special line with the NYPD, without the caller or sender being aware. It's like a tap. It allows us to be on top of any communication that might come from the bad guys. Say, a ransom call, or if your wife or son got to a phone and called for help. And we'll work with FBI for warrants on your hotel or home and work phones in Montana, all numbers associated directly with you or your wife, in case any calls go there."

"I want you to do everything that helps, yes."

"We want to be prepared," Cordelli said. "But the bad guys are smart. They toss the victims' phones. And they use prepaid disposables that are virtually impossible to track."

Hans Beck.

"Wait. There was a mix-up with Cole's bag at La-Guardia. I got a call from this guy, Hans Beck. We had his backpack, he had ours and we met near Penn Station late yesterday and traded them."

"Anything you can remember about him?"

Jeff described Beck and explained how he'd obtained Jeff's cell phone number. Ortiz made notes.

"He was kind of weird, nervous," Jeff said. "His number's on my phone."

Cordelli displayed the call list.

Jeff pointed to it.

"Did he threaten you, ask for money?" Cordelli asked.

"No."

"How was he weird?"

"I don't know—he seemed preoccupied, like something was on his mind. Maybe it was because he was rushed. He said he had to catch a train."

"Did you see what was in his bag, drugs, anything unusual?"

Jeff shook his head and Cordelli and Ortiz exchanged glances.

"He could've targeted your family for a robbery or ransom," Cordelli said. "Or it could be nothing. We'll check out the number but it could be a dead end."

"Well, what about all these police security cameras everywhere? Can't you use them to find my wife and son?"

"Yes, we can," Cordelli said.

"Then do it, goddammit! My family's life is at stake!"

The detectives let a few tense moments pass in silence as Jeff blinked back his fear, frustration and guilt. He shook his head.

"Jeff," Cordelli started, "you're upset, we understand. But we have people looking. We *are* investigating as we speak. But we need to be confident that you've given us all the information we need."

"I've told you everything I know."

Cordelli went back to examining the photos.

"Jeff, is Sarah under a doctor's care? Does she take any medication?"

"No."

"Does she use illegal drugs? Maybe gamble?"

"What?"

"We have to ask."

"No."

"Does she or Cole spend a lot of time online, chatting with strangers?"

"No."

"What was your wife's state of mind just before this happened? How would you characterize her demeanor?"

"What do you mean?"

"I'm looking at these pictures of you, of her, and I've got to tell you, your smiles look a little forced. I'm getting the feeling that there's some underlying stress in your family."

Jeff said nothing.

"Tell us about your family, your marriage. Is it all good out there in Big Sky Country?"

Jeff searched his heart for the answer.

"Who's this?" Cordelli turned the monitor.

The image nearly winded Jeff. He didn't know it was there—a beautiful shot of Sarah cradling Lee Ann, who was smiling up at her. Sarah smiled down at the angel in her arms. She'd obviously saved it on his phone.

"You said you have one child? Who's this, Jeff?"

Cordelli's eyes were like black ball bearings, shining hard.

"Our daughter." Jeff cleared his throat. "She died about a year and a half ago. SIDS."

"I'm so sorry," Juanita said tenderly as Jeff's attention flicked to the snapshot of Juanita and the girl with the butterfly.

"My condolences," Cordelli said. "But how would you characterize your marriage since then, up to the point these pictures were taken here, this morning? Would you say there was stress in your family this morning before Sarah and Cole disappeared?"

Jeff swallowed hard.

"Yes."

"Were you arguing?"

"Yes."

Cordelli shot a glance to Ortiz: *bingo*.

"What were you arguing about?" Cordelli asked.

Jeff stared at the image with restrained anger and said slowly, "I need you to help me."

"We are helping you," Cordelli said. "But we need the truth, all of it. What were you arguing about before Sarah left with Cole?"

"We'd been having a hard time since we lost our

daughter. Cole has always dreamed of seeing New York City, so we came here to give him the trip and to talk about our future."

"Were you going to stay together, or separate?"

Surprised at the accuracy of the question Jeff said nothing.

"Losing a child can lead to divorce—it happens," Cordelli said.

"It's what we were talking about this morning," Jeff said.

"So it would be fair to say your marriage was strained up to the point they disappeared?"

"I told them to stay right where they were while I bought new batteries for the camera."

"Jeff, is it conceivable that Sarah was a little ticked at how your conversations were going and needed some time alone?"

He stared at Cordelli, knowing how it looked to him, but knowing the truth, still feeling Sarah's arm around his waist, holding him tight.

"No."

"I need you to be honest with us, Jeff. Would Sarah have any reason to harm Cole?"

"God, no! I'm telling you, no. I told you at the start, she's a loving mother, a schoolteacher, a good person. She's incapable of doing any of the things you're suggesting."

Cordelli shot a glance to Ortiz, leaving matters open but signaling an end to the interview.

"Okay, Jeff," she said. "Be assured, we're on this, leave everything with us. Meanwhile, we suggest you go back to your hotel, in case Sarah returns. We'll stay in touch with you and we'll ask you to call us, should anything change."

"If Sarah shows up," Cordelli said, "please return to the station house with her and Cole so we can sign off."

Cordelli started repositioning file folders on his desk.

Clearing his desk.

That was all that Cordelli was interested in, Jeff thought later when he'd returned to the street and started looking for a cab.

Jeff would call the hotel and their room to check on Sarah.

But he had no intention of returning and doing nothing.

8

New York City

Time hammered against Jeff.

As his cab cut through the midtown traffic he watched the muted backseat TV monitor—reports on Broadway, the Mets, a triple murder in Brooklyn and more on the UN meeting in the Lower East Side.

Amid the horns, sirens, the chaos, he tried to think.

He called the hotel room, then the desk for messages—nothing.

His hope sinking, he turned to the city, the sidewalks, scanning the crowds, studying faces until details melted away. He understood the skepticism of the NYPD, knew how things looked to them.

Bad.

Because they *were* bad.

They'd said they were investigating but Cordelli and Ortiz likely thought Sarah took Cole for a few hours of shopping because she was pissed off. The detectives probably didn't put much currency in the witness, a street guy, and were reluctant to give it much effort. Deep down Jeff believed they had doubts about his report. He didn't trust them to make it a priority.

As his taxi rolled through the city, his misgivings resonated with his memories of himself at fifteen. His parents were killed when their tour bus crashed in the Canadian Rockies and he went to live with his grandfather near Billings.

In the months after the estate was settled, Jeff was given his father's Ford pickup truck. Traces of his cologne were still in the truck; the steering wheel was worn from where his big hands usually held it. Jeff cherished the pickup because it was his connection to his mom and dad.

Jeff got his learner's license, and when he drove the truck with his grandfather, it felt like his parents were in the cab with them. Jeff treasured the Ford, washing it and changing the oil himself. With that truck he learned how to fix things, to become self-reliant, to endure the deaths of his parents.

Then one day the truck was stolen from his grandfather's driveway.

Jeff was devastated. They'd reported the theft to police, who'd promised to "leave no stone unturned" in recovering it. But days, then weeks, passed with no news. Jeff convinced his grandfather to let him search for it by driving him to truck stops, auto shops, bars and diners in nearly every town in Yellowstone County.

Weeks passed. Then, as if guided by fate, they'd spotted a Ford pickup at a mall near Ballantine where they'd stopped to shop for shirts. It was Jeff's. It had a different plate and was all primed like it was going to be painted but it had the same tiny spiderweb fracture in the rear cab window and the chip in the left rear bumper.

After police and the court returned the truck, Jeff's grandfather told him something he'd never forgotten.

"The truck could never be as important to anyone as

it is to you, Jeff. There are certain things in this world that you just have to take care of yourself, or they'll never be done right. If you don't trust your gut in these matters, you'll have to live with the consequences for the rest of your life."

A horn blast yanked Jeff back to Manhattan's traffic and a decision.

So what am I going to do here, now?

He had no choice. He would search for his family on his own.

Where do I start?

He'd go back to the spot where it happened and start looking there.

He tried calling Sarah again and again. It rang to her message. Nothing. It had been about two hours since he'd last seen Sarah and Cole.

Where the hell are you?

Jeff stared at his phone, then, on impulse, he called the number for Hans Beck and got a recorded message saying the number was no longer in service. *That's strange,* Jeff thought, unsure what to make of it.

After the cab dropped him off, Jeff allowed himself a moment to entertain the belief that Sarah and Cole had returned. That they'd have some wild explanation and they'd all laugh it off. How sweet the relief would be. He'd admit to her that he'd been a fool, that he was wrong for wanting to separate—no, confused, stupid and so sorry.

He'd tell her that he wanted to keep their family together.

Hold them and never let them go.

But his hope was overtaken by reality as he came to the spot. There was no sign of Sarah or Cole. Freddie, the wheelchair panhandler, was gone. Jeff got out his

camera, cued the photo of Sarah and Cole and returned
to the ponytailed man selling souvenirs at the pushcart
where Sarah and Cole had been. Again, Jeff begged for
his help, showing him the photos.

The vendor shook his head, his face a mask of indif-
ference behind his dark glasses.

"They were right here," Jeff said.

"I told you, pal. I don't remember them."

Deflated, Jeff lowered his camera to grapple with a
million thoughts, horrible imaginings of what the phan-
tom abductors could be doing to his family at this very
moment. Slowly he turned in a full circle in the heart
of Manhattan, one of the busiest cities in the world.

He forced himself to remain calm, to think.

Retrace your steps. Re-create the scene.

His attention came to the store where he'd bought the
batteries, where it all started: Metro Manhattan Gifts
and Things.

He entered.

Not as busy as before. A few browsers checking out
the knickknacks; otherwise, a lull. Even the music was
subdued. He recognized the same girl at the counter.

A good sign.

She had her nose in her cell phone, thumbs flying.

He needed her. *Don't interrupt her. Not yet.*

He assessed the store again, locking in on the security camera mounted on the wall above the counter. It
was angled to the door, front window and the street.

Did it capture Sarah and Cole?

He had to see the camera's perspective.

"Can I help you?"

The clerk had finished with her phone. Her bejew-
eled nostril sparkled as she smiled—nice bright teeth,
sincere. He sensed a good heart.

"I was here a while ago buying batteries."

"I remember you."

"You do?"

"Your shirt, says Montana. I've visited Glacier National Park. It's gorgeous."

"Small world," he said. "Look, I was hoping you could help me."

"Depends on what you need."

"My wife and son, we got separated out front, and I was thinking that maybe your security camera—" he nodded to it "—maybe it recorded them."

She turned to it and back to him without speaking.

"I just need to see if it records the spot on the street where they were."

"Why don't you just look for them?"

"I did and a man who was near them told me they may have been abducted or robbed."

"What? That's a crazy scary."

"I'm worried. I need to see where they went or what happened. Can I just have a look at your camera's monitor, see it if picked up anything?"

"I don't really want to get involved."

"No, nothing like that. Just let me check it out, it won't take long. No one has to know and I'll pay you fifty dollars just to see. Just to have a look. If it doesn't get the angle, then that's it. If it does, I'll give you more money to rewind it back?"

"I don't know, I—"

"Excuse me," a woman said.

A middle-aged man and woman approached with T-shirts, key rings, postcards. Jeff stepped aside as the girl rang them up.

"Can you tell us how to get to Central Park from here?" the woman asked.

"Go right out front and catch a bus on Eighth Avenue," the girl said. "Or you can walk north on Eighth, but it's about sixteen blocks."

"Thank you."

Once Jeff and the girl were alone again, he pressed his case. He showed her his digital camera and the photos of Sarah and Cole. The girl blinked at them— a typical American family vacationing in New York.

"We were right out front a couple of hours ago," he said. "I just need to see what happened. I need your help."

"I think you should just go to the police."

"I did. I just returned from talking to detectives at the precinct."

"There you go."

"They said they're looking, but I'm looking, too. Please, put yourself in my shoes. Wouldn't you do everything you could?"

Considering his point and his plight, she glanced around, caught her bottom lip between her teeth. Jeff pulled out two twenties and a ten. She glanced at the cash.

"Just a quick look." He gave her his wallet, his phone, everything. "You hold this. I'm just trying to find my wife and son."

Searching his eyes she saw the emotion and desperation broiling behind them, his plea eroding her resistance.

"Please," he said.

After another glance around she put Jeff's items under the counter. Then she went to a wire mesh door that separated the counter from the rest of the store. She unlocked it and ushered him inside to the counter and the monitor on a lower shelf. The monitor screen was sectioned into quarters, four small clear color screens.

"It changes all the time," she said.

Jeff passed the fifty dollars to the girl and lowered himself. On one of the screens he saw a miniature, partial view of the ponytailed vendor and the street—it was very limited but it was something.

"I need to enlarge this one." Jeff tapped the top right quarter. "I need to rewind this one to the time I came in."

"I can't," she said. "It's locked so thieves can't take it. See?"

She tapped a steel mesh case around the control console.

"What's your name?"

"Mandy."

"Mandy, I'll pay you more. Is there anyone in the store with the key who can access the controls and can operate this? I need to see what happened to my wife and son. Then I'm gone."

Mandy took stock. The store was quiet. She looked to the rear.

"Chad has the key. He's in the back."

"Can you get him? Please, I just need to rewind it and see what happened."

Mandy pulled out her cell phone and sent a text message.

"Excuse me?" An old man rapped his knuckles on the counter and Mandy rang in his two sodas, two chocolate bars and two bags of chips, then came back to Jeff.

"Sit here and wait." Mandy pushed an overturned plastic milk crate toward him so he could sit behind the counter unseen. A few minutes later a lanky man in his early twenties appeared at the wire mesh door.

He was not the same young man Jeff had seen on the ladder a few hours earlier when he'd entered the store for batteries.

"What do you want, Mandy?" Then, seeing Jeff by the monitor, he said, "What the—? Who's he? What're you doing?"

She went to Chad, opened the door and updated him in a hushed tone loud enough for Jeff to hear. Chad's neck was tattooed with flames. He was harder than Mandy. Listening to her, his eyes narrowed as he gave Jeff an icy appraisal.

"Two cops were here," Chad said, "asking to see our surveillance footage. They didn't tell me why."

"When?" Mandy asked. "I didn't see them."

"It was twenty minutes ago when you and I were out on our break. Kyle told me when we got back."

"Did they find anything in the footage?" Jeff asked.

"They never saw it because Kyle doesn't have the key. I have the key. The cops told Kyle they'd be back later. Guess they're asking around at other places. It's probably got something to do with your situation."

"Will you help me?" Jeff asked.

"Maybe. You gave Mandy fifty bucks?"

"Yes."

"I want two hundred and all you get is a look. No copies."

"Deal."

"First, let me copy your driver's license, to cover my ass."

Jeff retrieved his wallet from the counter. Chad placed Jeff's Montana license on the small photocopier, then Jeff pulled out the cash, nearly all he had left. Chad shoved it in his pocket, then unlocked the console.

"What time do you need?"

Jeff consulted his receipt for the time and Chad expertly rewound the footage. Tiny people moved backward in fast motion. Then he enlarged the images and let the recording play at normal speed. A time and date stamp ran across the bottom.

The footage offered a clear color overhead view of the counter, the front area of the store, the door and suspect height marker. It also captured the front window, and the area above all the items on display. It only showed a limited view of the street.

People bustled by in both directions on the sidewalk, bordered by street vendors and vehicle traffic—but beyond the sidewalk the view of the vendors and the road was restricted. Jeff eyed every movement of every stranger when—bam!

"That's them!"

His pulse raced. There was Sarah taking Cole's picture, then Cole taking one of him with Sarah.

"Slow it down."

Jeff stopped breathing.

He concentrated on Sarah—feeling her slip her arm around him. Now the tourist was taking the shot of the three of them. The image tore at Jeff. *The tourist looks at the camera. Dead batteries. Jeff has the camera and leaves for the store. He stops to talk to Freddie with the beat-up wheelchair. Jeff gives him money.*

Behind them Sarah and Cole browse at the vendor's souvenir cart. They move closer to the road. Bit by bit they are exiting the frame.

"Can you slow it down some more?"

The footage slowed to near frame-by-frame speed.

Now, Sarah and Cole are almost out of the picture. All Jeff can make out are their feet, up to their knees, and the lower portions of cars passing by.

One stops near Sarah and Cole with such sud-denness.

It just appears.

Doors open, other legs emerge from it, shoes, black shoes, or boots. Military style? Three sets? They move fast, positioning next to Sarah and Cole. Right beside them. Too close. *A moment passes, then they all move to the vehicle two steps away.*

Doors open.

Sarah and Cole vanish.

Doors close.

The white vehicle pulls from the curb, the rear right quarter, rear bumper, plate flash. Then someone's head, a passerby, blocks the view; the plate is obscured. The vehicle disappears.

It's over.

"Hold it!" Jeff pressed his finger to the screen as if to grab the image and stop time.

Chad froze the frame.

"That plate. I need that license plate!"

"Hold on."

Chad froze the footage, then frame by frame he reversed and forwarded it until he had the best view on the plate.

"Hold on."

Chad enlarged the plate until it was clear enough to read.

"I need something to write with," Jeff said.

Mandy passed him a pad and pen and Jeff copied down the New York State license number.

"Can I use your computer to get online?" Jeff asked.

Chad and Mandy traded worried glances, obviously concerned that they were already too involved in what-ever was going on.

"No." Chad returned the security surveillance system to its normal state and his keys jingled. "That's all you're going to get from us."

"Please."

"We're done." Chad locked up the console.

"You saw what happened!" Jeff said.

"I don't know what happened," Chad said.

"Those people took my wife and son! I have to run this plate!"

"I don't know what I saw, but we're not getting involved."

"I just need a computer."

"We're done," Chad said.

Jeff looked at Mandy.

"There's an internet café three blocks west of here," she said. "I'll draw you a map."

9

New York City

In the minutes after Jeff had left the Fourteenth Precinct, Detective Vic Cordelli resumed staring at the pictures of the Griffins.

Juanita Ortiz stopped reading her notes and shifted her gaze to him.

"What is it, Vic?"

Cordelli brooded as mistrust gnawed at him and he shook his head.

"I just don't know about this one, Juanita."

Ortiz tapped her pen against her notes, sighing to herself.

"You got a lot going on—" Ortiz picked up her landline "—but I need you to help me get to work and run this thing, okay?"

Ortiz called the Real Time Crime Center downtown at One Police Plaza. The RTCC operated a vast computer network, including hundreds of surveillance cameras and plate readers in all boroughs. She'd requested all footage covering the time and location of Sarah and Cole Griffin's abduction.

While that was being processed Cordelli ran the Griffins through the National Crime Information Center, which held active records on millions of cases, ranging from thefts, to missing persons, fugitives and terrorists. The query rang no bells—no arrest, warrants, nothing.

As Ortiz checked with other local, state and regional databases, Cordelli got on the phone to Montana. He hooked up with Detective Blaine Thorsen of the Laurel Police Department, who was puzzled at why the NYPD was calling about Jeff and Sarah Griffin.

"No." Thorsen's keyboard clicked as he consulted local computer records for Cordelli. "There's no complaint history here. No custody orders. It's a damn shame that they lost their baby a while back."

"What was the cause?"

"The coroner said it was SIDS. We investigated and had no reason to believe otherwise. They're nice people. Why are you checking? What's going on in New York?"

"They're here on vacation," Cordelli said. "Jeff's reported that Sarah and Cole were abducted less than two hours ago near Times Square."

"Abducted? Shit, really?"

"We're looking into it."

"Do you have any suspects?"

"A witness gave us a couple of men and a vague vehicle description. Nothing solid. Does this sound out of character for the Griffins?"

"Completely," Thorsen said. "That family went through hell when they lost their daughter and now this. Lord Almighty. If you need anything from our end, anything at all, let us know."

Cordelli hung up.

His perspective was shifting.

He reviewed the report from the uniforms, the witness statement taken by Roy Duggan. He knew Duggan, knew he was a hard-ass who didn't trust many people. Duggan wouldn't waste his time if he didn't sense a case here. Cordelli would have to get down to the street and talk to Freddie.

For now, he returned to the family photos, the baby, Sarah, Jeff and Cole. Cordelli considered putting out an Amber Alert for Cole but they had nothing on a vehicle.

Juanita was still working her phone and the computer. These days an investigation entailed as much mouse clicking as shoe leather.

The more Cordelli looked at the Griffin family pictures, the deeper he'd looked into himself and how hollow his life had become.

Three nights back, in the case they'd just closed, a jacked-up addict had put a gun in his face but it jammed. Cordelli's "this-is-it" moment made him realize that nobody would mourn him because, after five years, he'd determined marriage wasn't for him. He'd told his wife that he couldn't breathe, that he was on a leash.

She got a lawyer and cut him loose.

The papers came through yesterday.

Seeing the Griffins underscored what he would never have.

It's what he saw with Juanita every day. He could never tell her how it ate him up. She had Lucy, her little girl, and Bert, her husband. He was a building contractor who often surprised her with picnics in Central Park or getaway weekends to Boston.

Cordelli figured these things were factors contributing to why he had been skeptical and a bit of a prick to Jeff Griffin. Yeah, maybe, he thought, downing the last of his coffee, maybe a little.

It was stupid.

He would correct it, starting now.

Going back over everything, one theory came to mind telling him that—

"Hey, you there? Vic? Hello? Did you hear me?"

Ortiz had yanked him from his thoughts.

"I said RTCC just came through. I think we've really got something here. Come around, you've got to see this."

10

New York City

The fleeting video images of Sarah and Cole vanishing with strangers were seared in Jeff's mind as he hurried through New York's streets to the internet café.

Seeing what had happened to them made it real.

Someone had taken them, pulled them from the street in a heartbeat.

Why? Who would do this? It's insane!

His scalp prickling, he glanced at the directions to the café while rushing through a crosswalk against a red light. A Mercedes bumper came within inches of his knee—the horn blast startled him as the driver spewed obscenities. Jeff waved it off, took a deep breath and moved on.

What was he doing running around like this?

He should call Cordelli and Ortiz, alert them to the surveillance footage and the plate. He'd do that. But not yet, because when he considered the slip of paper bearing the license number, he knew he had more than hope in his hand.

This was his thread to Sarah and Cole.

Nothing was going to stop him from following it.

* * *

It was called Virtual Connections Online Coffee-house.

Jazz music and the hissing gurgle of espresso machines filled the air of the packed café. At every table people had their noses in their BlackBerries, tablets, cell phones and laptops. All the rental computer terminals were in use. Jeff got his instructions and number from a girl in a white apron at the counter.

"Hit Enter, the rates come up. Swipe your credit card. Remember to log out. Three people are ahead of you but it won't be long—we have twelve terminals."

While waiting, Jeff went to the ATM next door for more cash. By the time he'd come back, a terminal in the corner had become available. The mouse was sticky and the keyboard was so worn off he had to strain to see what letters he was typing.

He took the half hour rate of seven dollars. He knew the detectives were monitoring his family credit card, so he used his company card for Clay Platt's Auto Service. He'd explain the charges to Clay later. Once he was online he searched Google services that identified license plates. He submitted the plate number for New York State, then his credit card information.

A few seconds later the monitor displayed the data. The vehicle was a white 2010 GMC Terrain, the registered owner was Donald Dalfini and his address was 88 Steeldown Road, New York City. There was a vehicle identification number, title, registration date and other information.

Jeff printed it all off, then searched the address.

It was in the Bronx. The map put it near Neverpoint Park in the southeast section of the borough. The estimated travel time from midtown was about forty minutes.

Jeff collected his pages, folded them into his pocket and debated his next step.

Call Cordelli and Ortiz, tell them I saw the recording and now had a plate and address.

He took out Ortiz's business card and pressed the number. The line rang, then went straight to her voice mail. He didn't want to leave a message and he didn't want to waste any time.

I'll follow this on my own. I'll take it as far as I can, then I'll alert them once I have something.

Jeff worked his way through the crowd to the street and flagged down the first cab he saw.

11

New York City

"Run it again but slow it down."

Cordelli rolled his chair beside Ortiz at her computer.

A few keystrokes and she replayed the video provided by the New York Police Department's Real Time Crime Center. The images covered Forty-fourth and Forty-fifth Streets near Seventh Avenue—at the time of Sarah and Cole's abduction.

It had taken time for the RTCC to gather the material but the number of angles, proximity and superior quality captured by its network exceeded anything from a single camera with a partial street view.

"Here we go." Ortiz's monitor offered an array of sharp perspectives as she zeroed in on what they needed.

Sarah Griffin emerges, taking a picture of Cole. Jeff joins them, his arm around her as Cole photographs his parents. Jeff approaches a tourist who takes a shot of the family, then looks at the camera. Jeff takes it, turns to the storefronts, talks with the panhandler in a wheelchair, then enters a store. Sarah and Cole move to a vendor's cart, looking at souvenirs. A white SUV with tinted windows brakes at the curb. Two men exit on the curbside, leaving passenger doors open. They're wearing ball caps, dark glasses, full beards, big, dark, front-button shirts loose enough to hide a weapon, dark jeans, dark boots, moving fast into Sarah and Cole's space. One leans to Cole's ear, telling him something, takes his arm, puts his other arm on Cole's shoulder and swiftly thrusts him into the backseat. Sarah reacts with the second man, who is trying to push her back. They appear to only want the boy. But Sarah battles her way into the backseat after Cole. The men overpower her, shut the doors, abducting her, as well. The SUV pulls away...gone like it never happened...no reaction from people on the street. Jeff emerges from the store searching, asking people, calling on his cell phone. Nothing...

The images froze: Jeff Griffin alone, helpless in the street.

The scene drove it home for Ortiz and Cordelli, briefly imagining the fear twisting in Jeff's gut before they'd kicked things into high gear. Cordelli tapped his pen to the monitor on the SUV's New York plate.

They wrote it down.

"Get the center to run the plate through everything," he said.

"Already on it." Ortiz had grabbed her phone.

"We want to get units rolling to the address of the registered owner ASAP. And," Cordelli added, "get them to track the SUV through the surveillance network. Can they tell us where it went? Where it is now?"

As Ortiz dealt with her call, Cordelli used her keyboard to replay the footage. He eyed every aspect, absorbed every detail of the chilling act that had played out in broad daylight on one of the busiest streets on earth.

"What do you think?" Ortiz asked after finishing the call.

"Who the hell are these guys? Why would they kidnap a Montana schoolteacher and her nine-year-old son?"

"It's hard to tell by her reaction if she knows them."

"Go back to this angle, on this one." Cordelli touched his pen to the monitor. "I can't make out any features on the suspects. Counting the driver, is it four men?"

"The SUV's got a little too much tint on the windows and that glare on the windshield doesn't help."

"We need to look into the family's finances, see if they had gambling or drug debts," Cordelli said.

"I thought the people in Montana said they were clean, upstanding."

"We'll check again and we'll get the FBI in Billings to assist. We'll request warrants on the family's computers, check their records. Maybe it's an online thing. Maybe she was having an affair that went bad."

"Or maybe the kid was chatting with a predator, told them about the family's vacation?" Ortiz said.

Cordelli went to his desk and made calls.

"I'll get things rolling to put out an Amber Alert."

He advised their supervisor, then started pulling together photos of Sarah and Cole, notes on the SUV—the plate, color—description of the suspects.

Ortiz's cell phone rang.

Her eyes widened slightly as she listened, then jotted notes.

"This is happening now?" Her voice betrayed a measure of incredulity before she said, "Got it," and hung up.

"Vic, you're not going to believe this." Ortiz stood, pulled on her jacket. "I'll tell you on the way. We've got to leave right now."

12

Neverpoint Park, the Bronx, New York City

The address for the SUV was in a corner of Neverpoint where faded Realtors' signs listed small, tired-looking houses as Must Sell or with Price Reduced.

"My stepfather lived here," Jeff's cabdriver said. "There was a landfill over there, that whole section."

It had taken about half an hour to travel from midtown to this part of the East Bronx, which was bound by Long Island Sound and the East River. After leaving the expressway, they'd driven through a mixture of warehouses, pawnshops, drugstores, hair salons and pizzerias.

They'd passed an assortment of low-income city apartment projects before coming to neighborhoods of shingle-roofed one- and two-story houses with small yards. On Steeldown Road, parked cars lined both sides of the street. A dog was in the middle of it, his head inside a fast-food take-out bag as he worked on the remains.

For the umpteenth time, Jeff glanced at the information on the printout, then back to the street.

Who was Donald Dalfini?

The Dalfini house at 88 Steeldown Road was a frame-and-stucco bungalow with a fenced yard. There was an older, dirty Honda with a dented rear quarter parked on the street out front, but the driveway was empty. The GMC Terrain registered to the address was a late model that would cost some thirty thousand dollars. Jeff didn't see how it fit with the income level of the neighborhood.

He told the driver to keep going.

The knot in Jeff's stomach was tightening, making it harder for him to concentrate.

Is this a mistake?

No, he had to do this. Too much was at stake.

"Pull over and let me out," he said when they were midway into the next block. Jeff paid the fare, tipped the driver, then gave him another twenty.

"Kill your meter and wait. I may need to return to Manhattan fast."

"Sure, pal. Out here to get some action, huh?" The driver winked at him in the rearview mirror and reached for his copy of the *New York Post*.

Walking to the house Jeff's breathing quickened, the horror rising. He couldn't believe the past few hours: Sarah and Cole abducted, the NYPD challenging his report, leaving him alone to track the people who took his wife and son to this street.

To this house.

This was beyond his control.

Suddenly, he was besieged with questions.

What are you doing? What are you getting into? You're not a cop. You should let Cordelli and Ortiz handle this, he thought as he came to the bungalow. *But what if Sarah and Cole are being held here, right now? What if they're being tortured, or worse?*

He couldn't live with himself if it turned out that he was this close but did nothing to save them. He'd already faced an unbearable loss. Standing in the street, in front of the house, Jeff had no choice.

My wife and son could be in there and I'm going in after them.

He wrote down the Honda's New York plate and scanned the interior. It had an overflowing ashtray. The passenger seat was covered with flyers and junk-food wrappers. Other than this car out front there was no sign of any vehicles at the house.

The curtains were drawn.

All quiet, except for the jets flying in and out of La-Guardia.

How was he going to do this? Call the phone number he obtained on the search record printout? Or ring the doorbell? A dog's distant bark underscored that he was losing time. There was a diffusion of light near a window. A shadow passed by a curtain.

Someone's in there.

Jeff stepped onto the property, walked to the side of the house, bent down and cupped his face to a basement window. His eyes adjusted to a double laundry sink, a washer and dryer, clothes heaped on the floor.

He flinched.

A child's earsplitting scream shattered the quiet.

Cole?

Something inside the house vibrated, someone moving around. Jeff started for the backyard but was stopped by a wooden fence and a gate that reached to his shoulders. He tried the handle; the gate was locked. He tried reaching over it for a latch but got nothing.

Gripping the top of the fence, he hefted himself over it, landing on a garden hose that snaked to the back.

Jeff followed it past a back door to patio steps, a small deck with lawn chairs and picnic table. It was a typical family backyard.

He stopped at the sight of two children standing in the grass, some fifteen feet away: a boy about Cole's age and a girl who looked to be four or five, both wearing swimsuits.

The hose meandered to the girl. She used both hands to hold the dripping nozzle, which she pointed at the boy, who was drenched. For a moment, water plunking from the boy to the deck was the only sound.

Then the boy, his blond water-slicked hair darkened, turned to Jeff at the same time as the girl.

The boy was not Cole.

The children's eyes widened slightly as they stared at Jeff, speechless until the girl said, "Hello."

At a loss, Jeff scanned the small yard when he noticed the children's attention shift a fraction to his left.

"I have a gun," a woman's voice said from behind him.

Jeff turned.

The woman's arms were extended; her hands were wrapped around the pistol aimed at him.

"Get on your knees and put your hands behind your head!"

Before Jeff could explain she shouted.

"Do it now, asshole! Or I swear to God I'll shoot you dead."

13

Neverpoint Park, the Bronx, New York City

Jeff raised his hands and lowered himself to the lawn.

The woman holding the gun ordered her children into the house.

Jeff got on his knees, his mind racing.

Are Sarah and Cole here? Where's the SUV?

The woman kept her gun on him and kept her distance.

A shrub of frizzy red hair haloed her face. She had to be in her late twenties but the lines carved deep around her mouth suggested an embittered life. She had an overbite. She wore jeans and a T-shirt showing a pit bull guarding a motorcycle. Tattoos swirled along her arms.

"Get out your wallet."

Slowly Jeff pulled it from his pocket and tossed it to her feet. Keeping her gun on him she retrieved it, examined his driver's license and fire department photo identification.

"Montana? Why the hell are you here, trespassing, threatening my kids?"

His pulse galloping, Jeff thought it odd she hadn't called the police. *Or maybe she has and I'll hear sirens?*

Her voice was throaty, she may have been drinking.
She looks like someone who has been arrested before.
If she's involved in the abduction she wouldn't want po-
lice coming to this place.

"Answer me, asshole!"

He tried to think.

"My wife and son were abducted a few hours ago near Times Square in an SUV registered to this address."

"That's a crock of shit!"

"It's the truth. Do you know Donald Dalfini? Where is the SUV? Are you his wife?" The woman didn't answer. As she considered his questions, Jeff kept talking. "Let me show you something?"

She took a moment, then nodded once. Jeff fished out Sarah's digital camera and Cole's key ring. He cued up the photos and held the camera to her with the ring.

"Look at these, please. Pictures we took today. I'm telling the truth."

Hesitating, she inched forward, keeping the gun on Jeff. She took the items with her free hand, then backed away. As she looked them over Jeff told her everything—about Lee Ann, the trip, everything. He explained all the events that brought them here, to this moment.

"Tell me where my wife and son are. I'm begging you."

Jeff saw that her eyes were blue, a bit glassy, as he searched them for her reaction. With each passing second her hardness started to fracture. As she blinked back tears her mouth began moving and she spoke, in a whisper, to herself. Jeff struggled to hear, certain she'd said, "I told Donnie it's freakin' wrong, stupid."

"Please," Jeff said. "I'm begging you. Are they okay? Are my wife and son hurt? Please."

On the verge of tears, she dragged the back of her hand across her mouth.

"Shut up! Your shit's got nothing to do with us!"

"It's your SUV. It's registered to this address."

"It was stolen three weeks ago when I went to the Neverpoint Mall. I've been scared the fuckers who took it would come here."

"Then we're on the same side. We both need to know what happened."

"Sheri, you need my help?"

A woman's voice came from just inside the sliding doors to the deck. A large woman in her fifties with long white hair stood in the dim light. She was wearing an oversize Mets T-shirt and tapped the tip of a baseball bat into the palm of her left hand.

"Did you call Donnie?" Sheri asked the older woman.

"I left him a message. Did you find out who this asshole is? Want me to help you with him?"

"No, I've got this."

But Sheri's voice quavered; her hands were shaking, signaling that she was losing her internal struggle to regard Jeff as a threat. He needed to search the house, then he'd alert Cordelli and Ortiz.

"Sheri, I told you the truth," he said. "If what you told me is true, let me look through your house for my family, then I'll go."

"I told you we got nothing to do with that."

"I need to look. Put yourself in my shoes."

As she weighed Jeff's argument, he pressed his case further.

"Sheri, listen to me—I need to find my family. Let me look and I'll go. No matter what you do, your SUV is linked to my family's disappearance and police will be coming here. I can let them know you helped, or I can let them know you hid something. I think you have a good heart. I don't believe you want to kill me because I'm telling you the truth. I need to find my wife and son."

After studying his face she swallowed, then lowered her gun.

"All right. Belva! Bring the kids out back. This won't take long."

"Are you nuts, girl?"

"It's my damn house. Do as I say!"

It was a small bungalow; the reek of cigarettes and stale beer hung in the air. The kitchen table was cluttered with plates, butter knives, an open bag of cookies, a loaf of white bread and jars of jelly and peanut butter. When Jeff entered the living room it became evident why Sheri might not call the police. The coffee table was lined with empty liquor bottles, beer cans and small clear plastic bags containing something organic.

There were newspapers open to want ads with jobs circled.

"Since Donnie got laid off at the plant, it's been hard," Sheri was almost apologizing to Jeff. "The mortgage, car and credit card payments are piling up. We're looking for jobs but it's hard, and then with the SUV stolen, that took the cake."

Holding her gun at her side, Sheri kept her distance as she escorted Jeff in his room-by-room search on the main floor bedrooms. He recognized the intrusive aspect of a stranger in her bedroom and those of her children but it was eclipsed by the outrage forced upon him. He looked in closets, under beds, in the basement and he tapped on walls until he was satisfied that Sarah and

Cole were not here. When they'd returned to the living room Jeff's cell phone rang.

The display showed a blocked number.

His heart rate soared when he answered.

"Jeff, this is Detective Cordelli. We've located the SUV."

"What about Sarah and Cole?"

Sirens and the rush of the road indicated Cordelli was in a car.

"No confirmation. We're en route to the scene now."

"What's the location? I'm coming."

"You sit tight at your hotel—we'll keep you posted."

"Tell me the location, Cordelli!"

"Jeff, look, we're not there yet. I don't know exactly what we have."

"It's my wife and son, tell me! I'm a firefighter. I've been to 'scenes,' Cordelli, bad ones. Other people will be gawking at the site. I have a right to be there, you know I do."

"Jeff, I'll call you back."

"No, I need to know."

At that moment Sheri and Jeff heard a distant siren that was approaching her area. Jeff figured that the police might also be acting on the Dalfinis' address. If that was the case, he didn't want to wait for them.

"Tell me the location now!" Jeff glanced out the window down the street. His cab was still waiting. "I swear I'll get it, one way or another."

Cordelli let a beat pass before relenting.

"Got a pen and paper?"

Cordelli recited the location. Jeff copied it on the newsprint border of a newspaper on Sheri's coffee table.

"What was that all about?" Sheri said.

"The NYPD have found something."

"What?"

"I don't know exactly but I have to go." Jeff collected his wallet and things from Sheri. "If it comes up, I'll tell the police that you tried to help me."

Sheri said nothing.

Concern deepened the worry lines on her face and she tried to absorb all that had taken place as Jeff hurried out of her home and trotted down the street to his cab.

14

Brooklyn, New York City

The 2010 GMC Terrain burned within sight of the Brooklyn Bridge, in the loading area of an abandoned warehouse at the fringe of a derelict industrial section of Brooklyn Heights.

Officers in a marked NYPD car patrolling the zone were first to spot it. They'd called it in with the plate number. By the time crews from Engine 205, Ladder 118, arrived the SUV was engulfed, the blaze blasting outward and skyward, turning the vehicle into a mass of ferocity.

The inferno crackled and hissed, discharging sparks and flakes of melted debris. Firefighters stretched a line, keeping a safe distance using the reach of the hose stream. Explosions can propel white-hot fragments with bullet force. Like all first responders, they knew every call could be their last. Their firehouse had lost eight members in the September 11, 2001, terrorist attacks.

Cordelli and Ortiz pulled up amid the sirens and lights of more arriving emergency vehicles. They were directed to Fire Lieutenant Van Reston. A crowd was collecting at the yellow tape that cordoned the area. Cordelli had to shout over the rattle-roar of the pumper.

"What do you have?"

"Arson, and given the intensity, I'm guessing they used an incendiary device."

Cordelli took down Reston's information in his notebook.

"Anyone inside?"

"Don't know yet. We'll know soon as we can have a look."

"Thanks." Cordelli and Ortiz scanned the area for surveillance cameras. It didn't look promising. They went to Officer Marktiz, the uniform who'd called it in.

"Any witnesses?"

"Naw." Marktiz shook his head as he retrieved more tape from the trunk of his car. "Nobody stepped up, nobody around. Nothing. We'll help with a canvass."

Cordelli and Ortiz knew coming into this that it didn't look good.

The vehicle used in the abduction of Sarah and Cole Griffin came up stolen, now it had been torched—all premeditated.

"They must've had a switch car ready," Ortiz said. "I don't like this, it's all too methodical. Now we could have homicides. I do not freakin' like this."

"Yup."

Thick smoke clouds churned from the wreck as crews doused the flames. Cordelli and Ortiz turned as a gust sent a choking column their way. When they turned back, Cordelli faced an old problem walking at him: Detective Larry Brewer.

"What the hell is he doing here?"

Cordelli had worked with Brewer a few years back. The guy's ego was bigger than Yankee Stadium and fit with his near-inhuman aura. Brewer's utter baldness accentuated his bulging black eyes and his pointed ears, earning him the nickname "Diablo."

"What're you doing at my scene, Cordelli?" Brewer's jaw worked a wad of gum.

"We're on a case."

"You're contaminating my scene. We've got an ongoing undercover operation with the task force."

"We're working an abduction—mother and son—and that's our vehicle."

"I saw your alert. My case takes precedence over yours, we're taking over. It's ours now. My captain will advise your supervisor to advise you to skip back to Midtown South and get me your notes."

"We're not going anywhere, Larry," Cordelli said. "We're going to wait here for Lieutenant Reston to give us the green light on *our* scene."

Brewer grimaced, twisting his neck until his Adam's apple popped. "You're in our way, Vic." Brewer stepped into Cordelli's space just as Brewer's cell phone rang. He answered it, pointed his chin to the other side of a patrol car and he and his partner stepped away.

"He's a piece of work," Ortiz said.

"He's a slab of misery."

With the sound of pressured water against metal, Cordelli turned sadly back to the smoldering ruin.

"I'll bet we have somebody in there, Juanita."

"I'm praying we don't. Look."

Beyond the tape, Jeff Griffin had stepped from a taxi to anxiously survey the scene. Cordelli cursed himself for giving up the address, but Griffin was right—he would've found out.

Cordelli had requested two cars be dispatched to the house of the registered owner on Steeldown Road in the

Bronx, and he'd hoped the units got to it before Brewer got a chance to claim it.

Now, a firefighter at the wreckage was shouting and signaling for Lieutenant Reston to look into the SUV's interior. Whatever was inside could not be viewed from a distance. Cordelli saw Reston lean in, saw his face crease before he directed his men to their next steps.

"Damn," Cordelli said.

It was clear to him what they'd found.

It was clear to Jeff Griffin, too.

He was experienced with these scenes.

From where he stood, he read Reston's face and it hit him.

Oh, Jesus.

The dread Jeff had locked in the darkest reaches of his heart lashed against the chains that held it there. He saw the fire crews unfold the large yellow tarps—the universal flag of tragedy, the confirmation of death. He watched them take care positioning the covering. Protecting the scene while respecting the dignity of the dead.

He was familiar with the funereal procedure.

He'd performed it himself.

He knew what happened to fire victims—how their skin cracked, how their bones broke, how the skulls could shatter and how the bodies could be burned beyond recognition.

Sarah and Cole.

He began shaking, pierced by one thought.

I have to see them. I have to see for myself.

Everything went white.

Time froze.

He could not immediately remember physically getting as close as he did to the SUV's charred remains before hands seized him and dragged him back while he screamed for Sarah and Cole. All he saw was the brilliant yellow sheet. All he could imagine was the horror under it. He didn't know how much time had passed or how he came to be in the rear seat of a police car with his hands covering his nose and mouth, blood roaring in his ears. For a moment or two he'd cried and when he dried his face, the clink of the handcuffs around his wrists alerted him to a man standing just outside the car.

"Mr. Griffin? I'm Detective Brewer. Can you hear me now?"

"Yes."

"Okay, I'm going to start again. You have the right to remain silent...."

15

Jeff Griffin was placed in a stark interview room at One Police Plaza.

He'd waived his right to an attorney.

Left alone to contend with the agony of no one confirming that Sarah and Cole were dead, all he could do was pray.

Please, tell me it's not them in the SUV, I'm begging you.

Adrenaline rippled through him.

He flattened his hands on the wooden table in front of him while memories strobed, snapshots of standing near Times Square with Sarah and feeling her arm around him. Tight. *We have to hang on and work this out.* Snapshots of the joy in Cole's face as he marveled at the skyscrapers.

They can't be dead.

By degrees Jeff regained the strength to keep from losing control. He had to hang on. He had to keep hoping, he told himself as events after the fire came into focus. Upon his arrest, Cordelli had rushed to the car, confronting the bald detective, demanding answers.

"Hey, Brewer! Where the hell are you taking him?"

Brewer had flashed his palm to Cordelli while he ended a cell phone call with "—okay, so we're good at Steeldown Road in the Bronx." Then he'd turned to Cordelli. "Step back, Vic. He's mine now. We've got two homicides, this is our operation."

"He's got nothing to do with this the way you think, Brewer."

"You don't know squat. Just get your notes to me or it's your ass!"

Brewer had gotten into the passenger seat of the unmarked Ford and closed the door. His partner, Klaver, was behind the wheel. The motor roared and its siren yelped as the Crown Vic left for the Brooklyn Bridge, Manhattan and NYPD headquarters downtown. They took Jeff up the elevator to a cell-like room where he waited.

Time swept by and he'd stared at the cinder-block walls and at his own reflection in the two-way mirror where he saw a man struggling not to fall into the abyss.

Sarah. Cole.

A click. The door opened. Brewer and Klaver entered.

They dropped file folders and notebooks on the table, dragged and positioned the two empty chairs opposite Jeff, then filled them.

"Are my wife and my son dead?"

The room went cold.

The detectives stared at Jeff.

Klaver was fair-skinned and wore the somber, pointed face of an undertaker. Brewer's expression burned with the intensity of an embittered cop bereft of compassion.

"The medical examiner and our people are still processing," Brewer said.

"You can tell me the presumed age and gender," Jeff said.

"Can't do that."

"Why not?"

"The remains are in bad shape. We're awaiting confirmation."

"Bull. You have an idea who's in that SUV."

"I know this is a horrible time," Brewer said. "We'll let you know as soon as we can. We've been reading your report and statement to Detectives Cordelli and Ortiz. We've made a lot of calls here and in Montana and right now we need to ask you a few questions."

"About what? I've been through this with Cordelli, he knows everything."

"The vehicle is linked to our operation."

"What operation?"

"We can't disclose details. A lot is in play right now."

"What does that mean? What the hell is this? My wife and son were abducted, they could be dead and you don't give a damn!"

"It doesn't get any more serious than this and we'll get through it faster if you help us to help you."

Blinking back his anger Jeff looked away, shaking his head in disgust.

"This won't take long, Jeff." Klaver spoke in the softer voice of the "good cop" and opened a folder. "There are a few things we need your help on."

Jeff's silence invited Klaver's first question.

"Take us back, step by step, to your arrival in New York, up to and immediately after you reported Sarah and Cole had been abducted."

Jeff inhaled and recounted every detail for the detectives. Afterward, he answered Klaver's follow-up questions, then Brewer weighed in.

"You and Sarah had lost a child. It took a toll on your marriage. You were planning to separate and were arguing about it at the time of Sarah and Cole's disappearance, is that correct?"

"What is this?"

"Is that correct?" Brewer said.

"Yes, I told Cordelli everything."

"Not quite everything," Brewer said.

"Did you accuse Neil Larson of having an affair with your wife?" Klaver continued.

Jeff was stunned at how they'd found out and how they were using it.

"Jeff?"

What was happening?

"Did you accuse Neil Larson of having an affair with your wife?"

Brewer watched Jeff swallow hard before answering. "Yes."

"And did you confront him in a school parking lot where he worked with your wife, to the point others had to restrain you?" Brewer asked.

Jeff hesitated at the twisting of the truth.

"Yes."

"And did that form part of your argument with Sarah just before you reported that she and Cole had been abducted?"

"Yes."

"So you confirm these facts?" Brewer said.

"Yes."

"What's your relationship with Donnie and Sheri Dalfini?" Brewer asked.

"Relationship? I don't know them. It's their SUV."

"How did you get their address in the Bronx?"

"I went to a store, Metro Gifts or something, and got them to let me look at their security camera. It was pointed at where Sarah and Cole were standing and I got the plate. Then I searched the plate online and took a cab to the address."

"Why didn't you check with the police first?" Brewer asked.

"I had the feeling that no one was looking for my family."

Brewer and Klaver paused to consider Jeff's answer.

"Jeff," Brewer said, "as a firefighter you've been to death scenes. You probably know a lot of people in law enforcement back home in Montana. You probably know something of investigative procedures."

Jeff said nothing, uneasy at the picture being drawn around him.

"You seemed to get out to Steeldown Road very fast to talk to Sheri Dalfini about her stolen SUV. Almost as if you wanted to get to the Dalfini residence before police *but* immediately after you'd reported Sarah and Cole's abduction. And then you got to the fire at the speed of light."

"I don't understand."

"It just doesn't look right to us at this stage," Brewer said. "It just doesn't add up."

The floor shifted under Jeff as realization rolled over him with seismic force.

"I don't like what you're implying."

Brewer shifted his lower jaw. In all his time and over all the cases he'd worked he'd come to respect one abiding rule: at the outset of an investigation everyone lies, and when the facts and pieces of evidence emerge, the lies melt like dirty snow in the rain.

"Jeff, I want you to be straight with me here," Brewer said. "When you believed your wife was maybe fucking Neil Larson and going to leave you I bet it hurt, what with just losing your baby and all. And I'm thinking that maybe you fantasized about making sure Sarah never left you, that maybe you came up with an elaborate fool-proof plan. You take her to a location, step away, the cameras record it—"

"What! That's crazy!"

"Maybe something went wrong, or you didn't know who you were dealing with."

"This is insane! Tell me who was in that SUV!"

Glaring at Jeff, Brewer reached for his BlackBerry, entered a command.

"This was in the SUV, Jeff. It matches the description in your report."

He slid the device to Jeff, carefully studying his reaction as Jeff looked at the crisp photograph of what remained of a New York Jets ball cap. Only a ball cap. Half consumed by fire, half scorched, but clearly identifiable, small, white with the green jet patch on white, familiar to Jeff as the one they bought for Cole.

Oh, Jesus. Oh, Christ, no.

Jeff looked at it until it blurred.

They're gone.

Jeff ached to pull Cole and Sarah from the darkness.

Sitting there in that small police room, the shock of seeing Cole's burned ball cap propelled him back to Montana and the morning he'd found Lee Ann.

Her little face all blue, her mouth a tiny O.

His futile efforts to save her.

He thought of his baby daughter with Sarah and Cole and that moment he saw the three of them through the window from his pickup in the driveway.

That perfect moment.

He struggled to hang on to those images but they were gone.

Jeff put his face in his hands and in that cold, hard room he never felt the heat of Brewer's and Klaver's stares as Brewer slowly slid back his BlackBerry. Chairs scraped; the detectives gathered their files.

"We'll leave you alone to consider matters," Brewer said.

The door opened to ringing phones, conversations and the squawk of walkie-talkies. Above the din Jeff recognized Cordelli's voice in a fragment of conversation. "Brewer! Did you get my message? My supervisor called yours and—"

The door closed, leaving Jeff alone, adrift in a sea of torment. Minutes passed with the same questions hammering against his skull: Who would steal his wife and son? Who? Why? His confusion and grief coiled into anger.

He would find them.

Whoever did this, he would hunt them down.

The door handle clicked.

This time Brewer entered with Cordelli.

"You can go now. Cordelli will take you out," Brewer said.

"What?" Jeff threw his question to Cordelli, then back to Brewer.

"Thank you for your help. We'll be in touch," Brewer said.

Jeff swallowed.

"What about my wife and son? Can I see them?"

"It's not them," Brewer said.

"It's not them?" Jeff absorbed the news.

"The medical examiner just confirmed the remains

belong to two adult males. We're still working on identifying them."

"What the hell is this? You show me my son's cap,
you lead me to believe my family's dead, you accuse me
of planning this whole thing. What is this?"

"It's part of an investigation," Brewer said.

Jeff pulled himself up to face Brewer.

"This some kind of sick joke for you, you prick?"
Jeff said.

Brewer stood his ground and Cordelli inserted himself between them to dial down the tension.

"Come on, Jeff." Cordelli put his hand on his shoulder. "Let's grab a coffee and I'll take you back to your
hotel."

In midtown Manhattan, not far from the Long Is-
land Rail Road maintenance yards, where Thirty-third
Street rolled down an industrial no-man's-land to the
Hudson, there was a twenty-four-hour diner called the
Terminal Café.

Cops liked it because it was quiet and out of the way,
Cordelli told Jeff after they'd taken a booth.

The soft clink of cutlery floated on air thick with the
aroma of onions and fried bacon. A bullnecked man
with a brush cut and white apron came to their table.
Cordelli got a coffee.

Jeff wanted nothing.

The man left and Cordelli looked at Jeff.

"You have every right to be pissed off."

"Don't tell me how I should feel."

Cordelli's coffee came; he dripped some cream in it.

"About ten years ago in East Harlem, a mother reported her five-year-old son abducted. Brewer caught
the case. She gave a description of a suspect. She had

everybody going in a million directions for four days until a janitor found the kid's body bound under a storage room staircase.

"The M.E. said the boy had been abused and was actually alive for two days bound under those stairs. Ultimately, evidence pointed to the mother but Brewer never, ever forgave himself for not going harder on her because he could've saved the boy.

"That's Brewer. Since then he doesn't trust anyone. That's all of us, really. Everyone's a suspect. People lie all the time. We see horrible things, it hardens you."

Jeff gazed out the window, across the Hudson at the lights of New Jersey, his emotions roiling.

"What's this got to do with me? What are you doing to find my family besides wasting time by dragging me through your police bullshit?"

"We're working with the FBI and every police jurisdiction in New York, New Jersey and Connecticut. And we're putting out an alert tonight with pictures and information. By morning, everyone in Greater New York will be looking for Sarah and Cole."

Cordelli's response gave Jeff a measure of assurance, but disbelief and fear twisted in his gut.

"There's a double homicide in the SUV, my wife and son are missing—I deserve to know more. What else do you know?"

"We think Cole's ball cap came off when they moved to a switch vehicle."

"But why take Cole and Sarah? They're from Montana. How is this connected to Brewer's operation and his task force, what is it?"

"The investigation is tight."

"Meaning?"

"No one will tell me much yet but that will change."

"This is bureaucratic bullshit! Is Brewer's operation more important than my family's life?"

"No, it's not like that. We're sorting everything out but our case will get rolled into his. Brewer is the lead on a major undercover operation that's been ongoing with about twelve local, state, federal and international agencies looking into organized crime."

"What kind? Drugs, human trafficking? I told you guys I haven't gotten any ransom demands. Sarah would've given them my cell number."

"The task force is investigating organized crime and ties to global networks. That's all I've got so far."

"So Sarah and Cole's abduction could be connected to anything. I read a news story about people in South America being abducted for their organs. Christ." Jeff ran his hand over his face, shaking his head.

"Don't do that. You'll make yourself crazy imagining the worst scenarios."

"The worst? It can't get much worse than it is now!"

"Look, Jeff, we'll concentrate on what we know. We'll do all we can to build on it and work with Brewer because we need one another's help on this. We've got the alert, we're processing the SUV. We're going flat out."

Jeff took in a long breath.

"I'll update you on everything that I can tell you."

Jeff nodded.

"Meantime, promise me no more amateur detective work."

"I'll keep looking for them. That's my promise. You would do the same and you know it."

Cordelli's pause confirmed Jeff's point.

"I'll drive you back to your hotel." Cordelli reached

for his phone. "I'll have one of our people bunk with you and put uniforms at your hotel."

"Why?"

"It's what we do."

"No, I don't want that. I'm not afraid of these assholes. Don't waste people on me. Put them on the street looking for Sarah and Cole. You've got the phone clone thing, so if I get a call, you guys get it at the same time."

Cordelli considered the need to man Jeff's hotel at this stage.

"You want me to set up anything with our support services? Want a shrink?"

Jeff shook his head.

"I don't need anything like that."

As they drove across midtown at night, a marked NYPD patrol unit stopped them at an intersection that was being blocked off. Cordelli tapped his horn and a uniform came to their car. Cordelli showed his detective's badge.

"Sorry, Detective, you gotta wait. Rules are rules."

Several minutes later the wail of sirens, the growl of police motorcycles, preceded the gleaming escort units of a VIP motorcade streaking by.

"Freakin' UN meeting," Cordelli muttered, waving to the cop who let him pass. "Yeah, yeah." Cordelli maneuvered through the intersection. They went another ten blocks before they stopped in front of the Central Suites Inn on West Twenty-ninth.

Jeff didn't move.

"You okay to go in?" Cordelli asked.

"No, but I'm going in."

"Just take it easy. Keep your cell phone charged. You can call me at any hour. Try to get some rest. I'll see you soon."

After Jeff got out and Cordelli drove off he stood alone in the street.

He stared at the hotel's entrance for a long, difficult moment as if watching a part of his life replay itself. It was only hours earlier that he'd walked through that lobby with Cole and Sarah, never dreaming that he would be walking back through it without them.

16

Jeff entered his hotel alone.

He kept telling himself this was not a dream, they were not out sightseeing or shopping and he would not meet up with them later.

Two murders, my God.

Reality stabbed at him with such ferocity he stopped to steady himself against a wingback chair. But the world still turned, evening life in the lobby was normal. With his pulse throbbing Jeff forced himself to stay calm and breathe evenly as he approached the girl at the front desk.

"Yes, sir?"

"Any messages for Griffin in 1212?"

Her name tag said Micki. She typed rapidly on her keyboard.

"Nothing, sir." She smiled.

Jeff noticed a small spike with paper messages near her keyboard.

"What about those?"

"They're old ones that have been relayed and en-

tered into our system. Is there anything else I can help
you with, sir?"

Can you help me find my family?

"No. Thank you."

Jeff went to the elevator. While waiting he was joined
by two women who were well into their sixties; they
chatted softly about their day as the elevator ascended.

"Did your group see Central Park, wasn't it lovely?"

"Oh, it was."

"This is such an exciting city, full of urban grit, isn't
it?" one of the ladies said to Jeff.

He forced a half smile. "Yes, it is."

The women stepped off on the third floor and Jeff
was grateful to be alone as the car droned to the twelfth.
The doors opened to two men, about his height, swar-
thy, unshaven, late twenties, early thirties. Surprised
to see Jeff, they were eager to get on and engaged in
some awkward sidestepping, brushing against him as
he got off, leaving a hint of mild cologne as he glimpsed
their reflections in the large mirror. They seemed to be
watching him with unusual intensity.

He shrugged it off.

A couple of weird tourists.

He walked down the hall to his room. The floor was
quiet but he hesitated at his door.

*Maybe they'll be inside with a wild story. Or maybe
I am really dreaming and this is the point where Sarah
wakes me up.*

His hand shook when he went to insert the plastic
key card. He inhaled and got it to work on his second
try, stepped in and hit the lights.

Empty.

The room had been made. The beds were turned
down crisply. Fresh towels were folded in the polished

bathroom. He conjured up memories of Sarah, Cole, himself, preparing to leave earlier that morning.

He stood there, unable to move, unable to think, and stared at nothing, like the sole survivor left behind in the aftermath. He began to inventory the room and noticed something was not right.

Their luggage.

Some of Sarah's clothes were still nicely folded, a ghostly reminder of her, but some of his clothes had spilled from their bags. Jeff allowed that maids repositioned items to clean but that was not how he and Sarah had left things. Was it? Or had someone rummaged through their clothes, looking for something?

Jeff went to the compartment where he'd left extra cash and traveler's checks, relieved they were still there. But soon unease pinged in the back of his mind.

What is it?

He detected a smell beyond the carpet freshener and disinfectant tile cleaner, something familiar, a weakening trace of cologne.

Where had he smelled it before?

The men at the elevator.

Was it the same cologne in his room?

Jeff's heart rate picked up before he recalled that he'd brushed against one of them. Did he smell it on his shirt? Maybe he shouldn't have refused Cordelli's offer to have cops stay with him. Maybe he should call him.

Maybe I'm just imagining everything?

Jeff started a shower to clear his mind.

He checked to ensure his cell phone's volume was up and set it beside the room's wireless phone, on a shelf near the shower. *Cordelli would have alerted me to any calls, right?* As steam rose around him, guilt and fear rippled through his body. He replayed the day, how it started in turmoil with Sarah before the vanishings, then Cordelli's suspicions, how he'd tracked the SUV to the Bronx to have a gun pointed at him, the fire, two murders and Brewer's accusations.

It's all too much.

It's my fault. Like it was with Lee Ann.

And like it was with Lee Ann, he was helpless again.

My daughter died in my care and I could do nothing.

Where are they? God, are they like that kid, bound somewhere?

Dying.

What should he do? What could he do?

Jeff made the water ice-cold to feel something other than useless and sorry for himself. His skin went numb.

But he endured.

He closed his hands into fists and hammered the walls.

He couldn't cry. He couldn't give up. He would never give up.

After the shower he checked his cell phone.

He checked it every minute.

Jeff thought about what Cordelli had said about the alert and reasoned that he should tell their family and friends back home because they were going to hear, if they hadn't already with all the police calls to Montana.

Sarah had an aunt and uncle in Billings. In Laurel, there was Sarah's principal. Jeff also needed to tell his boss, Clay, Sarah's friends, Alice and Val. He scrolled through their numbers.

What do I say? How do I begin to tell them?

His thoughts scattered beyond the horror he was facing, back over time, beyond the agony he'd suffered with his daughter's death, back to the moment he'd learned his mother and father had been killed.

It was the summer he'd turned fifteen and his parents were on vacation in Canada while he stayed with his grandfather, who'd given him a summer job helping him with his towing business.

It was the weekend and they'd gone to the fair in Billings to have some fun. Jeff loved the shooting gallery and the hot dogs. He remembered how he had just bought one for himself and his grandfather when a couple of highway patrol troopers, friends of his grandfather, appeared and took his grandfather aside.

The troopers' grave faces contrasted with the joyous air of the fair. They raised their voices over the noise and Jeff heard fragments as one of them told his grandfather, "We tried your radio in your truck...somebody told us you were here at the fair...so damned sorry..."

Their eyes turned to Jeff, and they removed their hats when they joined his grandfather to approach him. Something terrible was coming and he felt his body go numb.

"Jeff, son," his grandpa started, the tears rolling down his face, "your mom and dad... Oh, Jesus..."

Jeff let the hot dogs fall to the grass.

At fifteen, the world he knew had ended amid the deafening rock music, the diesel roar of the Scrambler and screams from the midway.

Jeff was at a loss then, as he was now, confronting the need to tell their people in Montana what had happened to Sarah and Cole. He thought hard about calling but he couldn't bear to hear their voices, their horror and their questions.

He wrote the same short text message to each of them:

Sarah and Cole are lost in NYC. Very worried. Police trying to find them. Tell you more when I know it. Please pray.

Jeff closed his phone, stood at his hotel window and searched the lights of Manhattan as sirens echoed in the night.

17

Nearly four miles south of where Jeff Griffin stood, Sheri Dalfini was on the brink.

At any moment this redheaded piece of work from the Bronx was going to give up something. Brewer was sure of it as he turned the laptop so she could see the arson-homicide photographs.

A little visual aid.

The two figures in the pictures were barely recognizable as human. Amid the two black masses there was a piece of shirt here, a shoe there, something that looked like a hand.

Sheri's gasp bounced off the walls of the interview room at One Police Plaza where Brewer had been questioning her relentlessly since they'd released Griffin. Brewer was using a different strategy with her than he'd used with Griffin.

"Take a good, long look, Sheri," Brewer said, "because if you don't start telling me what I need to know, things are going to get real bad for you."

Brewer showed her slide after slide.

The victims looked like charcoal mannequins. Their

hair and facial features had been burned off, leaving split skin and white teeth exposed in a death grimace.

"Who are these people, Sheri?"

She shook her head.

"Where are Sarah and Cole Griffin?"

She continued shaking her head, frustrating Brewer.

"We're talking about charges with four victims, Sheri—two dead and two missing."

Tears began rolling down her face.

"You're not telling me everything you know." Brewer shoved two sticks of gum into his mouth and stared at her impassively. She was something, all right, with that explosion of red hair, the T-shirt with the pit bull and the Harley. Butterflies, flowers, dragons and angel warriors swirled along her arms. Brewer never got the tattoo craze and never would.

While Sheri sniffled at the crime scene pictures he resumed flipping through his folder on Sheri Marie Dalfini, age twenty-nine, born in Brooklyn, married to Donald Dean Dalfini, age thirty-four. Two children: Benjamin, age eight, and Saleena, age five.

Sheri's occupation: mostly salesclerk. Donnie had been a factory worker at the Jebzite Foundry where they made sledgehammers before he was laid off about six months ago.

Sheri and Donnie were known to the police.

When she was nineteen Sheri was charged with shoplifting cosmetics. The charges were later dismissed. When she was twenty-two Sheri was charged with felony credit card fraud. She'd bought concert tickets, clothes and jewelry from someone who'd obtained them with a stolen credit card. Again, the charges were dismissed.

As for Donnie, two years ago he was charged with

assault after beating up a guy outside a bar in the Bronx. Donnie claimed self-defense. The case against him was dropped.

The handgun at Sheri's home was registered to Rosie Dalfini, Donnie's mother. Sheri said Donnie wanted it in the house because they feared the people who stole their SUV might come after their family.

The SUV, the white 2010 GMC Terrain, was the key.

Brewer's task force was alerted as soon as the SUV had emerged in Sarah and Cole Griffin's abduction. And when the Brooklyn patrol unit saw it ablaze a few hours later, a second alarm sounded.

The Dalfini SUV was listed with scores of stolen vehicles suspected of being tied to the major organized-crime operation under investigation by the task force. The operation involved a mind-boggling number of local, state, federal and international law enforcement agencies. It went far beyond stolen cars, and had been designated a classified priority reaching the highest levels of government security and secrecy.

As tragic as the abductions and homicides were, they had yielded Brewer his first solid leads.

Sheri and Donnie Dalfini were critical to advancing those leads, Brewer was certain of it. Clicking his pen and chewing his gum, he reread the file. Something about this pair didn't sit right.

Brewer saw a tiny red flag that went back almost a year.

At that time, Donnie had made an insurance claim after reporting that a large flat-screen valued at three thousand dollars was stolen from their home. He had a receipt from the New Jersey store where he'd said he'd purchased it. The store had since closed down, but while verification of the purchase was difficult, the insurance company paid out on the claim.

Not long after the payout, the New York State Insurance Frauds Bureau got an anonymous tip that Donnie had bought the TV at a garage sale in Connecticut for three hundred dollars, had staged the burglary and submitted a false claim. An investigation by Frauds Bureau investigators from General Unit was inconclusive, but Donnie Dalfini's file was flagged.

They were watching him.

Some six months ago, at the time Donnie lost his job, he and Sheri purchased a fully loaded 2010 GMC Terrain for $34,391. The financing they got, based on Sheri's job, meant high monthly payments, on top of all of their other bills.

It made no sense.

Not the brightest people in the Bronx, Brewer thought, *unless they had a plan, some sort of scheme.*

Three weeks ago, they reported the SUV stolen from the parking lot at the Neverpoint Mall. Donnie made an insurance claim. While it was being processed, the Insurance Frauds Bureau's Auto Unit was alerted and the SUV was flagged as a potential fraudulent claim. The NYPD Auto Crime and Insurance Fraud Unit were notified. That unit then alerted Brewer's joint task force.

And now here they were, with Brewer losing it with Sheri.

"Where are Sarah and Cole Griffin?"

"I told you, I don't know."

"Who are the dead people in the picture?"

"I don't know. Why do you keep asking me the same thing? I told you everything I know from the moment the police came to my home and asked me to come down here and help answer questions about our stolen SUV."

"We keep going around in circles."

"Maybe I should have a lawyer?"

"You waived your rights when we brought you in."

"That was when I thought you were treating me as a victim and not someone who is part of—part of this! Oh, Jesus, let me go home and see my kids."

"How do you know Jeff Griffin?"

"He's a freakin' stranger to me. I told you what happened."

"Where's Donnie?"

"I told you, he's looking for a job in New Jersey."

"Did Donnie kill the people in the SUV?"

"No. He's in New Jersey."

"Where? The numbers you gave us don't seem to work?"

"Bayonne, or Elizabeth. I don't know."

"Does he have Sarah and Cole?"

"God, no! We got nothing to do with that shit!"

Pages snapped as Brewer flipped through the file again. His jawline started throbbing.

"Do you know what insurance investigators at the State Frauds Bureau found out after you made the claim for the SUV?"

"How would I know?"

"They found that just before the claim you had an extra key made."

"So?"

"Mall security cameras show you touching a wheel before leaving the vehicle and then an unidentified suspect touching the same spot before driving off with it."

Sheri said nothing, then flinched when Brewer's hand whip-slapped on the table.

"We know what you and Donnie did! We know you staged the theft!" Brewer stood and raised his voice.

"Listen good, Sheri. As we speak we're preparing to execute search warrants at your house in the morning. You will be charged in connection with two homicides and the kidnappings of Sarah and Cole Griffin. You will sleep in a holding cell tonight, you will not go home and you will never see your kids again."

Sheri didn't move.

"Now, you can bring in a lawyer and we'll call the D.A. and prepare charges. Or, you can tell me who else is involved, help us and we'll tell the D.A. you're being cooperative. Sheri, you're facing a world of trouble and this is your last chance, the only way you can help yourself. Our offer is going to expire in about five minutes."

Sheri was frozen.

"Do you understand what's at stake for you? This is the end of the road for you, Sheri Marie Dalfini. You're going to prison."

She stared through Brewer to a lifetime of hard living, a lifetime of mistakes, bad choices and anguish. She couldn't take it anymore. Her chin began to quiver. Brewer had played his hand and at this point he'd let her have the quiet. The life she'd had, as sorry as it was, was over.

He had her.

"I told Donnie it was stupid for us to buy that goddamned SUV. We couldn't afford it. But no, he had to have it. He said he needed it after losing his job at the foundry so he wouldn't look like a loser."

Brewer slid a box of tissues to her.

"The payments were too much. We had to go to his mother for money, then for food. When it finally sunk in with Donnie, he started asking some of his asshole friends at the bar about people who could help us out of our jam.

"He found a guy who would pay us two thousand for the SUV if we left it in the lot. He'd make it disappear, then we could make the insurance claim and still be ahead to pay off some bills."

"Who is this guy?"

"I don't know."

"Think!"

"I can't remember his name exactly, but after the SUV was gone, Donnie never got the money. Donnie couldn't find the guy. Donnie's friends warned Donnie not to mess with the guy, to shut up about the money, which we would never see, and that if we told anybody we'd be ratted out to insurance. That's when Donnie got scared and got his mother's gun.

"Then out of the blue, friends get word to Donnie that the guy that owes him the money has a one-time high-paying job, or something, that was yesterday."

"Is this the Bayonne or Elizabeth thing?"

"I don't know, because I haven't heard from Donnie since the day before yesterday. I don't know nothing and I can't find Donnie. We got bill collectors calling, then this Montana guy scares me to death by showing up at our home looking for his wife and kid and I'm losing my freakin' mind and now our SUV is—" Sheri began choking on her words "—and those people in the pictures and, Jesus, I don't know anything…I swear."

"Who, Sheri?" Brewer said. "Who is the guy that Donnie went to work for, the guy who owed him for the SUV? Give us the names of the people involved, the people who wanted your SUV."

Brewer slid a pad and freshly sharpened pencil toward her.

"Give us names and if they're real I'll do all I can to help you."

Sheri nodded, brushed the tears from her cheeks, took up the pencil.

"I don't know—I'm not sure of the spellings."

"Give us what you can."

As her tears stained the paper she began printing, slowly and carefully.

18

Tranquil.

Acting on Sheri Dalfini's information, eight more unmarked police cars rolled into the crime-peppered enclave in the low hundreds, east of Morningside Park.

Would they find Sarah and Cole Griffin here?

Brewer watched from his window.

Despair permeated this corner of the city where living meant dying a little every day. Here, dreams twisted into rage against the system until they yielded the belief that to survive you have to take what you want. It was the same story in neighborhoods like this everywhere, Brewer thought.

This is how it was for Omarr Aimes.

His name was the one Sheri Dalfini had given them. All she had was "Omar Big Time," with Omarr spelled with one *r*. Brewer ran it through the computers searching variations, aliases, and sure enough, Omarr Lincoln Roderick Aimes, aka "Sweet Time," aka "Sweet Ride," aka "Big Time," came up. Age, thirty-two.

Brewer was surprised Omarr had lived this long.

He'd been shot four separate times. Started out as a juvie boosting cars; went inside and came out a hardened banger, working his way up the drug-dealer food chain. Omarr then took to a righteous cause with some "brotherhood," which was tied to international smuggling networks that had fallen under Brewer's investigation and the abduction.

Was Omarr a player in Sarah and Cole's kidnapping?

Klaver eased their Ford to a stop before a marked unit. Cordelli and Ortiz were behind them. A few hours ago the brass had folded Cordelli's case into Brewer's operation. Cordelli and Ortiz, who was easy on the eyes, were now part of the task force, assigned to work with Brewer and Klaver.

What a treat, Brewer thought before his concentration was broken by the crackle of the radio clipped to the uniformed officer standing point by the patrol car.

"Ever think of using your earpiece, sport?" Brewer kept his voice low. "They're not supposed to know we're coming."

Earlier, after Sheri Dalfini had given them Omarr, Brewer and Klaver worked the computers and the phones with their confidential informants. It didn't take long for their C.I.s to point them to Morningside, where Omarr lived under the radar.

They'd alerted their supervisor, who got things moving on a warrant, identifying Omarr as a wanted suspect in the homicides of two unidentified males and the kidnapping.

Given the magnitude of the offenses, the NYPD's Emergency Service Unit and scores of other police were dispatched to the marshaling point two blocks from the location. Brewer saw all the u-cars but lost count. Uniformed patrols had set up the outer perimeter, deflecting traffic, while the tactical squad set up on the building.

Out of sight, down the block from the building, squad Chief Lieutenant Clint Gatlin locked onto Omarr's apartment through his binoculars.

Third floor, unit 12.

His team of heavily armed officers had already studied the building's floor plan. They had, in near-silence, swiftly evacuated people from the line of fire in the surrounding residences and now waited inside.

Paint blistered along the walls where Gatlin's squad had taken positions on the stairs leading up to unit 12, on the landing above it, the fire escape behind it and on the roof.

Gatlin's information showed that the subject possessed automatic and semiautomatic guns and should be considered dangerous.

His team would make a forced rapid entry.

After a final round of radio checks, Gatlin gave the green light to his squad sergeant.

Within seconds, the team smashed through the apartment's door and rear window; their helmet lights raked the darkness as they swept the living room, kitchen, stormed down the hallway to the first bedroom where they found an elderly woman awake, alone and afraid in her small bed.

In the second bedroom they found a girl, about six or seven years old, alone in her bed, holding a stuffed teddy bear and crying at the big gun-toting men stampeding through her home.

The third bedroom was empty, but men's boxers, shirts, pants, were strewn about the floor and the bed. Clothes spilled from the dresser.

The bathroom was checked, closets were checked;

special equipment was used to scan the walls and ceiling for body mass. The entire unit was inspected three times before it was cleared and declared safe.

The squad leader radioed Gatlin, who alerted Brewer.

Brewer, Klaver, Cordelli and Ortiz donned body armor and headed down the street. By the time they'd entered the apartment building, Louella May Bell, the unit's rent-payer, was in her robe and seated at the kitchen table under guard by the ESU.

"Ma'am, are there any weapons in this home?" the officer asked her.

"I don't have any guns. You're the people with the guns."

When Brewer arrived, he waved the ESU away. He and Cordelli sat with Louella at the kitchen table while Ortiz and Klaver stayed with the little girl in the living room. Ortiz looked around as Klaver tried to calm the child by showing her a game with butterflies on his BlackBerry.

"Don't worry, everything's okay," Klaver said. "What's your name, sweetheart?"

The girl didn't respond. She watched the game without smiling.

In the kitchen, Brewer placed the warrant on the table next to Louella, snapped open his notebook and began jotting the date, time, address.

"Miss Bell, we understand you're Omarr's grandmother. We'd like to talk to him. Could you tell us where we can find him?"

Her mournful eyes reflected a life of struggle, an uncomplaining endurance of police trouble concerning her grandson.

"I done told the other men and I'll tell you the same, Omarr's not here."

"We've figured that out. Where is he?"

"Why you got to trouble him? He's doing the best he can. He's had a hard, hard life. He never knew who his father was. Did you know my daughter was raped at fifteen when she had him? A year after he was born she was murdered. Omarr's daughter Shereesa means the world to him."

"That's the little girl who lives here also?"

"Yes, sir, she's seven, and Omarr loves her to death."

Taking stock of the apartment, Ortiz thought it was well-kept with modest dignity. The sofa, coffee table, area rugs, lamps, were immaculate. Framed photos of people and keepsakes were lovingly displayed on the shelves.

Ortiz inspected each of them.

Many were of older men and women, looked like they were on vacations, a few of younger people, including a good number of the little girl.

Ortiz stopped at one framed picture: a birthday picture.

The little girl was smiling before a huge cake with seven candles and the words *Happy Birthday Shereesa* iced on it.

The man standing behind her, smiling with his hands on her shoulder, was Omarr. Ortiz's attention went to Omarr's hand.

She concentrated on the ring he was wearing.

Oh, Jesus.

In the kitchen Brewer would not let up with his questions for Louella Bell.

"I told you I don't know where Omarr is." Louella's eyes shifted to the doorway where Ortiz was standing.

When Brewer and Cordelli turned, Ortiz tilted her head and they joined her in the living room.

"Look at this one," Ortiz pointed her BlackBerry at the birthday photo. "Look at his ring." Ortiz then turned her small screen to show Brewer and Cordelli the color picture she'd cued and enlarged.

It was the same ring.

The photo was among dozens provided by the crime scene people.

It was the ring found on one of the victims at the SUV fire in Brooklyn.

"Well, well, well," Brewer said.

Ortiz glanced back toward the little girl, a gesture that suggested Brewer be careful. Then he took Ortiz's BlackBerry and returned to the kitchen.

"Miss Bell." Brewer showed Louella the enlarged picture of the ring from the crime scene. "Omarr wears a ring just like that, doesn't he?"

She stared at the ring in the picture for the longest time, not moving, not saying anything until her tired eyes brimmed with tears.

"Miss Bell—" Brewer cleared his throat "—does Omarr have a dentist?"

Louella closed her eyes.

She was not a stupid woman.

The day she had dreaded was here.

The day part of her had died when her daughter was killed had come again with an armed invasion and four grim-faced detectives standing in her home at four in the morning.

Louella May Bell knew.

"I have a card in my purse."

She swallowed and went to stand but her knees gave out.

Brewer and Cordelli caught her, set her gently back in her chair.

Suddenly Shereesa flew to her and the two held on to each other.

"It's just us now, child, just us."

19

Jeff Griffin was too tense to sleep.

He dozed, awakened and then drifted into that torpid state between consciousness and fantasy.

In his darkest hour he found a flash of happiness: a vision of himself with Sarah, Lee Ann and Cole together. It passed in brilliant light like a dying star before the horror descended, crushing him until he woke to the nightmare.

On the luggage rack at the foot of their bed, he saw Sarah's sweater, a folded top and pants. On the neatly made bed beside him, Cole's underwear, shorts and T-shirts.

These were the remnants of yesterday.

He was alone in the aftermath.

It was 6:20 a.m.

He grabbed his cell phone from the nightstand, thankful it was fully charged.

No messages. No texts. Nothing.

He called down to the front desk. A man answered.

"No, sir, there are no messages for 1212."

Jeff placed the handset back in the cradle. Pain hammered from the inside of his skull; his stomach was cramping from having not eaten for some twenty-four hours.

They need you. Get to work.

He started the room's coffeemaker, then took a shower. Images of the car fire and corpses swirled in the water's rush until he remembered Cordelli's caution.

"You'll make yourself crazy imagining the worst scenarios."

Stepping from the shower he thought, *first things first*. His stomach roiled to the point of nausea. He had to eat something. Sarah, a believer in contingency, had put a couple of apples and granola bars in her bag.

Okay, that was breakfast.

Jeff ate the food and drank black coffee, deciding he would call Cordelli for an update. Maybe the cops had a lead from the fire victims? As Jeff reached for the hotel phone, it rang.

His heart skipped. *Please let it be Sarah.* He grabbed it.

"Is this Jeff?" a woman's voice asked. "Jeff Griffin?"

It was not Sarah.

"Who's calling?"

"Melissa Mason from the *New York Post,* I'm trying to reach Jeff Griffin. Would that be you?"

Melissa Mason was caffeine fueled and fast-talking, with a New York accent. Cordelli had told him that police were going to put out a public appeal for help on the case late last night.

"Yes, this is Jeff Griffin."

"Jeff, I'm writing a story for the *Post.* Have you received any word on the whereabouts of your wife and son?"

"No."

"Do you any idea who would do this?"

"No."

"Can you detail for me exactly what happened near Times Square yesterday?" Jeff hesitated, then told her. Melissa punctuated his recounting of events with "uh-huhs," then asked more questions and went over their background. "Sarah's a teacher? And you're a mechanic and a volunteer firefighter in Montana? And Cole is nine? Is he your only child?"

That one stopped Jeff cold. But he answered.

"We had a daughter, Lee Ann. She died at six months."

"Oh, my God, I'm sorry," Melissa said. "This whole ordeal has gotta be horrible for you. What thoughts are going through your mind?"

"I want them back. I don't know who did this, I don't know why. I want them back."

"I understand. Um, Jeff, I'd like to come to your hotel with a photographer to take your picture, would you agree?"

"I don't know, I—"

"We'll go big with Sarah's and Cole's pictures. It'll help find them, Jeff. It'll go on our site, and on the streets, everywhere. It won't take long. We can be there in forty-five minutes, maybe sooner. We'll try sooner."

"All right."

"Do you have a cell phone number, an email address?"

Jeff needed to keep his cell phone clear.

"Just use the hotel number."

After the call Jeff switched on the TV in time to catch a local New York City morning newscast. Sarah and Cole stared back at him.

He didn't move except to adjust the volume as the female anchor read the news.

"We start off this morning with this breaking story of two dead men and the brazen abduction of a schoolteacher from Montana and her nine-year-old son. Tyko Sanderay has more. Tyko?"

The story cut to a reporter in his twenties downtown.

"Yes, thank you, Maria. Police say this strange case all started here, yesterday morning on the fringes of Times Square, when Sarah Griffin and her nine-year-old son, Cole, were abducted by as many as three men in a white SUV. Detectives and FBI agents say this brazen criminal act was caught by security cameras."

Stop-action images of Sarah and Cole being taken quickly into the vehicle played as the reporter's voice carried over them.

"The woman's husband, the boy's father, reported his family missing to the NYPD yesterday morning. Detectives determined it was a stranger abduction. Now, here's where the story gets even more troubling. Within hours of the kidnappings the vehicle was driven into Brooklyn. The vehicle, a 2010 GMC Terrain, was discovered in Brooklyn on fire by an NYPD patrol unit. And we obtained this footage from a viewer who was passing by when firefighters arrived."

The report showed shaky cell phone video of the SUV burning.

"There were several small explosions. When the fire department finally doused the fire, they found the bodies of two males, burned beyond recognition inside, in what has been classified as a double homicide. Maria."

"Tyko, Action News *has just learned that police may have tentatively identified one of the victims as Omarr*

*Lincoln Roderick Aimes, aged thirty-two, after an early-
morning raid on his home near Morningside Park?"*

*"Yes, Maria, our sources have just confirmed that.
Now, police don't know, or aren't saying, who is behind this series of crimes. Nor are they saying why a
schoolteacher and her son on a family vacation to the
city were targets. One source told me this morning that
there's every indication that they're still alive and may
be being held somewhere. The NYPD is working with
the FBI and a multitude of other agencies on this case.
Sources say investigators would not rule out anything
at this stage and they're asking that anyone with any
information call the hotline immediately."*

"And you'll keep us posted, Tyko."

"We will, Maria."

Jeff sat down on the bed, not listening as the news
continued.

*"Thank you. Now in other news, the yearly United
Nations General Assembly Meeting gets under way,
and with more than one hundred and fifty world leaders come the usual traffic headaches...."*

As Jeff struggled to absorb everything, the hotel
room phone began ringing again and he got up to answer it without adjusting the TV.

*"A chief concern for security officials is the planned
visit to Battery Park for the 9/11 memorial by the Russian president and the president of Mykrekistan, the
troubled Russian republic. Officials are bracing for
what could be violent protests against the Mykrekistan
government for alleged human rights...."*

The hotel phone continued ringing until Jeff shifted
his attention from the TV and answered.

"Good morning, this is Russell Powell of the *New
York Times*. May I speak with Mr. Jeff Griffin please?"

"I'm Jeff."

"Mr. Griffin, the *Times* is preparing a story on the abduction of Sarah, your wife, and Cole, your son. Would you agree to an interview now over the phone?"

"Yes."

"Thanks. I'd like to start by confirming names and ages—"

Jeff's attention shot to the nightstand as the keypad lights on the cell phone illuminated as it began ringing.

"Wait," he told the *Times* reporter, and put the hotel phone down.

His heart began racing. The number was blocked. Was it Cordelli? Another reporter? He answered and pressed it to his ear.

"Hello?"

Static crackled. Then: "Jeff! Oh, God, Jeff, help us!"

His skin tingled at the sound of Sarah's plea.

"Sarah! Where are you?"

More static and commotion.

"Daddy! Please come and get us! Please hurry!"

"Cole! I'm coming, son! Where are you, tell me!"

The line went silent. Jeff kept the phone welded to his ear, his digital lifeline, his only hope to see his family. For that moment all he heard was the small tinny voice of Russell Powell from the *New York Times* on the handset on the nightstand.

"Hello, Mr. Griffin? Are you still there? Hello?"

Jeff ignored him and hung up.

The cell phone connection was unbroken. As Jeff called into it for Sarah and Cole, it clicked with a deep robotic voice, filtered through a scrambler.

"If you want to see your wife and son again, do as instructed. Your son's bag was mixed up with ours at the airport. When we arranged to have the bags exchanged an item was missing from our bag. We want our property."

"What? I don't understand. Is this Hans Beck? Everything was in the bag! Please, this is a mis—"

"We want our property returned. It is a small toy airplane. It is only of value to us. Find it, bring it with you and leave now on foot for Grand Central Terminal. Keep your phone on for instructions. If you fail, if you inform police, your family will die. We are watching. *Leave now!*"

"Please, let them go! This is mistake! I'm begging you, please let them go!"

The line went dead.

20

They're alive.

For now.

His heart racing, Jeff scanned the room.

A toy airplane?

His family had been abducted for a toy?

This is insane.

He couldn't make sense of the absurdity. Time pummeled him. Each second was a fist striking him with desperation, demanding action.

Concentrate.

Cole had dumped the bag's contents on his bed. A vague memory of him playing with a toy surfaced, then Jeff recalled Cole telling Hans Beck about the airplane.

Maybe it fell out, got misplaced.

Immediately Jeff sifted through Cole's clothes but found nothing. He ran his hands swiftly over the bedspread. Nothing. He dropped to his knees and looked under the bed, no sign of a plane.

What if I can't find it?

He pressed his face to the room's carpet and inspected the area around the bed, the dresser, the desk, then saw the curtains.

The curtains! Cole was playing near the window behind the curtains!

As Jeff searched the area on the floor, the interior windowsill, his cell rang. He kept searching. As he moved to the area behind the chairs and table near the window he heard a slight rattle coming from the curtains.

The cell phone rang a second time.

I'm losing time!

Jeff ran his hands along the hem of the curtains, pockets formed at the bottom of the folds. Suddenly, miraculously, he felt something hard in one of them and inserted his fingers, feeling a plastic casing.

Got it!

He retrieved the toy plane Cole had been playing with, then answered his cell phone.

"Jeff, this is Cordelli."

"Did you guys get that call? They're alive! I'm going to get them back!"

"We got it but I need you to listen to me!"

"Did you get a name on the phone? Was it Hans Beck?"

"No. They're using an untraceable cell phone, a throwaway. Listen. Don't move. We're scrambling to set up."

"Christ, didn't you hear them? No police, they'll kill Sarah and Cole!"

"Jeff, we can't take any risks. We don't know who we're dealing with or what they might do."

"Yes, we do! They've already killed two people!"

"Don't go anywhere, don't give anyone anything. Wait for us to come to you!"

"No, I'm going now and I'm going alone!"

"Jeff, wait! Listen to me, there are things we can do that no one will see. We can put plainclothes people on the trains. We can stop the trains if we have to."

"No! They said no police. Cordelli, they already killed two people. I'm not going to risk my family's life!"

"Jeff, you're not thinking this through. We've got people rolling to positions now. Wait in the hotel lobby. Don't move!"

"There's no time, Cordelli!"

As Jeff headed for the door, the hotel phone rang. Jeff got it.

"Mr. Griffin, Russ Powell from the *Times*. I think we got cut off. What just happened there? Did you get a call from your wife?"

"I can't talk right now."

Jeff hung up, slid the phone in his shirt pocket and rushed to the elevator. As he jabbed the down button, his heavy breathing filled the hall. The elevator car was empty. On the way down, he looked at the plane.

It was a 747 jumbo jetliner, made of hard plastic a couple of inches long. He activated the lights and jet engine sound. He rolled the wheels in the palm of his hand. It had no markings, other than a Made in China sticker on the bottom of the battery compartment.

This was his key to getting Sarah and Cole back.

The elevator stopped on the fourth floor.

Jeff shoved the toy into his jeans pocket.

The doors opened to four people, each with a large suitcase—a man and a woman, both older than Jeff, a teenage boy and teenage girl. The girl was squatting, fussing with her bag's contents.

"Come on, Ashley, hurry up!" the woman said.

The dad reached in to hold the elevator doors.

"It's stuck! The zipper's stuck," the girl complained as time slipped by.

Without a word, Jeff stepped around them and headed down the hall to the stairs, rushing to the lobby within a minute.

Outside he surveyed the street for any sign of the kidnappers, Cordelli, the NYPD or the press.

Nothing.

Using his map he checked his bearings.

As horns and traffic noise rose from the city around him, Jeff set out for Grand Central.

21

Manhattan, New York City

Grand Central was a thirty-minute walk from Jeff's hotel.

Jeff ran.

He darted through traffic and weaved around work-bound New Yorkers. He would not take a cab. The caller had been explicit that he travel by foot. Jeff had gotten as far as West Twenty-ninth Street and Broadway when his cell phone rang. The robotic voice gave him further instructions.

"Go to Big World Gifts on West Thirtieth Street, in the forties. The clerk is holding a purchase to be picked up by 'Jeff.' Give him twenty dollars. Take the package, open it and continue to Grand Central!"

"Let me speak to my wife!"

The line went dead.

Jeff hurried around the next block.

He was on West Thirtieth and moving fast when his cell phone rang.

"It's Cordelli, are you at your hotel?"

"I can't talk right now."

"Tell me where you are. I'm sending an unmarked. We have to set up!"

"I've got to do what they say."

"Jeff! You don't know how this is going to go!"

"I can't talk!"

Rushing down Thirtieth, Jeff scanned the storefronts: the jewelry stores, import-export outlets, the vans and large delivery trucks being unloaded. He pinballed among sweating workers, expertly wheeling dolly carts laden with boxes.

Big World, Big World, where is it?

He was in the high thirties when he came to a busy sidewalk display of new luggage at Discount Prices! and tables overflowing with towers of Cheap T-shirts! The store's window was curtained with a spectrum of novelty T-shirts on hangers, along with a placard that said Jewelry, Electronics, Cell Phones, Coffee, Snacks.

There it is!

The sign over the narrow storefront: Big World Gifts. It was in a three-story building, rust-stained brick, open steel-grated fire escape. The upper level windows were sealed with plywood.

A wave of stale air hit him when he entered.

The place was cramped, cluttered. A balding man in his seventies, wearing a white shirt, loosened tie and unbuttoned vest, bifocals, was leaning over a newspaper on the counter case. A small Asian woman standing beside him was tapping the keys of a calculator. Other customers entered behind Jeff. He dug out his cash quickly.

"I'm here to pick up a purchase for Jeff?"

The man eyed Jeff, the cash, Jeff again, then turned to a messy storage unit and got a small box with a picture of the Empire State Building on it.

Jeff handed the man a twenty and took the box.

"Who gave this to you?"

"A very polite gentleman came in this morning and took care of it. He said Jeff would pay a little something for holding it and pick it up for his son."

"Do you know this man? Have you seen him before?"

"No." The old man nodded to the box. "It's good to go, all set."

"What do you mean? What's good to go?"

"I don't know. Sir, please." The clerk indicated the other customers behind Jeff; a woman crossed her arms and jingled her keys.

Then it struck Jeff that the kidnappers may have handled the box.

They'd leave fingerprints.

"May I get a bag, please?" he asked.

"Sir, you have a box."

"Please." Jeff put a dollar on the counter.

The old man sighed, reached for a paper bag and slid the box into it.

Jeff returned to the street, found an alcove to examine the item. Before he could open it, it started ringing. Carefully holding the box by its edges, he saw a cell phone inside, nothing more. He tried to be as prudent with the phone but it was impossible.

The ringing underscored the urgency.

He handled the phone normally.

The number was blocked.

Jeff answered.

The robotic voice resumed.

"Police cannot track this phone."

"Please, release my family!"

"Throw your other phone away!"

Jeff scanned the street, trying to see if he could spot the caller. He pulled his personal phone from his pocket, took the few steps to the nearest sidewalk trash can and dropped his hand into it.

"All right, I tossed it," he lied, palming his phone. "Let me speak to my wife!"

"There's a new plan. A change in direction. You are not going to Grand Central. To the right of the Big World store there is an alley. Take it to West Thirty-first Street." The caller hung up.

The darkened, cool alley reeked of urine and the odor of a dead cat. Moving along the Dumpsters and bags of neglected trash, Jeff searched for options. He didn't find many. His personal phone was his lifeline to Cordelli. He hadn't thrown it away and he would not lose it.

He felt the toy in his pocket, took it out, looked it over.

Why is this so important? Who would go to such extremes over a toy?

This little airplane was his only hope of ever seeing Sarah and Cole.

Cordelli was right. There was no way to know how this would go, or what these bastards would do once he gave them the toy.

This toy plane was his bargaining chip—his insurance.

By the time Jeff had reached the end of the alley, he had a plan.

He had to move quickly.

At Thirty-first Street he hurried into a coffee shop that was jammed with men in suits and ties, women in blazers, people anxious to get to their jobs. The air smelled of cinnamon, bread, perfume and brewed coffee.

"Can I help whoever's next, please!" a man at the counter called.

"Next!" a woman behind the counter called. "Can I help you?"

Jeff took his place in line with people reading Black-Berries, or folded copies of the *Daily News* or *New York Times*.

The staff was fast, the line moved.

"Excuse me, can I use your washroom," Jeff asked.

"It's occupied and it's customers only, sir. Your order?"

"Small black coffee. With a lid." Jeff put two dollars on the counter.

"There you go," the clerk said, handing him the key from the returning customer.

Jeff went directly to the washroom.

It was small: one urinal, one stall and a sink. Reasonably clean. He locked the door, took stock, then looked up. He got into the stall, stood on the toilet and lifted a foam ceiling tile. In the ceiling he concealed the paper bag containing the toy plane, and empty box that had held the cell phone.

As he replaced the tile, his cell rang—the one the killers had given him.

Quickly, Jeff returned the key to the counter.

The cell phone rang a second time.

Jeff rushed to the street—"Sir, your coffee?"—and answered the cell phone on the third ring.

The robotic voice resumed.

"Listen carefully…"

22

Manhattan, New York City

The brakes creaked when Cordelli and Ortiz's unmarked Impala halted outside the Central Suites Inn on West Twenty-ninth Street.

No marked NYPD units or uniforms, nothing to betray that police were racing against time. That was good. Cordelli didn't want the suspects to know they were in pursuit.

But he remained anxious.

They saw no sign of Jeff Griffin in the street or in the lobby.

They showed ID at the front desk and the clerk led them into the office of the manager, Kim Cameron, who was on the phone contending with an erroneous order. When Cameron saw their shields and her clerk's worried face, she ended her call and stood.

"We need your help," Cordelli said.

"Concerning?"

"We're pursuing a felony in progress that poses a risk to a number of people and the possible destruction of evidence. We need immediate entry to the room of your guest Jeff Griffin."

"You need a warrant."

"No, we don't."

"But, I—"

"Ma'am. We need this now! We can do it with a key, or we can have ESU lock down your hotel. I advise you not to consider obstructing us."

"I'll get a key."

In the elevator, Cordelli and Ortiz tugged on blue latex gloves. Cameron took a breath, not knowing what to expect.

At 1212 she knocked and, as Cordelli had requested, asked for Jeff Griffin. No response. She opened the door.

"Please remain in the hallway and let no one enter," Ortiz said, shutting the door.

As they inventoried the room Ortiz got a call with updates from the Real Time Crime Center.

"Vic, they're trying to triangulate Griffin's location now from the last call he received. They say he's close. We've got unmarked units looking."

Cordelli squatted at the clear plastic wrapping, backpack and clothing heaped in a far corner. He mentally replayed what they'd learned listening to the kidnapper's call to Jeff on the cloned phone. Bags had been mixed up at the airport; their interest was in a toy plane.

What the hell could it be?

Using his pen, he poked through the belongings on the floor.

"Juanita, we'll need a warrant to continue processing this room and that bag for any trace to the guy he exchanged it with."

A commotion had arisen outside the door just before it opened. Brewer and Klaver pushed past the hotel manager.

"Nice work, Vic." Brewer entered with Klaver and took stock of the room. "You should've had someone here with Griffin the whole time. You fucked up. Now we've got a mechanic from Montana running helter-skelter in the city at the behest of murderers."

"We've got the RTCC on his trail. We know he's headed to Grand Central. We've alerted everyone there. Jeff could lead us to the suspects."

"Or we get another hostage, or another homicide. Real nice work, Vic."

"Why don't you shut the fuck up, Brewer!" Cordelli said.

"Hey!" Klaver tried to defuse the mounting tension.

"Hold it! Vic, Larry. Hold up!" Ortiz had her phone to her ear. Her expression indicated critical information was coming in now. "An unmarked unit has a lead. Griffin was at the Big World gift store on West Thirtieth less than twenty minutes ago."

At Grand Central Terminal, NYPD transit police and members of the counterterrorism division maintained a nonstop vigil for suspicious activity.

The most recent alert was the low-key search for Jeff Griffin.

Thousands of people streamed through the main concourse with its cathedral-like sky ceiling. Officers posted throughout the sprawling system had been equipped with photos of Jeff and studied the faces of white males fitting Jeff Griffin's description.

Transit officers posted in small guard stations on the platforms at Grand Central's fourteen subway tunnels kept close watch on video monitors of security cameras.

No reports of anyone matching Jeff Griffin's description or of any suspicious incidents at Grand Central.

Cordelli and Brewer left Ortiz and Klaver at Jeff's hotel and took Cordelli's car to the store, a few blocks away. Two plainclothes officers had been canvassing the street with Jeff's photo when they'd got a lead.

"Mr. Feldman and his manager, Karen Lee, are certain Griffin was here half an hour ago, maybe less," one of the officers told Brewer and Cordelli when they'd arrived. "Isn't that right?"

"Yes, he picked up a package," Karen Lee said.

"What sort of package? What's in it?"

The couple was silent for a moment.

"Like this." Karen Lee showed the detectives a box containing a souvenir of the Empire State Building.

"Is that it?" Brewer and Cordelli sensed they were not being told everything. "You know, this case is very serious. We need the truth or anyone connected in any way could be in a lot of trouble."

Feldman removed his glasses, ran a hand over his moist brow.

"Earlier this morning, a man came in and paid cash for a prepaid phone, like this one." The man pointed to a packaged phone. "The man set it up and said Jeff would be in to pick it up. That's it."

Brewer took the package of the phone. He took a photo of it. "Are you sure it was just like this one?" Brewer pressed the man.

"Yes."

Brewer emailed the photo from his phone, then made a call to request analysts contact the cell phone company to see if any phones of this model had been recently activated in their location. Brewer provided the bar code and other information.

Cordelli continued questioning the couple.

"Do you know the man who bought the phone for

Jeff? Is he a regular? Has he ever paid for anything
with a credit card?" Cordelli then glanced at the security camera above them.

"No. We've never seen him before," the man said.

"Will you volunteer your surveillance tapes?"

"Of course, we want to cooperate, right, Karen?"

"For sure we will help police, for sure."

At that moment in downtown Manhattan, near the
Brooklyn Bridge and city hall, detectives and analysts
assigned to the case were going all-out at the NYPD's
Real Time Crime Center.

In a softly lit, windowless room on a midlevel floor
of One Police Plaza, they were using every high-tech
resource they had to pinpoint Jeff Griffin's location.
They worked at rows of computer stations and screens
before a massive two-story array of flat video panels,
known as the data wall.

One displayed enlarged recent photos of Jeff Griffin so everyone at the RTCC and police on the street
could identify him.

It was here at the center that they were also monitoring all calls on Jeff Griffin's personal cell phone. They
could not yet locate the origin of the kidnapper's calls
because they were coming from a prepaid phone without any personal information. So far they had nothing
specific on the phone being used by the suspects to
contact Jeff.

One detective was processing the information Brewer
had just relayed from the package of a phone identical
to the one left for Jeff at the gift store.

At the same time, Renee Abbott, one of the RTCC's
top analysts, was welded to her work on Jeff Griffin's

personal phone. Thank God Jeff had left it on. The roaming signal was good.

As long as you keep it on, I can find you.

Renee, tracking Jeff's roaming signal using satellite mapping, was able to narrow the signal location down to the block he was on. She could also determine the direction Jeff was moving. Renee could then tap into more detailed city maps to display nearby landmarks, then employ the surveillance cameras.

We're one step behind you.

The challenge was to not let Jeff or the kidnappers know how close they were behind them. The NYPD could not use marked units with lights and sirens to block streets, not with two hostages, one a child, at risk. And Renee knew Jeff's trail would die if Jeff switched off his personal cell phone and removed the battery.

She concentrated on the latest signal flash on her computer screen, then the data wall and geocode maps.

All right.

Her keyboard clicked.

This is it.

Renee dispatched an update to the lead detectives and plainclothes units on the street.

"Heads up. We have a new location."

23

Manhattan, New York City

The caller's machinelike voice gave Jeff detailed orders.

"Go to the Thirty-fourth Street subway station. Take the Seventh Avenue express line south to Fourteenth Street. You will get further instructions there."

As Jeff took notes on a hotel message pad, the hotel pen kept slipping through his sweating fingers. He stopped and used the top of a city trash bin to steady his writing.

The call had come through the new phone, the one they'd said police could not track. As he resumed jostling through the city's busy streets, new fears gnawed at him.

New York was overwhelming.

He didn't know the city, let alone the subway system. *What if I can't find the right train, or get on the wrong one?*

He drew the back of his hand across his mouth, fumbling with his maps, trusting he was moving in the right direction as another fear bit at him.

The plane.

God, did I make a mistake? Without the plane I have nothing. I should go back and get it. No, the plane is critical. It's all I have to bargain for Sarah's and Cole's lives.

Jeff ran along Seventh Avenue by Madison Square Garden and Penn Station. The Seventh Avenue subway line was also known as the Broadway Line. The subway stop at Thirty-fourth Street and Penn Station extended over Thirty-second, Thirty-third and Thirty-fourth streets, according to Jeff's map.

Which one do I take?

He stopped in front of the Thirty-second Street entrance to Penn Station, one of the busiest train stations in the world. Rivers of passengers flowed in and out of the building under the neon sign promoting a rock concert at Madison Square Garden. Jeff was unsure of the best way to go. Before descending the stairs into the concourse, he asked for help from a gray-stubbled man giving away commuter newspapers.

"I have to get on a train going south on the Seventh Avenue Broadway Line, is this the fastest way?"

"Naw, take the Thirty-fourth Street station." He nodded to the stop a few blocks from where they stood. "See, that's the best one for the Broadway Line."

Jeff set out for the station. As he threaded through the pedestrian traffic his personal cell phone rang.

The number was blocked.

What if the killers were calling to check that he'd tossed the phone; or Cordelli had news; or it was Sarah or Cole? It rang again. He couldn't let it go. He answered without speaking.

"Mr. Griffin?" a familiar voice asked. "Hello, can you hear me?"

"Yes."

"It's Russ Powell at the *Times*. We were talking earlier."

"How did you get this number?"

"Mr. Griffin, I just need a moment."

"I can't talk to you now."

"Sir, I get the sense you've just had contact with your abducted wife, Sarah. Can you confirm that?"

"I'm sorry, I have to go."

Jeff ended the call, shut off his phone, knowing he may have shut off his lifeline to Sarah and Cole. *Just for a few moments,* he told himself as he entered the station at Thirty-fourth Street and Seventh Avenue. The stairway shuddered as humid air with a trace of sewer smell carried the clamor of trains. Inside, he found a station booth, thankful there were only seven people ahead of him. His turn came fast.

"Next." The agent's voice sounded like it came from a tin can.

"I'm a first-time user of the subway—"

"How nice."

"I need a southbound express train on the Seventh Avenue Broadway Line."

"I'll need $2.25 from you. Or, you can get a seven-day MetroCard, unlimited train and bus, thirty bucks."

"I'll take the card."

The agent took Jeff's cash, passed him the paper card.

"Slide the black strip through the slots at the turnstile. Follow the signs to the island platform, take a number 2 or 3 and get off at Fourteenth."

Jeff hurried to the platform. It was crowded with commuters. He went to the midway point, kept close to the tiled wall, avoiding the edge. He'd read news stories about people getting shoved in front of trains.

He could hear the faded rumblings of the other trains at Penn Station. While waiting for his he looked into the black tunnel, the yawning jaws of the abyss, and thought of Sarah and Cole.

Will I ever see them again?

White lights shot at him from the darkness, bringing a screeching sound that turned into the hum of an approaching train. Its brakes moaned as it settled into the station. The doors opened and passengers getting off did a sidestep shuffle with those getting on.

Jeff found a seat between a woman reading the *New Yorker* magazine who smelled like an ashtray, and a man in a suit who must've doused himself with cologne, to counter the subway air.

The doors closed, the train jerked, tilting everyone, then gathered speed. The platform's brightness gave way to the drab walls racing by. As Jeff assessed the other passengers he wrestled with more questions.

What if the killers are on this car, watching me?

At one end, a group of teenagers, mostly girls, yakked at high speed while hypertexting. Business types in suits, their noses in cell phones or tablets, were sprinkled throughout the car, along with tradesmen in paint-stained jeans. Other riders slouched over packs, eyes heavy, nodding near sleep.

As the train rocked and yawed, the lights of local stations strobed and Jeff's mind flashed with memories.

Sarah glowing on their wedding day...letting go of Cole's hands as he took his first steps...holding Lee Ann seconds after she was born....so tiny...so perfect... carrying her coffin in the cemetery at the edge of town... the mountains...the crying wind...the ache in his heart that would never go away....

The train lumbered to a stop at the Fourteenth Street

station and the doors opened. Jeff took the stairs two at a time, surfacing to morning in Chelsea and the West Village.

Standing at West Fourteenth Street and Seventh Avenue, with time slipping by, he scanned the streets for any hint of Sarah, Cole or his next move. He looked at the deli, the flower shop, the grocery store. He searched the area's tree-lined sections that fronted a pizza place, a smoke shop, shoe repair outlet, nail salon, dress store, check-cashing store. As he glanced up at the red-and-gray stone tenement buildings rising over the neighborhood, his fear mounted.

Sarah or Cole could be in any of these buildings.

He looked at the traffic, at the people coming and going as if today was normal.

How can the world keep on turning?

Where is my family?

He stared at the phone the killers had put in his hand, attempted to redial but got a busy signal. The knot in his gut tightened and he wanted to scream at them.

I'm here! Dammit, I did what you wanted! Give me my family!

He was done waiting for them to call and took out his personal cell phone from his pocket, turned it on and redialed.

It was futile.

Another busy signal.

When he ended the call his personal cell phone rang in his hand.

Hope surging, he answered without checking the number.

"Jeff, this is Clay at the shop."

"Clay."

"Listen, son, we're just hearing the news here in town about Sarah and Cole. Is it true?"

"Yes. They're lost."

"I don't understand. What happened?"

"Clay, I have to go."

"But is there anything we can do to help?"

The kidnapper's phone began ringing.

"Clay, thanks."

Jeff ended his call and answered the ringing phone.

"State your location," the robotic voice demanded.

"West Fourteenth Street and Seventh Avenue."

"Get back on the subway at Fourteenth. Take a number 1 local train north to the Eighteenth Street station. Get off and start walking east on West Eighteenth Street into the three hundreds. Don't stop."

"Let me speak to my wife and son now!"

The caller hung up.

Jeff rushed down the subway stairs, swiped his MetroCard, followed the signs to the local platform and boarded a northbound number 1 train. Eighteenth Street was the next stop, so he remained standing.

As the train jerked forward and gathered speed, he made a rough count of the other passengers in the car. About a dozen. He kept close watch until the train decelerated and clattered to a halt at the Eighteenth Street platform.

A few people got off, a few got on. He worked his way around them and rushed to the stairs and surfaced. He followed the caller's instructions and headed east on West Eighteenth Street.

Parked cars lined both sides of the narrow street.

Traffic appeared nonexistent, as if this part of Manhattan had been abandoned. He walked steadily, taking inventory of the stone buildings, small walk-up apartment blocks, the art deco–facade of a health center, a few arching trees, the plywood-sheltered scaffolding of segments under renovation and businesses shuttered with roll-up steel doors.

Something was catching up to him.

A tidal wave of emotion and fear.

Why is this happening? Am I being punished for what happened to Lee Ann, for wanting to destroy what remained of my family? How could I have been so blind, so stupid? I need them now more than ever.

His anger mounting, his heart pounded in time with each hurried step. He was fighting his urge to cry out for Sarah and Cole when he heard the tick and purr of an engine.

A van was rolling along the street behind him.

He dismissed it as a delivery truck.

But it didn't pass him. Instead, it slowed, matching his speed.

Jeff took a quick look: a white GMC cargo, with dark windows up front. No commercial markings on the panels. It was a Savana, maybe 2010, 2011, in good shape.

A bearded man wearing a ball cap and dark glasses was in the passenger seat with his window all the way down.

"Excuse me, Mr. Griffin? We need you to step over to the van." The man tapped a leather wallet to his door frame. A badge glinted.

Cops, Jeff thought, *not good. Not now.*

"No, you guys take off, I'm handling this!"

The van halted in protest.

"Get over here! We've got something to show you!"

Jeff stopped, glanced up and down the street, then, as he neared the van, the side door swung open and his knees nearly buckled.

It was Sarah.

Her mouth and hands were bound with duct tape.

Two men on either side of her wore distorted white ghost masks. One of the men was pointing a gun at him. The other was holding a knife to Sarah's throat.

Her eyes were huge with terror as they found Jeff's.

24

At the Crime Center, analyst Renee Abbott reached for her World's Greatest Mom mug, took another hit of strong coffee and whispered another prayer.

It'd been a long time—*too darned long*—since they'd lost Jeff Griffin near Penn Station. That's where the roaming signal from his cell phone had vanished. Since then, Renee kept a vigil on her monitor and the huge flat panels on the data wall. She was in direct contact with the IT wireless guys who had cloned Griffin's personal cell. Renee hit a button on her console.

"I still got nothing, Artie," she said into her headset's microphone.

"Yeah, not a bleep, nada," Artie said. "He must have it off."

"The leads said Griffin picked up a new cell at the gift shop on West Thirtieth—the suspects left it for him."

"Yeah, these guys are smart. We can't find him," Artie said.

"This is not good. I don't like it."

As they spoke, Renee clicked through the new images

of Griffin that had been captured by the security cameras at the gift shop. They'd been circulated to everyone operational. These pictures were less than an hour old. Renee zoomed in on Griffin's face. A handsome, decent-looking guy, under colossal stress, she thought, going to the photos of his wife, Sarah, and son, Cole.

"Heads up." Artie's voice betrayed an urgent tone.

Renee's monitor showed a blip on the map.

"Is that him, Artie, at West Fourteenth and Seventh Avenue?"

"Bingo. He's back on the personal. He tried a call, now he's taking a call from a Montana number. I'll get back to you. I've got to advise the leads. We're so close now."

Renee checked satellite mapping, geocodes and alerted people in the sector. She'd barely finished doing that when Artie came back on.

"He's on the move again. Going north, signal strength is spotty," he said. "I think he's on the Seventh Avenue Line going north. Yes, it was the subway. He's already off at Eighteenth. Signal is good."

"I can see he's moving," Renee said. "I'll get units rolling, stand by."

Detectives Joe Finnie and Sean Maynard were fresh this morning. First shift on after a few days off, following five nights on.

They'd closed a carjacking beef and an assault in Clement Clarke Park. They were heading out of the Tenth Precinct for a follow-up interview on the assault when their lieutenant reassigned them to the kidnapping. That was just under an hour ago.

"The mom's a looker. Nice-looking family." Maynard was behind the wheel of their unmarked unit. He'd glanced again at the photos on the screen of his partner's netbook. "What do you think?"

"I always wanted to go to Montana," Finnie said.

"They've been circulating this stuff for nearly an hour now. It's a needle-in-a-haystack thing." Maynard bit into a bagel as he drove. "What are the odds we'll see action on this down here, Fin?"

Finnie studied updates on his small computer.

"Better than you think. Turn this thing around."

"Why?"

"They got something on our guy, on West Eighteenth and Seventh. We're almost there. No lights, no siren."

Finnie's cell phone rang. It was Renee Abbott at the Real Time Crime Center, confirming that their unit was live and unmarked in the hot zone.

"We are," Finnie said, "and I've got your photos and description of the subject."

"He's proceeding eastbound on West Eighteenth Street, in the three hundred block. By your twenty, you should have a visual."

Maynard wheeled their unmarked Crown Victoria onto West Eighteenth Street. They slowed to a near-stop, creeping along in the three hundred block, scrutinizing the sidewalks of the narrow street.

Traffic was nil.

All seemed sleepy here. A van was stopped at the end of the street.

"Who's that?" Maynard indicated a man approaching the van.

Finnie took small binoculars from the console. He focused on the man and van down the street. He glanced at the photos from the gift shop. Shirt color, pants, body build, all matched.

"That's him, Sean." Finnie grabbed his phone, which was still open to Renee at the center. "We've got him, please advise?"

25

Jeff froze.

Time stood still.

In one surreal instant he inhaled every detail he could.

The van's rear had no seats, or windows. Sarah was sitting on the carpeted floor between two masked captors near the rear doors with her back against the wall on the driver's side.

The man in the ball cap and dark glasses in the passenger seat repeated his order.

"Get in!"

Jeff hesitated, wishing he could reach inside and pull Sarah out.

But where's Cole?

He considered calling 9-1-1 or Cordelli, anybody, but there was no time. The driver had glanced nervously at his side-view mirror. Jeff glimpsed a sedan approaching slowly from some distance behind them. The street was too narrow for it to pass. They'd soon be blocking its path.

"Get in now!"

As Jeff stepped up into the van, one of the masked men tucked his gun, grabbed Jeff's shirt and yanked him inside before pulling the door shut.

The van proceeded down the street.

Jeff got on his knees opposite Sarah.

She was gaunt. Fear had gouged stress lines into her face. It shone with sweat, snot and tears.

"Where's Cole?" Jeff asked.

His question triggered an explosion of muffled crying and as he moved to comfort Sarah the gunman shoved him down, searched him for weapons, found none, but seized his phones and passed them forward. The gunman moved back beside Sarah and held Jeff at gunpoint.

"Where is our property?" the man in the passenger seat asked.

Keeping half a block behind the van, Detectives Finnie and Maynard followed in their unmarked Ford sedan for the next few moments.

They'd already sent in the van's license plate.

"Subject is now eastbound on West Eighteenth. Traffic is light," Finnie said into his phone.

"The tag comes back out of Hockessin, Delaware, registered to a 2010 Ford Mustang," Renee Abbott responded. "R.O. reported plates stolen two weeks ago."

"It's a stolen tag," Finnie said.

"Big surprise." Maynard kept a lock on the vehicle.

"How do you wish us to proceed?" Finnie said into his phone.

"Stand by," Renee said. "We'll go to the leads— they've been monitoring."

* * *

As the van rolled through midtown, Jeff continued his rapid inventory.

Remember every detail.

Sarah was wearing the same clothes she'd worn for their walk to Times Square. *That was yesterday. That was a lifetime ago.* Aside from her anguish, Jeff could not tell if she'd been hurt as alarm screamed in the back of his brain for their son.

God, where is Cole? Don't let him be dead! Please!

He looked into Sarah's eyes and battled to let her know.

I'm here with you. We're going to be okay. We're going to fight.

There were four captors. Two were in the back: one holding a knife on Sarah and the other pointing a gun at him.

In the front, the bearded man in the passenger seat, who'd so far done the talking, had an accent. His English was good but he sounded European.

He was in charge.

The driver had a ball cap, full beard, dark glasses, practically a twin to the leader. The driver was smooth at the wheel, vigilant, constantly scanning the traffic and mirrors. Drawing on his expertise as a mechanic, Jeff figured the van had a powerful Vortec V8 motor.

On the floor behind the console dividing the two front bucket seats, he noticed a duffel bag, partially opened. He saw and heard a digital emergency scanner squawking with police dispatches. There were walkie-talkies, his phones and others, folded maps, along with other items.

Were those bullet tips?

Sarah's masked captors had dark sweatshirts, with

their hoods up, dark pants, work boots. They were wearing earpieces. At times Jeff heard leaked dispatches in a foreign language. The air smelled of strong cigarettes and spicy food. The van was clean other than some take-out food wrappers and empty take-out coffee cups with colorful logos. The van creaked as they traveled through the West Side. In the fraction of a second Jeff had to think, he tried to retain every detail before time ran out.

"Where is our property?" the leader demanded again.

"I have it," Jeff said.

"You lie. Cut her!"

"No! Wait! Please! I put it in a safe place! You said I would see my wife and our son! What have you done with him?"

"He is insurance. We want our property now! Or we will kill your son and wife in front of you, starting with the boy!"

"This is a mistake! Return my family and I will tell you where to find the plane. Please, we've already suffered so much."

"You have suffered?" The man in charge whirled to face Jeff. "*You* have suffered?"

The man's dark glasses and full beard concealed his features but his nostril's flared with rage. A gold filling from his yellowed teeth glinted.

"You know nothing of suffering. Very soon we will show the world what it is to suffer—to lose what you love."

Across town in One Police Plaza, Brewer and Cordelli's task force lieutenant, Ted Stroud, had been alerted to the unfolding situation. In all his years on the job, he'd made many split-second calls.

Some ended well.

Some didn't.

The bad ones haunted him. But Stroud had no time to dwell on win-loss columns. He needed to advise his team now. He reviewed the circumstances one more time. This was a tentacle of their investigation that had involved a double homicide, the brazen abduction of a mother and her son, and now the husband attempting an unassisted ransom operation.

It was live, mobile, risks at every turn. A hell ride.

"Advise the unit to continue following the suspect vehicle and get other unmarked units rolling into position to box him. If he runs before we set up, pursue. *Do not lose him.* Alert all marked units in the sector but keep it off the air," Stroud said.

Renee Abbott checked with Finnie and Maynard.

"We got it." Finnie, phone to his ear, eyes forward on the white van, then advised Maynard, adding, "Better tighten up on him, Sean. He's getting some distance on us."

The van's driver adjusted his grip on the wheel and eyed his side mirrors, concentrating on that white Ford sedan.

Still there, nearly half a block behind them.

The driver had first noticed the sedan when they'd stopped on West Eighteenth Street, how it had materialized and moved slowly toward them from the distance. At the time, he thought the car was looking for a parking space, or checking an address.

His assessment had changed.

For now, after several minutes and several blocks, that white Ford sedan continued trailing them. The driver watched with increasing nervousness until he was convinced.

"We're being followed," he said.

The man in charge studied his passenger's side mirror.

"See?" the driver said. "That white car to the right, the Ford."

The man in charge looked hard into the mirror, then ahead to the next cross street.

"Slow down and stop for the yellow light, then go through it."

The driver eased the van to ensure it was clear while approaching the next intersection as the green turned yellow. Just as the yellow signal turned red, the driver accelerated, drawing horn honking from opposing vehicles green-lighted to advance through the intersection.

A siren screamed behind the van.

The unmarked white Ford had activated the emergency lights concealed in its grille and threaded through stopped traffic. The Ford's siren gave several loud yelps as it cut through the intersection, weaving in leaps against the red light in pursuit of the van.

The van's driver shoved the gas pedal to the floorboard. The V8 roared and the van sailed west on the cross-town street, its speed climbing as it knifed through traffic.

Jeff braced himself while watching the captors strain for balance. As the van rocked violently he saw the pistol slip in the gunman's hand.

This is my chance.

Jeff slammed his fist into the gunman's face, then instantly smashed the face of the man holding the knife to Sarah.

The gun clattered out of reach.

As the dazed gunman clawed for it, Jeff elbowed

his face hard, then grabbed the second captor's head, twisted and cracked it against the van's steel ribbing.

Jeff hooked his arm around Sarah's waist and dragged her to the back, praying the rear doors were unlocked. His attack took them all by surprise. Before the men in front could react he'd worked the rear latch.

The doors opened to pavement blurring a few feet below, the rush of air loud, chaotic with sirens and horns, brakes.

Sarah was quaking; he had no time to pull off her bindings, they had to escape and find Cole.

"Drop with me and roll! Keep your body loose!"

He pulled her close to go but she froze, eyes bulging. One of the captors had her foot and was reaching for the knife. Jeff moved back, delivered several kicks to his head, prying Sarah from his hold.

Gripping one of her hands and squeezing his arm around her waist, they inched out the rear and were hanging over the bumper.

The unmarked police unit was a few car lengths directly behind them, siren wailing, lights wigwagging, when the second captor and the man in charge pounced on Sarah, engaging Jeff in a life-and-death tug of war.

Jeff crushed her bound hand in his. Sarah groaned, Jeff lost his grip. The men pulled her back into the van. The force sent him farther over the bumper.

He was faceup, his back arching, his hair brushing against the asphalt, which passed under him with the speed of a power grinder.

One captor had Jeff's leg and was dragging him back into the van. Jeff held on to the door, writhed and kicked himself free and over the edge.

He fell from the van and hit the speeding street, not feeling his skin tearing as he rolled and bounced in a dizzying whirlwind of buildings, sky, pavement and traffic. Then came the flashes of emergency lights, the thud and squeal of brakes and burning rubber as the unmarked Ford swerved and stopped within inches of hitting him.

Jeff was on his stomach and conscious as Detectives Finnie and Maynard rushed to his aid.

"We need an ambulance!" Maynard shouted to a uniformed patrol officer who was running to the scene. "Get someone on traffic control!"

"Damn, we lost them," Finnie said.

On the street as blood webbed into his eye, Jeff saw the van doors close, saw it weave neatly around a large rig.

His heart hammered against the pavement.

He watched the van disappear into New York traffic and was overcome with defeat.

26

Jeff Griffin's scalp was still prickling as he stared at the ceiling from his hospital bed at Bellevue.

He'd never lost consciousness.

He recalled the ambulance *whoop-whooping* as it blurred across town. The EMS tech in the jump seat had watched over him until they arrived at the hospital where a nurse and senior resident assessed him. That was some ninety minutes ago.

Now they were waiting for the attending physician to sign off.

Jeff lay there, his eyes fixed on nothing. The back of his head was numb. Adrenaline was still rippling through him; his ears were ringing and his face was pounding from the blood rush of his futile battle to rescue Sarah.

He was so close.

He'd touched her, held her and then he'd lost her again.

I'm so sorry.

God knows where Cole is or what they'll do to Sarah now that I failed. I should've picked up that gun and shot them all. I should've waited for Cordelli and the cops to take over. I screwed up. I'm so goddamned sorry, Sarah. Oh, Jesus.

His eyes stung, his body shook, just as the door opened and the doctor, a balding man about Jeff's age, came in with a nurse.

"Hello, Mr. Griffin," the doctor said, picking up his digital chart while the nurse removed the ice pack from the back of Jeff's head so the doctor could check the small laceration.

"The swelling is not too bad," the doctor said. "It seems you don't have a concussion and the X-rays indicate no broken bones. Let's give you the once-over."

The doctor leaned forward and shined a penlight in Jeff's eyes. He had minty breath. The nurse took Jeff's temperature and vitals. The doctor put on his stethoscope and listened to Jeff's breathing. Then he assessed his neck, chest, abdomen and compressed Jeff's pelvis.

"Aside from some scrapes and bruises, you're in good shape. Your adrenaline was going full tilt. You were in 'fight mode.' You're lucky—"

Lucky?

Jeff shot anger at the doctor, who was aware, because of police and news reports, that Jeff's wife and son had been stolen by murderers.

The doctor adjusted his tone.

"Jeff, under the circumstances it could've been worse."

"Did they find my wife and son?"

"We don't know but two detectives have been waiting to talk to you."

"Send them in."

The nurse rolled the tray and IV stand aside and

a moment later Cordelli and Brewer were standing at his bed.

"They tell us they're going to discharge you," Cordelli said.

"Did you find Sarah? It was a GMC Savana, 2010."

"No," Cordelli said. "We're checking all surveillance cameras we can and our people in the car behind you may have gotten a few photos."

"And that helps, how?"

"Jeff," Cordelli said, "we asked you to hold off for us to set up."

"You took a stupid risk," Brewer said.

"I got closer to them than you guys! Christ!"

Jeff cupped his hands to his face, feeling the raw sting of cuts, scrapes and helplessness.

"Where does that leave us now?" Brewer said. "You should've let us handle it. This hero crap only works in the movies."

"You think I was trying to be a hero, Brewer? That what you think?"

"Hey!" Cordelli tried to dial down the tension. "This won't get us anywhere, let's get to work."

Cordelli set a digital recorder on the bed and opened his notebook.

"Tell us how many people were in the van, what they looked like, what they said, how they said it. Accents, tattoos, weapons, what you saw in the van. Everything."

Jeff gave them details while they still burned in his mind.

"They said, 'Very soon we will show the world what it is to suffer—to lose what you love.'"

Brewer and Cordelli exchanged glances at what they characterized as a terrorist threat.

"Did they elaborate, offer any details, like a target, address, location?" Cordelli asked.

Jeff shook his head.

Again and again Cordelli and Brewer went over every aspect of the incident with Jeff.

"We'll have you talk to a sketch artist to get more, anything that can help," Cordelli said.

Brewer pressed Jeff on "the small toy airplane."

"On the call the plane was their priority—what is it?"

"It's just a toy plane," Jeff said, describing it.

"Did you give it to them?" Brewer asked.

"No, I hid it."

"We need it."

As soon as Jeff was discharged Brewer and Cordelli drove him to the coffee shop on Thirty-first Street. He went to the washroom and retrieved the bag with the toy plane, and empty box for the cell phone.

Brewer put the items in a larger bag and started making calls.

"This could be our key."

27

Lori Hall, a criminalist at the NYPD crime lab, had been up late for the past five nights writing her research paper.

In addition to her full-time job, Hall, a thirty-three-year-old single mom with a four-year-old daughter, Carrie, was working on her master's degree in recombinant DNA technology at New York University.

Shortly after Hall's divorce a year ago, Carrie was diagnosed with a rare and dangerous lung disorder. She needed specialized treatment with expensive drugs not covered by Hall's work health plan. Hall needed her master's degree to be upgraded from 1B to a level 2 criminalist. It meant a raise, which would help pay for Carrie's treatment.

It also meant Hall faced the added pressure of her university work and her growing caseload at the lab.

This morning she'd hoped to wrap up analysis of trace from an assault in the Bronx and move on to analysis for a homicide in Bed-Stuy when Gil Doddard, her unit supervisor, put a brown paper bag on her workstation.

"Hold up, Lori, got a hot one for you."

"What's this?"

"A mystery we need you to unravel."

Hall glanced at the accompanying paperwork, tugged on fresh gloves, withdrew a small toy airplane and gave it a cursory inspection.

"Take this thing apart, analyze every component."

"What am I looking for?"

"Anything unusual. Anything that shouldn't be there. It's already been processed for latents and trace."

"And it's a hot one?"

"You heard about that case that just happened, about the tourists from Montana? A mom and her son abducted near Times Square?"

"Yes, something on the news this morning, might be tied to our double homicide in Brooklyn."

"This toy is part of it and your analysis is the number-one priority in town right now. So get going."

"All right, I'm on it."

Hall inhaled deeply, then let it out slowly.

No pressure. Stay calm. Do the work.

She cleared her other case, set out dating the proper paperwork for the new one. She adjusted herself on her chair at her bench and began examining the toy.

A jumbo jetliner made of plastic. She measured it at four inches long with a three-and-a-half-inch wingspan. Hall then weighed and photographed it. Then she activated the features and the red lights on the nose, tail and wing tips flashed and jet engines sounded. She rolled the plane back on its wheels, released it and it rushed forward, tilting for takeoff. It was absent of any markings, other than a Made in China sticker on the bottom and a tiny bar code on the side of the base.

Hall placed the toy under her illuminated, German-made wide-angle magnifying lamp and recorded the code. She then went online and submitted the code to a number of secure databases.

Results were instant.

This was a common pull-back novelty toy. They are often used for promotion with airline logos and markings. Hall noted that they were manufactured around the globe in India but chiefly China. This one was made in the Chenghai district and shipped around the world from the port at Shantou, Shenzhen. This one was model number F-SE23679C.

The dominant material was non-phthalate PVC.

With the toy enlarged under the lamp, Hall set out to disassemble it, evoking her days when she'd dissected frogs in high school. But as she went to separate the fuselage from the chassis, she caught her breath.

Tiny scratches along the seam.

She went to her forms. The latent and trace process did not involve any disassembly.

Who made the scratches?

She adjusted her magnifier.

These were not marks from the manufacturing process.

This thing's been opened before.

Hall pried the base from the fuselage to reveal the tiny casing for the motor and batteries. She was gentle, as small wires were tethered to the section.

She examined the motor and tiny gearbox, reviewing how pull-back toys operated on Newton's third law of action and reaction. The toy was powered by springs and gears through a basic gear train. It could be put in neutral, backward and forward modes, and had the ability to store energy.

Hall got all that.

Nothing out of the ordinary here, she thought, taking photographs and making notes.

She moved on to the housing for the batteries. The sound and lights features were powered by four common AG13 batteries that looked like tiny buttons, or pills. Using tweezers, Hall removed the batteries and examined them until she was satisfied that there was nothing unusual about them.

What is the deal with this toy? I don't see anything.

She continued analyzing the battery housing, the tiny metal contacts.

Sticking out her bottom lip and shaking her head, Hall was moving to the conclusion that there was nothing suspicious about this item when something caught her eye.

She repositioned the housing under her magnifying lamp.

Something strange about the contact clips.

More microscopic scratches. The clips seem to have been "thickened." Hall took more photos, then found the right tools and with surgical precision removed the clips.

She held them under the lamp.

Early in her career, Hall had worked in explosives. She'd gone to Hazardous Devices School at the FBI–U.S. army facility at the Redstone Arsenal in Huntsville, Alabama. She was posted in Iraq and became an expert on bomb components. When she returned she rode with the NYPD bomb squad.

Hall knew that she was looking at something remarkable.

A microscopic wafer detonator.

She set it under her microscope.

Its components were characteristic of a ceramic substrate with a glaze of polyimide but reengineered with radio static chips the diameter of a human hair. This device could function flawlessly using a dedicated current pulse that fired with a preset or dialed-in frequency.

Nothing could jam it or stop it.

I've never seen anything like this before.

Hall had read speculation that some groups were on the cusp of developing microscopic detonators that were virtually invisible to detection by traditional security measures like dogs, swabs scanners and X-rays at airports.

These new devices could be fired through a wireless device like a laptop or cell phone. They were fail-proof.

They could detonate the most powerful explosives one could build.

Hall licked her dry lips and reached for her phone.

"Gil," she said, "you'd better come see this."

28

Is this my hell?

To live a never-ending nightmare in the futile hunt for Sarah and Cole?

"Did you hear me, Jeff?"

Numb and skewed, Jeff stared at the fresh cuts and scrapes on his hands. He'd flattened his palms on the polished table of a boardroom at NYPD police headquarters.

It was early afternoon, a few short hours after he'd seen Sarah.

Will I ever see her and Cole again?

Ice cubes clinked as Lieutenant Fred Ryan, spokesman for the department, poured a glass of water, then passed it to Jeff.

"Have some water and we'll go over everything one last time."

The lieutenant swiveled in the chair next to Jeff and flipped through pages on his clipboard.

"This will be broadcast live online and with major news networks. You'll read the brief statement and that's it. Stick to the statement. Say nothing about the toy air-

plane or mixed-up bags at the airport. You must not release any details that could further endanger your family
or damage the investigation. The press will want to
focus on you but do not take any questions," Ryan said.

"We'll handle that," Lieutenant Ted Stroud, with the
task force, said.

FBI Special Agent Steve McCallert, from the FBI's
New York headquarters, agreed. "This is chiefly an appeal for information."

Ryan's cell phone rang. He took the call and Jeff
glanced around at the people in the room. He knew
Cordelli, Ortiz, Brewer and Klaver. The others were
strangers.

"They're ready downstairs," Ryan said. "Let's go."

"Wait," Cordelli said. "Remember, Jeff, the kidnappers will be watching. You should know that by talking to the press you're talking to the men who have
your family."

"And—" Brewer stood "—they've already murdered
two people."

The press auditorium was on the second floor of
One Police Plaza.

It was a room befitting the nation's largest police
force, with stone walls, rows of chairs, waxed and polished hardwood floors, a stage with a podium bearing
the NYPD shield.

Jeff estimated well over a hundred news people were
clustered around forests of cameras and tripods in front
of the stage. Crew members adjusted lenses and micro-
phones. Reporters made calls, gossiped or scribbled
notes while Jeff and the officials took their places, lining up abreast behind the podium.

He had wanted to do this, make a live statement to the press.

Investigators agreed that having him make a heart-felt plea for help was critical. This would be New York City's top news story; it would go national and around the world. Tapping into his anguish could yield a break.

As Ryan began, Jeff slipped into a surreal state.

Sarah and Cole are gone. I battled for Sarah and I lost. Cole's missing. Two people were burned to death in the SUV used to abduct my family. Why is this happening? The kidnappers' ultimatum roaring: "We want our property returned…. If you fail, if you inform police, your family will die!" God, please help me….

Lieutenant Stroud took over for Ryan.

"We'll provide you all with pictures," Stroud said before starting a slide show presentation on a large screen behind them. He summarized points of the case, chronologically with dates and locations, but would not discuss certain key aspects.

"I want to stress that this investigation is ongoing, and we continue to pursue a number of leads," Stroud said.

Massive photos of Sarah and Cole appeared alongside locator maps as Stroud started with how yesterday Jeff had reported Sarah and Cole's abduction from the Times Square area, how surveillance footage led to the stolen SUV and the double homicide in Brooklyn.

"Omarr Lincoln Roderick Aimes of Morningside Heights, Manhattan, has been identified as one of the victims in the SUV. His involvement is under investigation but he is known to police. Identification of the second victim is still pending. The SUV had been reported stolen from the Bronx, an aspect under investigation," Stroud said.

"We found evidence that indicated Sarah and Cole Griffin had been in the SUV. Subsequent to the homicides, the kidnapping suspects contacted Jeff and arranged a meeting this morning. Jeff was directed into a suspect van bearing stolen license plates. Jeff's wife, Sarah, was being held in the van and Jeff attempted to free her. During his struggle, the van led police on a high-speed pursuit. It ended on the West Side when Jeff fell from the fleeing vehicle directly into the path of the pursuing police unit, forcing it to stop. Sarah Griffin remained captive in the van. The suspect vehicle eluded arrest. Jeff was treated at Bellevue for minor injuries and released. NYPD detectives in the pursuing vehicle managed to take three photographs of the incident in progress."

Whispering rippled among the group when three large color photos appeared on the screen. They showed the van doors open, with Jeff and Sarah, her hands and mouth bound, hanging out of the speeding vehicle, fighting men in dark clothing with macabre ghostly masks.

They were stunning images.

"We're sharing these with the press. We're asking anyone with any information about this case to contact us. Our priority is the safe return of Sarah and Cole Griffin and the arrest of those responsible for these acts. Now, before Jeff makes a short statement, we'll take just a few quick questions."

FBI Apecial Agent Steve McCallert joined Stroud at the podium and took the first question from a woman in her twenties who identified herself as Rachel Glass with *Newsday*.

"Do you consider this a terrorist act?"

"Nothing's been ruled out at this point," McCallert said. "Especially in light of the fact we have a major

United Nations event ongoing now. A host of agencies, departments and individuals will be sharing all information."

"Sam Howe, *NBC News*. What are the kidnappers demanding?"

"We're not prepared to go into that sort of detail," McCallert said.

"But you are confirming that there are demands?" Howe said.

"Sam, we can't discuss that aspect of the case, period," McCallert said.

"Vicky Knoller, *ABC News*. What exactly happened inside that van?"

"That's under investigation," Stroud said.

"Anne Paige, *FOX News*. Have you identified the suspects in the van?"

"We are working with our law enforcement intelligence partners to uncover all possible ties to these crimes," McCallert said. "That includes any radical extremism or terrorist organizations, both at home and overseas. We're pursuing every lead in that regard."

"So that's a no?" Paige said.

"I think I answered your question," McCallert said.

"Tony Hicks, *Star-Ledger*. Can you tell us why the Griffin family is the target? From the information you put out last night, why would the suspects target a small-town mechanic, schoolteacher and their son, on vacation in New York?"

"We cannot answer that question," Stroud said.

"Fay Taylor, *News One*. Does Jeff Griffin know the victim, Omarr Aimes?"

"We can't answer that at this time," Stroud said.

"Ed Cruickshank, *Associated Press*. What sort of evidence have you collected so far?"

"Ed, all we can say is we continue to process all evidence collected by NYPD," Stroud said. "We'll transfer it for further forensic examination at the FBI laboratory in Quantico, Virginia."

"Kevin Fallon, *Daily News*. Lieutenant Stroud, you head the task force on organized crime. By implication, then, I would think organized networks are behind this. Can you elaborate on that?"

"We're examining a variety of things in connection with the crimes, Kevin," Stroud said, then held up his palms. "Now before we close this conference, we'll call on Jeff Griffin to make a statement, but we want to emphasize that he won't be taking questions. Jeff?"

Jeff heard his name but didn't move.

"Jeff?" Stroud nodded encouragement. "Would you step up, please?"

Suddenly he felt the folded sheet of paper in his hand as he moved to the podium. The camera lights were blinding; he could not discern faces, only the silhouettes of still photographers, their cameras clicking. The fresh bloodied cuts on his jaw and cheekbones made strong news pictures.

Jeff opened the page, stared at the enlarged bolded words, cleared his throat and began reading.

"I don't know why my wife, Sarah, and our son, Cole, have been taken. I'm—" he saw the word *pleading* but continued with "—begging that they be returned unharmed and for anyone anywhere who knows anything about this case to please contact police. Thank—"

"Jeff, Vicky Knoller, *ABC News*. A quick question—"

"Vicky, we said no questions." Ryan joined Jeff at the podium to shut Knoller down but Jeff had indicated he would answer.

Ryan shot a look to Stroud. They did not want to risk further antagonizing the suspects. Stroud mouthed "One," giving the okay for Jeff to answer a question. Ryan then placed his hand over the podium microphone and whispered a caution in Jeff's ear to be careful and brief.

"This will be the final question," Ryan said.

Grumbling rumbled through the press crowd.

"Sorry, guys, that's how it is," Ryan said, pointing to Knoller.

"Thank you," she said. "Jeff, looking at the photos of you and Sarah battling the kidnappers, I can only imagine the horrible agony you're enduring. If you could speak to Sarah and Cole right now, what would you tell them?"

As Jeff looked into the lights, images of Lee Ann, Sarah and Cole flashed before him. He reached into the deepest regions of his heart and spoke slowly.

"A year and a half ago we lost our six-month-old daughter, Lee Ann. It tore us apart. We made this trip with our son to help us deal with her loss and the fact we were blaming ourselves for it. I swear to God, I don't know what's happened here. I don't understand why someone would take my family and murder people. I'm begging whoever did this to let them go and take me. If you need a hostage, take me. I mean, what kind of people terrorize women and children?"

Soft murmuring rose from the reporters, pages in notebooks rustled crisply as they were turned. Stroud, McCallert and the others exchanged looks of concern.

"Jeff." Ryan kept his voice low over Jeff's shoulder. "Careful."

"You ask me what I want to say, it's this—I love you, Cole, more than you'll ever know. I love you, Sarah, and want you to know that you were right. We have to fight to hold this family together and I swear to you—"

"Jeff, okay." Ryan tried in vain to cut Jeff off.

"—that's what I'm going to do—"

"Jeff."

"—I will never give up. I'm coming for you."

Ryan got control of the podium.

"I think we're done, folks. Okay. Thank you all very much."

29

Somewhere in New York City

The old casket factory was an anomaly.

In a city with some of the most expensive real estate on earth, abandoned buildings were quickly sold, renovated or demolished.

But this aging four-story stone complex, standing forgotten near the East River, had changed hands many times over the years. Various permits had been issued, only to expire, with new ones reissued as the property fell into a bureaucratic black hole.

Established in 1896 to build coffins, the factory's business peaked during the 1918 flu epidemic. After the Second World War it became a furniture warehouse that went bankrupt. Now it was a tax shelter for a numbered corporation—an absent landlord.

The corporation had contracted a property management agency with a record for violating local codes. Long ago there was talk that the agency was a front for a global money-laundering operation.

That was the history.

Rumor had it that several months ago the empty structure had been rented to an international production company. The company had paid in cash and intended to use the building for a movie, but the windows and doors remained boarded up. The rust-stained wrought-iron gate was padlocked. It was opened for the few vehicles that appeared and disappeared into the rear loading bays.

No one paid much attention to the place where Sarah and Cole were being held.

And today, at the very moment investigators were appealing to New Yorkers for help in their case, Jeff Griffin's voice spilled from the large TV their captors were watching in a far reach of the factory. Sarah and Cole could not see Jeff but his words carried hope through the taut, foul air.

"I love you, Cole...I love you, Sarah... You were right...we have to fight to hold this family together...."

A great sob rose at the back of Sarah's throat. Tears rolled down her face. She ached to break free of her binding and hold her husband. When the press conference ended she spoke in a quavering tone to Cole.

"See, honey, Daddy's doing all he can to help us. We have to be strong."

Cole didn't react.

Sarah's heart sank and her chain made a soft *clink-clink* when she brushed at her tears. Her pulse was still racing and she couldn't stop trembling, for now things were worse after Jeff had tried to save her earlier that morning. *Much worse.*

Their captors were enraged.

In the aftermath, after the van had vanished into traffic, they'd replaced the hood over her head and began arguing with one another. Again, she guessed at their language: Russian, something Slavic, or Eastern European.

When they'd returned, and replaced her next to Cole, they'd removed her hood and the tape over her mouth. Once more they locked one handcuff around her wrist and threaded the second cuff to a long chain, as was the case for Cole.

Their chains were fastened to a steel beam.

Sarah and Cole had been put on ripped, stained mattresses that reeked of urine. They were given torn blankets, bags of chips, doughnuts, bottled water.

Their chains reached into a small bathroom. It had a battered, ill-fitting swinging door that shut, offering some privacy, but the handle was missing so it wouldn't lock. Inside, the cramped room had filthy walls and an air vent the size of a milk crate wedged into patched-over, crumbling drywall. There was a discolored toilet that still flushed, a sink with running water, paper towels and several bars of soap still in their packages.

Their mattresses were pushed against a wall.

Sarah found a broken broom handle to fend off the rats. The floor was encased with bird shit from the pigeons that had entered through the holes in the roof. Often the birds made aggressive raids for their food.

Across the vast factory floor, dirty with islands of crumbling half walls, were steel drums of trash and scraps of rotting lumber. Forests of cracked concrete columns and rusting steel beams rose from the waste. Webs of wiring and broken light fixtures drooped from the great ceiling. Daylight dimmed because it was filtered through the lines of weathered factory windows yellowed with age, filth and bird droppings.

Sarah and Cole could see their captors in the far section. Twenty in all, she guessed. There was a lot of movement and Sarah saw an array of new computers and electrical equipment along with crates of components, supplies, weapons.

She also saw what looked like wardrobe racks with official-looking uniforms, and the wheels of several vehicles that were covered with tarps.

There were tables bearing maps, charts, books, binders, cell phones, walls with more maps and radios kept low with emergency chatter. She knew from Jeff's firefighting work that they were police scanners. There were fridges, large TVs and cots.

The few times the leaders spoke to her it was in accented but strong English. They were disciplined and intelligent men. This was a small army, she thought, and they continued to terrify her as they did since that moment they stole them from the street.

At first they were only interested in taking Cole. Sarah fought them but her struggle ended as quickly as it began when they took her, too.

"I have a gun pointed at your son's head! Say nothing, cooperate and no one will die!"

It had all happened so fast.

Inside, they'd handcuffed them, put hoods on their heads and pushed them down to the floor of the vehicle as they drove through New York City. Twice they'd switched vehicles before they arrived in this hellhole.

Sarah was certain they were plotting something massive, something terrifying. Her fear deepened when the news conference ended and their arguing intensified.

A glass was smashed.

Now, some of the men began shoving others until a small group started directly toward Sarah and Cole. You did not have to understand the language to know the worst was coming.

"Mom?" Cole said.

"Shh, shh, honey. It's going to be okay."

Several men, with full thick beards, dark pants, T-shirts, their eyes bulging with rage, stood over them. One had a large flag, which Sarah did not recognize. One had a video camera. One seized Cole from the mattress. Cole's chains jingled as the man positioned him before the flag. One of the men held Sarah down.

"Mom!" Cole's eyes filled with tears.

The fourth man, the leader, kept his hands behind his back.

"Your husband failed to obey our instructions."

The leader nodded to the cameraman, the red record light came on and Sarah's heart nearly exploded. The leader suddenly displayed his pistol, prepared it for firing and pointed it at Cole's head.

Sarah screamed and struggled in vain. Cole cried out.

"Your husband gambled with your lives and lost."

One of the men began reciting a manifesto in a foreign language as they prepared for the first execution.

30

As Cole's death sentence was read out the gunman pressed the muzzle against Cole's head.

Cole shook as he cried. His eyes found Sarah's.

She screamed and fought against the captors.

"This execution is the result of failure," the man with the gun told Sarah.

"No! He's just a boy, an innocent boy!"

"It is a result of your husband's failure to return our property—" the man raised his voice "—the failure of your government and all governments to—"

A boot kicked the man's hand, sending the gun scraping across the floor.

A larger group of men had materialized and overtook the others. Cole was released, Sarah was released. She scurried to Cole, held him tight and calmed him as they watched.

The men of the execution effort were punched and kicked by the others who then hauled them before a line of men brandishing guns.

The beaten men were forced to their knees.

All attention went to one man. Sarah had not seen him before.

His head was shaved clean. He had a bushy black beard and a commanding presence, as if he were supreme leader.

He stood a few inches over six feet. He had a muscular build that strained his New York Yankees T-shirt. The grip of a pistol was visible from his shoulder holster. He wore blue jeans and an ice-cold expression as he looked down upon the man who was going to kill Cole.

"Tell me, Zama," the new leader said in clear English to the ringleader. "Was it not your responsibility to secure the component?"

"Yes, Bulat, but—"

"Stop. Your job was to secure the component and help with the setup, correct?"

"Yes, but circumstances changed."

"Stop. I am informed that your courier picked up the wrong bag at LaGuardia, is that not a fact, Zama?"

"Yes, as we reported. But we terminated him and took corrective action, sir. Immediate corrective action."

"Corrective action? Is that what you call it?" He threw the printed pages of an online news article at Zama's face. "You've alerted U.S. law enforcement to our presence! This changes everything! But that is not all, Zama. Is it?"

"I don't understand."

"Of course you don't because you've proven yourself a fool."

"I am dedicated to the mission."

"You have jeopardized our entire operation!"

"No."

"It changes everything!"

"I should never have allowed our sponsors to convince me that you should be part of our brigade."

After a long silence, Bulat lowered himself, looked the frightened ringleader in the face and adjusted his fury to a whisper.

"All of the dying, the souls of our children and martyrs, all are now at risk of being meaningless because of you, Zama."

"That is not so. I give my life to our mission."

"No, Zama, like your courier, you are a liability."

"Please."

"Don't worry. I need you."

"Thank you."

"We are now forced to scramble to change our operation completely in order to salvage it. But I still need you."

"Thank you, Bulat."

Zama tried to show his gratitude by kissing the back of Bulat's hand but the leader withdrew it.

"I need you to be an example to others that fuckups like you will be erased."

Bulat unholstered his pistol, took one second to prepare it for firing, drilled the gun into Zama's skull. The sound—like an enormous firecracker—was deafening. Sarah and Cole flinched.

The body fell forward to the filthy floor.

Bulat regarded Sarah and Cole for several seconds before stepping over the corpse and lowering himself to face them. Their chains chimed softly as they trembled.

Bulat inhaled deeply and let his breath out slowly.

"It is futile to fear what is inevitable." He tapped the still-warm muzzle of his gun on Cole's head. Then he tapped it on Sarah's head. "Sooner or later, we all must die."

31

Sarah's eyes were ballooned in a silent scream as her face filled the large flat-screen TV in Jeff's hotel room.

Her mouth was sealed with tape, her hair snaked wildly. Fear creased her face as she struggled between her captors with their gruesome masks and Jeff in the back of the fleeing van.

Detective Lucy Chu, an NYPD forensic artist, typed again on her laptop keypad. The image on the screen shrunk, the focus zoomed out and Chu continued displaying the three photos taken by detectives from the pursuit earlier that morning.

Frame by frame, section by section, Chu enlarged them, examined them intensely with Jeff, striving to pinpoint any identifying details. The photographs were helpful but so far had failed to yield a lead. The kidnappers were silhouetted or in shadow.

And they stayed that way.

The technical experts had already gone full bore to enhance the images but with little success. Chu repositioned her chair so that the TV screen was behind her and Jeff was looking at it while facing her.

Chu picked up her drawing pad, eraser and graphite pencil.

"All right, watch the pictures," she said, "and take me back inside the van." She left the three-photo slide show flowing, to keep Jeff's attention on the interior of the van. She'd already interviewed him at length. Her goal was to use composites, image modification, whatever it took to mine Jeff's memory for potential evidence.

"Let's start with hands."

Again and again Chu asked him about body parts, necks, hair, tattoos, jewelry, scars, clothing, footwear, characteristics of the van and items in the van. Over and over she drew, erased and redrew each time a nugget of detail surfaced.

It was painstaking, exhausting work and they pressed on.

Jeff took brief breaks by glancing around his new room. After his clash with the suspects, the NYPD and FBI moved him to this hotel, near Grand Central, in the shadow of the Chrysler Building. The location was undisclosed, for security reasons, they said, while they processed his old room for evidence and leads to the suspects.

This was a larger, more luxurious hotel. The task force had arranged to have Jeff's original hotel room number deflected to a phone they'd set up here, and they'd given him a new cell phone that maintained the Griffin family's cell number, in case Sarah, Cole or the kidnappers called him.

Detectives Cordelli and Ortiz were there observing but revealed nothing whenever Jeff plied them for details.

"What's so important about the toy plane?" he asked.

"I don't know. That's still being analyzed," Cordelli said. "Everything's still being processed for any possible trace evidence from Hans Beck."

Jeff sensed an undercurrent of anger toward him because he had disobeyed police orders and set out on his own to meet the suspects.

They would've done the same thing I did. Any man would have.

"Let's go back to what items you saw in the van," Chu said.

"There was something in there but I can't remember."

"I know it's hard but you said something about takeout?"

"A bag and a cup, maybe two cups."

A cell phone rang, breaking Jeff's concentration.

As Cordelli turned to take the call, Chu frowned and Jeff used the interruption to go the bathroom, locking the door behind him.

Inside, he turned on the cold water, letting it fill the sink.

He met himself in the mirror. The tiny veins in his eyes were red with strain. Anguish carved deep into the wounds on his face. He hadn't slept. He was still shaky from his fall. Adrenaline still rushed through him. His head throbbed and he shook out three aspirin from a new plastic bottle and swallowed them.

Events replayed before him.

Everything.

Holding Sarah. Holding Lee Ann. Losing Lee Ann. Losing Sarah.

Was I wrong? Did I make a horrible mistake not giving the killers their property? But they did not show him Cole. Where was Cole? Oh, God, tell me what to do.

It was all Jeff could think of as he emptied the sink only to refill it again and again.

"Jeff." Chu was knocking on the door. "Are you well enough to resume?"

"Yes," he said. "I need a minute."

He splashed cold water on his face, dried it and returned to his chair.

"Good. Now, you were recalling details of items in the van."

Jeff took a moment as his thoughts veered.

"There was something about the shoes. One man had a fine, bright red line where the top was stitched to the sole."

Chu flipped to a new page. She knew to go with the flow of her witness's recollection, to not disturb it but guide it, coax it along. Her hand whisked over the paper, working fast as Jeff described the dark round-toed boot with the bright red stitching.

"Like this?" Chu flipped a sketch.

"Yes, that's it."

"Anything more on the boots?"

Jeff shook his head.

Chu made notes, then went back to her pad and flipped to a new page.

"What about the items in the van, the take-out bag and cups?"

"They were coffee cups, like paper or Styrofoam coffee cups."

"Were they from one of the big fast-food chains, or coffee chains?"

Jeff concentrated, slowly shaking his head.

"I don't think so."

"Anything distinctive you can remember?"

"An *L,* a stylized *L.*"

"Printed or cursive?"

"I think cursive."

"Any other letters, symbols, colors?"

"I'm thinking a word, a partial word, like *Lasa,* or *Laksa.* Blue lettering or black letters in a white or yellow-colored cup, I think. I can't be sure."

"Okay, what was the attitude of the cups and the bag? Standing up, on the side, crushed? Were there lids?"

"Black lids, they were on their sides, like they were empty and the bag was tossed on its side, a used white napkin at the top. I think that's it. Everything happened so fast."

"I understand." Chu nodded, concentrating as she drew.

She and Jeff worked that way for the next ninety minutes, going over detail after detail, and one by one, Chu's images piled up.

32

Sheri Dalfini was at her kitchen table, raking her fingers through her red frizzy hair and going out of her mind.

Damn you, Donnie. What the hell am I supposed to do, huh? Saleena can't stop bawling. "Where's Daddy?" Benjamin thinks we're getting a divorce. Quit being an asshole and call me.

Sheri lit another cigarette, dragged long and hard on it. The smoke filled her lungs, helping her relax, but not enough.

It had been too long since she'd last heard from Donnie. Those NYPD pricks had threatened to take her kids.

This was serious shit.

Sheri calculated the time before her next shift. She needed another beer to help her think. She'd seen the latest news, how their SUV was tied to this double homicide and kidnapping.

Beside the overdue bills and collection notices were copies of the *Post* and *Daily News*. This Omarr Aimes, who died in their SUV, had to be Big Time, the name she'd gotten from Donnie, the name she'd given up.

That guy—Jeff Griffin—who was in her yard, was on TV. It was all part of this big case with his wife and son.

Oh, Jesus.

Sheri was scared.

She took a long pull on her beer and tried to relax.

A few reporters had called her. She told them to go to hell and took Saleena and Benjamin to Belva's place. But what was she supposed to do now? Get a lawyer? She'd helped police, told them what she knew. That should be the end of it.

Oh, God. I told you this was a stupid, stupid idea, Donnie.

To have the truck stolen for the insurance and some cash to get out of debt? Dumb. Donnie's jackass friends didn't have a clue who this Omarr Big Time was, or how dangerous this guy could be.

The doorbell rang.

From the side window Sheri recognized the detectives on her doorstep. The quiet one and that prick Brewer.

Sheri cursed, then took a long drag on her smoke, stubbed it out and went to the door.

What do these assholes want now? Can't they leave me alone?

"Hello, Sheri," Brewer said. "Can we come in?"

"This is not a good time. I got to go to work."

"It's important that we talk to you."

"I told you everything I can tell you, Brewer." Sheri sniffed. "I helped you, so back off and leave us alone."

She started to close the door. Brewer stopped it.

"We think it's very important right now that you let us come in, Sheri."

"Did you come to charge me?"

"No."

He looked at her, steady, resolved. And in that moment she knew.

A chill coiled up her spine, cutting through her beer-induced haze. It was Brewer's tone, almost human, and his face, almost compassionate. It was the same with his partner, Klaver. With him she found a weary sadness.

"Please," Brewer said.

Sheri surrendered the door, her thoughts racing as she managed to make it to the sofa.

Brewer sat beside her; Klaver sat in the chair, holding a file folder.

The two cops exchanged cool, clinical glances that touched on concern.

"Sheri," Brewer began, "this is the part of our job we hate."

She clasped her hands in her lap, hard, and stared at them, bracing for the worst.

"Remember those pictures we showed you of the victims of the fire in your SUV?"

Sheri would never forget the awful images.

"As you know, we identified one, Omarr Aimes, the man whose name you gave us."

She didn't move.

"We've identified the second victim."

Sheri's knuckles whitened.

"Our crime scene people and the medical examiner's office were able to get a few fingerprints. Sheri, I'm so sorry but the prints are consistent with your husband, Donald Dalfini."

Sheri did not react.

"I have material from the victim for you to confirm."

Brewer took the folder from Klaver, opened it to several enlarged photos of a tattoo, a small tattoo that said

SD & DD Eternally, and a man's gold wedding band engraved with the same inscription.

"Will you confirm the deceased as being Donald Dalfini, your husband?"

A great bubbling groan erupted from the pit of Sheri's stomach with such volume Klaver would later tell other cops that he swore it rattled windows.

"Yes, that's Donnie," she managed before sobbing. Brewer attempted to console her for several minutes.

"We're so sorry for your loss," he said. "Is there anyone we could call to be with you?"

Sheri did not respond.

She hugged her midsection indicating she was about to vomit and did so as Klaver got a large potted plant under her chin. Brewer helped her to the bathroom. Klaver then called Sheri's mother-in-law while Sheri cleaned herself and regained a degree of composure before returning to the sofa.

Klaver had taken the plant outside and hosed it for her.

Brewer and Sheri waited in the awkward silence until Brewer spoke.

"Forgive me for asking you at a time like this," Brewer said, "but is there anything more you can tell us about Donnie and Omarr, about any other people who may have been involved in any way?"

Sheri was pressing clouds of tissues to her face.

"Are you going to charge me? Because I won't survive now, not without my kids, I just won't."

"If you continue to cooperate, I give you my word I will do all I can to ensure the D.A. knows."

Klaver returned and passed Sheri a glass of cold water. She thanked him.

"Before this happened, Donnie called me and said

he was going to make ten thousand dollars if he helped Omarr."

"Helped him with what?"

Sheri stared at her tissues, then at a picture of her and Donnie with the kids at Coney Island.

"Help him with what, Sheri?"

"I had nothing to do with any of it."

"Sheri."

"That job I told you about was to help pick up something for some foreign guy."

"What foreign guy? Did he say who, or where, or have a phone number?"

She shook her head and sobbed.

33

Manhattan, New York City

The pressure to clear the case was mounting.

Under the media glare it was growing into a hydra.

Several aspects worried investigators: the murders, the brazen abductions and the chase. But most troubling was the discovery of the microdetonator, made all the more chilling because it had surfaced when more than one hundred and fifty world leaders were in town for the UN General Assembly.

But NYPD Lieutenant Ted Stroud remained calm.

He'd faced nightmares before, he thought a few short hours after the press conference when he'd arrived at the FBI's New York headquarters at Twenty-six Federal Plaza in Lower Manhattan where he showed his ID at the FBI security window.

Riding the elevator up to the case-status meeting, he glanced at the photo he'd tucked in with his own: U.S. marine corporal Kirby Stroud in his dress blues. Killed in Iraq in 2007 at age twenty-five and buried in Arlington.

He blinked at it for several floors.

Kirby was his son.

Yes, Stroud thought, drawing inspiration from the picture, he'd faced nightmares in his life and he was still standing.

He closed his wallet, stepped off at the twenty-eighth floor and headed to the boardroom. It was a large one with a view of the Brooklyn Bridge. Already, some thirty people had taken their seats around the cherry-wood conference table.

Stroud knew most of the players with the NYPD, the FBI, the Secret Service, Homeland, Port Authority, State Police, ATF, Customs and the TSA. He nodded to them, settled into his seat and reviewed his files when Ken Forsyth, FBI supervisory agent with the NYPD–FBI Joint Terrorism Task Force, entered.

It was determined that because the case was deemed to be related to terrorism, the JTTF, with the support of all other involved agencies, would control the investigation.

"Let's get started." Forsyth began the meeting with introductions of those at the table and those on the line in Washington, D.C., and other locations. "We believe we have discovered the threads of a plot," Forsyth said.

"First, I'll state the obvious—absolutely no information on this case is to be released without authorization." Forsyth's eyes went around the table. He knew many investigators had cozy relationships with members of the press. "Everything said in this room and subsequent case-status meetings is classified. If certain facts were passed to the public they'd give rise to alarm, create panic, weaken our case, which could thwart us from saving lives. We must maintain the integrity of the investigation. Is that understood?"

Throats cleared but no one spoke as Forsyth continued.

"Interest in this case is intensifying minute by minute," he said. "The White House has just informed this office that the State Department has received a number of 'inquiries of concern' from several foreign governments. At this stage no major events will be canceled."

Forsyth moved on with an update. The detonator had been flown to the FBI lab in Quantico where it would undergo further analysis.

"In relation to the detonator, the FBI is pursing the information passed to us by the NYPD concerning Hans Beck, the subject who made contact with Jeff Griffin over the mixed-up luggage. We've determined through passport tracking that in the past seventy-two hours, a Hans Beck of Munich, Germany, flew from Paris, France, to Montreal, Canada, to LaGuardia. We suspect the passport was forged using the identity of a Hans Beck, a civil servant in Hamburg, Germany, who'd reported the theft of his passport and wallet four months ago from a hotel in Vienna, Austria. We'll continue working with the Royal Canadian Mounted Police and Interpol on the subject. I'll move on to you first, Adam."

Concern was written on the face of Adam James, a senior agent with the Secret Service, the agency in charge of security for all world leaders attending the United Nations General Assembly. James had already made extensive notes, punctuated with cross-checks with his own files.

"The detonator is key," James said. "We're damned lucky that Jeff Griffin did not hand it over to the suspects. Second, it was an excellent catch by the people at the NYPD lab."

James removed his glasses before he continued.

"This is obvious, but the discovery raises so many red flags. That someone is plotting an attack, that they are either here or on their way. And if we've caught this one, how many are out there that we haven't caught? We've got one hundred and sixty-two world leaders in town. Most of them are in the crosshairs at home. Any one of them could be a target here."

James replaced his glasses and returned to his notes.

"Thanks, Adam," Forsyth said. "We're working with other national security agencies, examining all intelligence and all known groups for any links to the case. We'll share a key-points summary as soon as possible."

Forsyth said the task force was running down leads on international elements of the investigation.

"We are also following up on all credible tips that have come since the press conference ended," Forsyth said, then checked off other areas, before going around the table.

The ATF was working on the arson homicides with the fire department's Bureau of Fire Investigation, the NYPD's Arson Explosion Squad. They each gave brief reports before Forsyth came to Stroud, whose team played a leading role.

"We're looking for connections," Forsyth said, "connecting evidence to the suspects to give us the full picture. Ted will give us the foundation as to how all of this surfaced with the abductions."

Although Adam James came close, Stroud was relieved that there was no armchair quarterbacking, or criticism on their handling of Jeff Griffin, the contact with the suspects and the chase. Too much was at stake.

Since September 11, 2001, there had been more than a dozen plots by extremist groups to kill New Yorkers. Everyone knew the challenges and the risks. Unlike TV shows, movies and books, nothing in a real investigation was simple or uncomplicated with all loose ends coming together nicely. No, it never, ever worked that way in the real world.

For the benefit of all investigators, Stroud quickly outlined the chronology of the Griffin abductions and homicides, contact, the chase, the airport bag mix-up and discovery of the microdetonator.

"Bear with me," he said. "I'll explain how this is connected to the major ongoing undercover investigation by my task force, which was formed primarily with the D.A.'s Organized Crime and Rackets Bureau, the NYPD Auto Crime Division and the Insurance Frauds Bureau.

"Well over a year ago, through confidential informants and intel from the insurance industry, we'd learned about a highly sophisticated, international criminal enterprise. Suspects would steal cars in all five boroughs and neighboring states. In some cases, they worked with legitimate car owners who agreed to have their car stolen, so they could make an insurance claim. In most cases, the cars were new.

"We've made no arrests so far, as our work is ongoing, but this is what we suspect happens—once a vehicle is stolen, the suspects wash its title clean by checking the vehicle identification number of a similar make. Then they create fake documents from out of state to create a new VIN plate and stickers, then reregister the vehicle out of state to sell them offshore, shipping them from various U.S. ports to Africa, Central America, the Middle East, Russia and Eastern Europe.

"The white 2010 GMC Terrain used to abduct Sarah and Cole Griffin, and which was subsequently the site of two arson homicides, was registered to Donald and Sheri Dalfini of the Bronx. Their reported theft of the SUV was red-flagged and a target of our task force because Donald Dalfini had a history of suspected fraudulent claims. Sheri Dalfini is cooperating with our investigation and acknowledged her husband, who has just been identified as the second homicide victim, did intend to defraud the insurance company by having it stolen by Omarr Aimes, the first victim.

"Our intel indicates Aimes was associated with the criminal networks stealing the vehicles and that tentacles of those networks are connected to Middle Eastern and Eastern European organized-crime groups."

A silence went around the table.

"Some of these crime groups," Stroud said, "are known to supply resources to terrorist organizations."

"Ted," James said, "is it possible that a terrorist group used the Dalfini's stolen SUV to go after the Griffins for the detonator?"

"That's possible," Stroud said.

"Then they could have hired, or forced, Omarr Aimes and Dalfini into helping with the abduction, then murdered them to cover their tracks?" James said.

"That's one theory," Forsyth said.

"But to be so bold with a daylight abduction?" A Port Authority investigator was doubtful. "Then a chase. Wouldn't that blow any operation?"

"It could be a risk they were willing, or needed, to take," Forsyth said. "It could mean that the people behind it are prepared to be martyrs for their operation, which likely involves that microdetonator."

"I agree and I don't like where this is going," James said. "We've got the president and the first lady due for arrival in less than forty-eight hours."

34

Somewhere in New York City

He was going to kill Cole.

In the hours after the man was shot dead before their eyes, Sarah was still trembling. Her breathing had leveled as she held her son, feeling his adrenaline rippling through him. She brushed her tearstained cheek on his head and tried to understand all that had befallen them.

Why is this happening?

The question haunted her.

As Sarah and Cole waited in the awful dread, Sarah's thoughts pulled her back to that day when she was ten years old, sitting at her desk in school in Billings.

Mrs. Millet had rolled down the big map and tapped her pointer on Antarctica. Tyler Memford whispered, *"I'd never go there because it'd be like falling off the bottom of the world."* The vice principal appeared at the classroom door, all stern-faced, asking for Sarah, giving rise to giggles and whispers—*You're in trouble.*

The vice principal escorted Sarah to the office. She thought it strange that he'd put his hand on her shoulder but it was a good thing because seconds later everything turned into a dream and she couldn't remember if she'd remained standing for much longer.

The principal's office was a forest of people. When she'd entered they'd ceased talking with the words "…they can't reach any relatives yet…" hanging in the air. Principal Whittle kept rubbing his hand over his chin. The school nurse, her face wrinkled with worry, clutched her own locket. There was a police officer and two state troopers who kept twirling their hats in their hands. Sarah felt everyone's attention on her, transferring the weight of impending doom. As one of the troopers squatted down, his utility belt gave a leathery squeak. The nurse joined him and tenderly brushed Sarah's hair while searching her eyes as if the words she needed were there.

"Sarah, sweetheart, we have some very, very bad news.…"

The nurse took Sarah into her arms. Sarah stared at the flag, then the room turned red, white, then blue with blazing stars like heaven, spinning and spinning as the nurse and the trooper told her how a tanker truck had crashed into her parents' car at the edge of the city where they'd been shopping for a new fridge.

"God took them, Sarah. They were killed. I'm so sorry."

The funerals, the cemetery, the strangeness of her mom and dad's untouched bed, clothes, dishes, the streams of relatives, friends of her parents, church ladies—the aftermath was all one long blur, so intense she could not remember moving to Laurel to live with her uncle Burt and aunt Ginger.

Like falling off the bottom of the world.

Sarah's aunt and uncle were kind and loving but for

the first few years Sarah felt incomplete, like part of her had been amputated.

She was a shy student in high school, but through her part-time waitressing job at the mall, she had a lot of friends.

She started going steady with Kenyon Rupp.

In her senior year, Sarah secretly dreamed of becoming a teacher, marrying Kenyon and starting a family. But that dream ended here in New York on the class trip when Kenyon broke up with her in Central Park.

Then, like an answered prayer, Jeff Griffin saw her crying and started talking to her. Jeff was in her class. He was a nice guy, sensitive. In Central Park he'd confessed to her that he'd always liked her and told her to forget Kenyon.

"Don't worry, Sarah, everything's going to be all right."

And it was.

Jeff had rescued her.

In many ways, Sarah believed the rest of her life started at that moment in Central Park with Jeff.

When they'd returned to Montana, they started dating and eventually Sarah became a teacher and Jeff became a mechanic and firefighter. They got married, had Cole and they saved for their dream home. Then she had Lee Ann, their little girl. Sarah's life was perfect. She was so blessed, so buoyant with joy, she was walking on air.

But their world exploded when they lost her.

Why is this happening?

That question had haunted Sarah again as they struggled through the excruciating pain, the utter desolation and emptiness, the guilt and anger.

In the weeks and months after Lee Ann died, Sarah

fell into the habit of sitting alone in the dark aching for her daughter to come back. Sarah could still smell her, hear her in the night crying for her; she could feel her in her arms.

But her arms were empty.

Sarah was convinced that she was cursed. She'd lost her parents. She'd lost her baby. Was she going to lose Cole and Jeff? For months she feared that each time Cole or Jeff left the house, she would never see them again.

Lee Ann's death had consumed Jeff, too.

Weakened by grief and guilt, he'd grown distant and paranoid over Neil Larson, over everything. Jeff the fixer, the rescuer who saved lives, was helpless and so blinded by pain he was willing to destroy what was left of their family.

But now, with everything they had left at stake, they had to fight.

Sarah believed with all her heart that her last-minute plea to Jeff in their hotel restaurant had worked. She believed it because she saw it in his eyes in the van when he risked his life to save her. And she believed it because she heard it in his voice echoing through this hell. *"I love you, Cole... I love you, Sarah... We have to fight to hold this family together...."*

That's right, she thought, stroking Cole's hair.

Now she had the answer to her haunting question.

Why is this happening?

To make us stronger.

We can never surrender.

We have to fight.

Again she glanced over to the area where some of the men were quietly working.

They're planning something huge, something horrible.

We have to get out of here.

We have to tell people what's coming.

35

Somewhere in New York City

Flames burned in Bulat Tatayev's eyes.

The fire reflected his hell and his will to be delivered from it.

Even if it meant killing one of his men.

Zama.

Bulat's memory traveled across the Atlantic and across time to a troubled region of the Northern Caucasuses where he and Zama had grown up, like many of his men under his command.

There, as boys in the mountains, they'd played football together, chased the same girls, went to the same schools and dreamed the same dreams.

Bulat was born in Mykrekistan, a small Russian republic slivered between the tinderbox republics of Dagestan and Chechnya near the Caspian Sea. Bulat's father, a chemist, and Bulat's mother, a teacher, had joined Mykrekistan's long-standing rebellion against Russian rule.

But the struggle to create a free and independent nation was always crushed.

After a failed uprising, Bulat's father and mother had

taken him to gather with others to line the streets of their town to protest a passing Russian military convoy.

Bulat's father stood in the path of a tank and held up the sign he'd made on their kitchen table opposing the Russian occupation. The tank's gunner shot him. When Bulat's mother rushed to his aid, the gunner shot her, too. Before anyone could move, the tanks rolled over their bodies as if they were animals.

Bulat was fourteen.

He ran to them but others held him back to save his life. He fought, screamed, then fell to his knees in the snow-soaked dirt, his body quaking, tears running down his face. The foul-smelling diesels growled and steel clanked as he mourned the rag dolls that were his mother and father.

In the days and weeks that followed, Bulat remembered nothing.

But the seeds of vengeance had been planted in the blood-drenched mud where his parents had died.

Bulat had been taken in by relatives and passed to various homes. He was always the outsider, the loner.

"You are an orphan of the revolution," one uncle told him, "perhaps you are destined to lead it one day."

As Bulat became a young man he joined the struggle with a vow to honor his parents by winning freedom.

The Republic of Mykrekistan was divided between the loyalist minority, which ruled as a Kremlin puppet, and the resistant majority determined to break free of its Russian yoke. Mykrekistan was a region of unrest. For years across the land there were enclaves of separatist fighting and talk of unifying insurgent movements for a revolutionary war.

After graduating from school with high grades and the ability to speak English and some French, Bulat became a junior engineer in a chemical factory. He also secretly trained with the underground militia and helped lead attacks against Russian military targets.

By the time he was nineteen he had killed fifty men.

Impressed by Bulat's zeal, a wealthy warlord with international links arranged for him to study in Europe, Canada, Australia and the United States.

"You are a true son of Mykrekistan, you carry our plea and hope for our emerging nation," the warlord said.

For the next six years Bulat was away. He lived in London, Paris, Hamburg, Sydney, Toronto and New York City. He studied engineering and improved his English, his French and learned to speak some German. But the goal of his education abroad was to gather intelligence, establish cells and strengthen "freedom" networks in Mykrekistani communities around the world.

In New York City, he fell in love with Leyla, a pretty NYU student from Mykrekistan. They returned to Mykrekistan where they married and started a family, first with Lecha, their little boy, then Polla, their little girl.

Back in his homeland Bulat was embraced by rebels as if he were a returning prophet. During the years that followed he'd become a professional soldier and resumed his role leading missions against the Russian occupiers that were devastatingly effective as the potential of a revolutionary war increased.

Beyond the bloodshed, Bulat saw the future in the faces of his children, the promise that a free Mykrekistan was within their grasp. He felt it when he took them to the cemetery to kneel at the graves of his parents—to remind Lecha and Polla that his life, like those of their grandparents, was devoted to the struggle.

One year, after a brutal winter, the spring brought hope when Moscow announced free elections and the start of peace talks aimed at the transition of power and independence.

It was a lie.

The move was a ploy meant to end the toll exacted by the insurgent attacks. The election was rigged, resulting in another government that kowtowed to the Kremlin. Anger ignited unrest on every street of every village, town and city. Within weeks Mykrekistan was engulfed in war.

For weeks Moscow hammered Mykrekistan's rebel forces with its overwhelming military might. Rockets, bombs, tanks and ground troops razed entire towns.

Bulat took his family to a safe house in one of the rebel-controlled mountain villages, but the Russian military tortured prisoners for information on rebels, then unleashed relentless attacks on their strongholds.

One night Bulat woke to the sound of distant thunder. It was approaching. Dishes and cutlery began clinking because the earth started shaking.

Bulat knew what was coming.

He moved quickly to get his family to safety just as the sky shrieked with such ferocity Bulat feared it was being ripped apart. In an instant the air spasmed with a deafening roar and great wind, then everything flashed white as though the sun had hit the earth.

Bulat was hurled into blackness.

He awoke to the smells of earth and charred meat. He called out to his family in vain, then heard strange voices. Flashlights pierced the night as rescuers extracted him from the rubble.

Then in the dust-filled blackness they found Leyla.

Eyes and mouth open, only her head was exposed.

Bulat called her name and prayed as he frantically removed the debris around her.

It was futile. She was dead.

Leyla's hand had a death-grasp on a foot. *Lecha's
foot.* A flashlight beam followed it into the rubble as
Bulat dug savagely to Lecha's knee, his thigh, then to...
nothing but bloodied flesh, veins and tissue.

They found the rest of his son's remains across the
room.

Bulat and the rescuers searched for Polla.

He called out to her, his shattered heart clinging to
the hope that she had survived. Then they found her.

Above them.

Entangled in the roof's wreckage.

Dead.

Bulat got her down.

Her body was intact and warm as he carried her from
the horror to the tiny meadow near the house where the
rescuers had arranged Leyla and Lecha. Their bodies
had been wrapped in sheets.

As Bulat held Polla in his arms something inside him
cleaved, separating him from this world and his connection with humanity.

*They don't kill you, they kill what you love, which is
far worse than death,* he thought.

From the mountainside, among the dead, he saw the
distant bomb flashes and the tracer fire of the Russian
onslaught across the region. Bulat had no time to mourn.
He fought the enemy as the war raged for months. Thousands of Mykrekistanis died before Russian forces had
regained control of the republic.

"They invade our country, murder our children, our
families, and the United Nations does nothing," Bulat

told his men. "We must plunge our sword deep into Russia."

In the months after the war, Bulat led a number of strategic strikes against Russian institutions in Moscow and Saint Petersburg. However, the FSB, Russia's security service, paid informants to lead them to most of the rebels. They were captured and their families were located, arrested, then tortured before their eyes.

Then they were all executed.

Bulat and his surviving loyalists had escaped.

Soon, the Kremlin declared an end to hostilities and installed a puppet regime whose new president proclaimed victory.

"They have won nothing but a death sentence. We will never surrender," Bulat told his men.

Bulat's struggle had been crippled but his mission still burned. He would honor the dead with a free Mykrekistan by forcing the world to drink the blood of injustice.

"They can only understand once they feel what we feel. We will exchange pain for pain on the largest stage possible."

Bulat drew upon all of his resources and global connections and began planning a mission that would guarantee world attention to Mykrekistan's plight.

He would bring his struggle to the United States.

Everything had gone smoothly until Zama fucked up.

Zama was part of the advance team. Bulat had just arrived from Paris, where his forged passport had been produced.

Bulat shook with anger.

This operation had been painstakingly planned for more than a year and now it was in jeopardy. It did not involve hostages, car chases and news conferences with the FBI. All Zama had to do was to oversee the pickup of the component from LaGuardia, bring it here and help set up.

That was it.

The expensive component was rare and critical because it was undetectable by any means of security.

Without it the operation could not happen.

Everything was at risk because of Zama.

Bulat stared at his corpse burning in the furnace in the grim, lower bowels of the old casket factory.

Zama's incompetence was unforgivable.

The furnace flames reflected the determination burning in Bulat's eyes. He had shown the others that failure was not tolerated.

"Scatter his ashes over the East River. We leave no traces, just like you did with Hans Beck, or whatever that idiot's name was," Bulat instructed his men before he returned to the upper level operation planning table.

He glanced at his watch.

Less than thirty-six hours to go.

"Yannov," Bulat called to one of the men. "We will not dispose of the woman and boy. Not yet. Is that understood?"

"Yes, Commander."

"We are changing the operation in order to save it. I have a new plan that will include the woman and the boy. With them we'll get even closer than we first thought. Did you enact the backup?"

"Yes, Commander, a second device. It is en route from Amsterdam."

Bulat scanned the maps, photos, monitors, the muted news channels.

"Good, we will salvage the mission. All is not lost. This operation will seize the world's attention." Bulat turned to the direction of the factory where Sarah and Cole were being held. "We need the woman and boy. They're going to be a big part of it."

36

What am I missing?

Jeff drew his face to within inches of the flat-screen TV in his hotel room. He examined the millions of tiny pixels that formed the three pictures of Sarah in torment as he'd fought to free her from her captors.

But he no longer saw his wife, himself or the kidnappers.

He saw nothing but liquid crystals rotating polarized light.

It had been more than three hours since he'd started working with Detective Lucy Chu, the forensic artist, and some thirty-four hours since Sarah and Cole were stolen. Events bled into one another, with this morning's call from the kidnappers leading to his failed rescue bid, the hospital, the press conference and now his work with Chu.

In all that time, he'd barely slept.

Jeff blinked several times and rubbed his face.

Chu and Ortiz traded glances.

"Maybe you should knock off for a bit?" Ortiz said.

"I had her in my arms," Jeff said to the TV. "I had the door open."

"Jeff," Chu said. "You should take a break while I work on images."

"I was so close to getting her back."

"Let's get out of the hotel," Ortiz said. "So you can clear your head."

"We have to find a detail, a lead," Jeff told the TV.

"Come on, Jeff, let's go out for a bit." Ortiz took his arm gently but he shook her off.

"No! Did you hear me? I can't! I don't even know if Cole's alive!"

In the tense silence he saw the two detectives looking at him with pity and concern, the way sane people look at someone who is losing their hold on reality. Through his anguished exhaustion Jeff recognized this and after a long moment said, "All right, I'll go out by myself."

"I have to go with you," Ortiz said.

"No." He collected his cell phone and room key. "I'll go alone."

"That's not possible," Ortiz said.

"Am I under arrest?"

"Of course not." Ortiz handed him a Yankees cap and dark glasses. "Here, people might recognize you after the press coverage. Your face is out there."

Jeff stared at her.

"You guys are pissed at me. You don't trust me."

"Jeff, it's for your safety, in case contact is made again," Ortiz said.

He glanced around the room.

Cordelli had left after his call. Brewer and Klaver were following leads.

"All right," Jeff said, "there's a place I need to go."

Over twenty city, state and federal police agencies

were working on the case, Ortiz told Jeff on the way to her unmarked car.

"There was a case meeting at the FBI's office downtown. People from D.C. were on the call."

Jeff looked at her.

"Washington? Do *they* know what the toy airplane has to do with all this, can you tell me?"

"No, because I don't know. All I can tell you is that everyone's looking at all angles of the murder case and the abductions—" she nodded to a helicopter and a passing motorcade "—because of the UN meeting going on in town right now. And, at last count, we're following sixty tips called in since the press conference."

"Sixty?"

"A handful could be credible leads. Everyone's going flat out, Jeff." They'd reached the car parked near the hotel entrance. "Where did you want to go?"

"Central Park."

"That's not far, which entrance?"

"South."

"What's in Central Park?"

"Hope."

As they drove across midtown, Jeff scoured vehicles and faces in the street for Sarah, for Cole, for the kidnappers.

"You know, anyone would have done what I did, Juanita. They would've gone out on their own if it meant getting their family back."

She looked at him, at his face laced with cuts, scrapes. He looked as if he'd been at the losing end of a brawl. He was beat up physically, emotionally, but he was not defeated and she admired that about him.

"I know, Jeff."

"I remember seeing a picture of a little girl on your desk," he said. "You have kids?"

"Our daughter, Lucy, is six."

"Tell me about her?"

Ortiz's face softened into a smile.

"She's perfect. She's everything to us and I would die without her."

Jeff nodded, narrowing his eyes as he searched the streets for a way out of his nightmare.

"Tell me about Cole, Jeff?"

"He's my buddy. He has a heart of gold. When—" Jeff swallowed. "When Lee Ann was born all he wanted to do was hold her and look after her. You know what he did before we brought her home from the hospital? He took his favorite old toys, lined them up in her nursery, to welcome her and watch over her."

Jeff shook his head, glowing at the memory, then his face slowly darkened.

"I've got to find them, Juanita."

Central Park gave Jeff sanctuary from his nightmare.

Here, the boiling chaos of the city melted into the peace of the creeks, waterfalls, vast green expanses and sheltering trees.

Central Park was an island of calm.

Jeff and Ortiz found a bench near the Gapstow Bridge at the northeast end of the Pond.

"This is where Sarah and I met, really got to know each other," Jeff said. "We went to the same high school and I sort of knew her. I liked her and thought she was nice but she was dating a farm kid on the basketball team. Then we came to New York City on a school trip, about fifty students.

"We were in the park, around here, and Sarah was off by herself crying. She looked so sad and alone. I'd learned that her boyfriend had broken up with her and all I could think was who would be dumb enough to break the heart of such an angel. So I started talking to her. I told her not to worry, that what happened was the best thing because I was going to marry her one day and we would have the greatest life and come back here with our kids and tell them about it and laugh at the day her idiot boyfriend broke her heart."

Ortiz smiled.

Breezes fingered through the trees and Jeff looked up.

"Lee Ann's death undid us. We came here a broken family and I wanted to smash what was left. Sarah wanted to save it. But by the time I realized she was right, she and Cole were gone."

Jeff leaned forward and cupped his battered face in his hands.

"I can't stop believing that this is my fault."

"You can't blame yourself," Ortiz said.

"It started here. I'm the one who wanted to come back here. I'm the one who let Lee Ann slip away from us. I'm the one who wanted to destroy what was left of our family. I had Sarah in my arms this morning, now she's gone again. And I don't know where Cole is."

They sat without speaking for a long stretch. Jeff's knuckles whitened as he tightened his grip on the bench and the muscles in his jaw bunched as his anguish turned to rage.

"If those fuckers harm my family, I will find them and I will kill them."

Ortiz said nothing and they sat there watching the wind ripple the glass surface of the water.

37

Quantico, Virginia

The most advanced forensic laboratory in the world was located at the sprawling FBI Academy in the Virginia woods, fifty miles outside of Washington, D.C.

When the traffic was good, Special Agent Wilfred North could make it to his suburban district home in thirty minutes. He was collecting reports and contemplating the drive at the end of his day when his cell rang.

It was the deputy director.

"Glad I caught you, Will. We need an immediate assessment of a component related to a live credible threat in New York. I'll send you the report from the preliminary work the NYPD did earlier today. We've just flown the device to Quantico. I've told Chuck I want you and your people to process it. We need to know who made it, who is using it, where it came from, everything you can tell us ASAP. You should have it in minutes."

North set aside his reports, then emailed several ATF colleagues, as well as scientists, engineers and technicians who worked with him. He requested that they stand by to consult. Then North texted his wife he'd miss dinner.

It wouldn't be the first time.

As one of the FBI's top veteran forensic investigators at the Terrorist Explosive Device Analytical Center, his work often involved cases where lives were at stake.

North was six months from retiring. He and his wife were to meet a Realtor this evening to discuss purchasing a cabin near Canmore, Alberta, in the Canadian Rockies. But North shoved personal matters out of his head while he waited for the device.

Seated at his workstation, he cleaned his glasses with a soft cloth and reflected on his career. A former U.S. marine before he joined the FBI, North was a certified bomb technician and a crime scene investigator. He'd then worked in counterintelligence before he played a key role at the TEDAC.

The center was a multiagency branch where North's team analyzed bomb fragments, components, data and intelligence from explosions, plots and investigations in the U.S. and around the world. The team alerted its domestic partners and international allies with data they needed to find those responsible for an attack, or to prevent one from happening.

Over the years, North's work included investigations related to Oklahoma City, the USS *Cole,* attacks against the World Trade Center, the U.S. Embassy in Tanzania, the London subway attacks and terrorist incidents in Madrid, Athens, Tangiers, Kuwait City and Istanbul.

North's computer chimed with an email from the deputy director; a classified copy of the NYPD's assessment of the device. North had just enough time to read and circulate it to his colleagues when the package arrived.

He slipped on his lab coat, latex gloves and began.

He kept his workstation with its multifaceted computer system and various scopes and monitors spotless.

North activated the secure encrypted online system, then connected his headset. This accelerated analysis enabled his colleagues in the TEDAC and in labs across the country to see everything he saw in real time while allowing them to simultaneously access their systems to conduct research and offer live commentary.

Because of the superb preliminary work by Lori Hall at the NYPD, they were up to speed on the item.

North placed the component on a tray and positioned it with one of his powerful microscopes, equipped with HD webcam capabilities. He brought everything into focus for his colleagues online.

"What we have," North said, "is a wafer detonator, microscopic in scale, that was concealed by affixing it to a contact clip in the battery housing of a plastic pull-back toy jumbo jetliner. Can everyone see that?"

North waited for confirmation before resuming.

"Now the toy itself was manufactured in China's Chenghai district and the dominant material was non-phthalate PVC. We need the signature of the component maker. The detonator is a state-of-the-art, highly sophisticated device. Let's look at all aspects. I haven't seen anything like this before. Time is working against us. Everyone knows the drill, so let's get to it."

The experts undertook a number of procedures using an array of top-secret databases, secured with layers of passwords.

They looked into bomb-tracking systems containing more than two thousand reports detailing components used in improvised explosives and incendiary devices in the U.S.

Repositories on tracing the chain of manufacture, import and sale of industrial explosives and components nationally and globally were scoured. Sister databases recording thefts and losses of materials were checked.

The TEDAC had received and stored components from bombing attacks made around the world and created a computerized searchable data bank that was a critical tool for all investigations.

International bomb data centers were accessed and case studies were consulted for telltale elements. They studied global computer banks that monitored patterns and trends of terror networks and internationally known bomb makers.

An hour later, North received everyone's assessments. But before he completed drafting a preliminary analysis, his deputy director called.

"FBI HQ needs to know now, Will," the deputy said. "The White House is pressing with concerns, specifically because of the UN General Assembly in New York where the president is going to participate in forty-eight hours."

"I understand," North said.

"So give me a verbal and I'll call HQ."

North repositioned his glasses.

"Bottom line—we've never seen anything like this. Something similar has surfaced in an assassination attempt in Pakistan, attacks in Syria, Yemen."

"What exactly is it?"

"The NYPD had it right. It's a microscopic detonator—advanced, state-of-the-art stuff."

"Who made it? Who do we go after?"

"A number of possibilities. The North Koreans may have developed it, or Iranian scientists. We've got some word that it could've been Russian made and tested in Syria, before it was offered for sale to terror networks.

"This device can be used to deploy a powerful non-nuclear bomb and it's virtually invisible from detection using the normal security procedures."

"This isn't good, Will."

"No, and we don't know how it got here, if there are others already here, or en route."

"There are about one hundred and fifty world leaders in New York and each of them is a potential target."

"Or all of them," North said.

38

Amsterdam, the Netherlands

Aleena Visser was lying to herself.

With her passport and ticket clamped in her straight white teeth she locked the door to her apartment.

She adjusted her shoulder bag, hoisted her small wheeled suitcase, with its vibrant zebra pattern, and hurried down the stairs to the street in time to board the tram as it lumbered through the bohemian district of de Pijp.

She tried to deflect the worry that was nagging her.

Looking out the window at the long, narrow streets, she was glad she'd moved from the crowded, expensive insanity of Jordaan. In de Pijp she was more at home with artists and students. She had a grand apartment. She could breathe here and it was better for her work as a travel writer for an online magazine.

That's what I am, she kept assuring herself, *a travel writer and nothing else. Sometimes I help Joost, that's all I do.*

Earlier in the day, Joost Smit, her editor, had summoned her into his glass-walled office.

"I have an urgent assignment and you're just the

person to do it for us." He printed off a sheet, gave it to her and looked up over his bifocals. "We've landed major advertising for an American hotel and restaurant chain and we need a special edition on New York. We're bumping up the deadline, so you leave today for a week in Manhattan."

"Today?" Aleena's bracelets jingled as she swept back her blond hair.

"We've booked you on a flight from London that gets into Newark in the morning, New York time. Here's your ticket and a cash advance. Use the company card for other expenses."

"What do you need for the edition?"

"A feature on Central Park, the status of Ground Zero and whatever else you like. And—" Joost reached into his valise and put a small wooden box on his desk "—would you please deliver this for me in Manhattan?"

It was a ballerina music box.

"Who's it for?"

"My niece. It was handmade in Zurich and belonged to my great-grandmother. I don't want to risk shipping it because it has tremendous sentimental value." Joost removed his glasses, then lowered his voice. "It's very important that it be handled with the utmost care and is delivered successfully. You are the only person I can trust to do this, Aleena. Will you do it?"

She shifted her attention from him, glanced around the office, then shifted it back and in a near-whisper said, "No."

"Aleena, it is imperative this be delivered. We'll triple the payment."

"I don't care, I can't do this anymore."

"Last one, I promise."

"That's what you said the last time."

Joost let the warmth in his face melt as he squinted through the glass toward Aleena's desk and the framed photo of her with her family.

"Tell me, how are your mother, your sister and her sweet children?"

"Don't do this."

"If there were another option, I would use it but we don't have time."

Aleena swallowed her tears and nodded.

"Good," Joost said. "I'll call you with instructions later."

That's how it went with Joost: an assignment somewhere around the globe and a delivery.

Aleena left the tram and got on the subway. It whisked her to Schiphol Airport where she checked in and passed through security screening smoothly. She bought an herbal tea, settled in at preboarding, then texted Joost.

Seconds later, he called.

"Do not write any of this down. You are to make no record of what I am going to tell you, and memorize your emergency contact number, is that understood?"

"I know how it works."

Not long after Joost gave Aleena details on delivery of the music box in New York, she boarded. And as her jet climbed over the North Sea, she resumed trying to convince herself she was a travel writer doing a small favor for a friend, the last favor.

The first leg of her trip took her to London where she needed to change planes at Gatwick for a direct flight to Newark, New Jersey.

As Aleena's bags rolled along the conveyor and into the X-ray scanner a stern-faced female security agent requested her passport and boarding pass. The agent, who had the shape of a male bodybuilder, eyed her with a coolness that bordered contempt.

At twenty-seven, Aleena was beautiful. With her blond hair, ice-blue eyes, some tattoos and a pierced left nostril with a diamond, she embodied a free spirit.

Satisfied that Aleena matched her passport photo and everything was in order, the agent returned the documents and Aleena passed through security. As people located their seats on the jet, Aleena assured herself she was not doing anything wrong by helping Joost.

Just believe what he told you.

As the 747 lifted off and greater London unfurled below, Aleena's stomach knotted. She pressed her head back into her seat, blinked at the ceiling.

I can't keep doing this.

Aleena wrestled with all of her rationalizations until her conscience forced her to admit the truth. She was not a travel writer. Not really. That life ended long ago.

Aleena Visser was a professional smuggler.

I admit it.

I am an international criminal.

How did this happen to me?

She'd met Joost Smit at a conference for journalists in Madrid, *oh, so many years ago.* He was a seasoned reporter who'd worked for *Le Monde, Reuters,* Interfax and AFP. He was retiring to launch a travel magazine and offered Aleena a position that paid her double what she was earning as a general assignment newspaper reporter in Rotterdam.

Joost had huge financial backing and incredible contacts around the world. In a few short years, Aleena had set foot in most every country on earth, writing wonderful travel features and loving her life.

While on assignment it was common for her to deliver an item or two to one of Joost's ex-news pals, an ex-cop, diplomat, professor or some all-around shadowy figure. If the contact failed to show, she called the emergency number she'd memorized. Aleena was impressed by how many people Joost knew in exotic places from his journalist days. Joost paid her well for the favors. Of course, she'd heard the nasty rumors and jokes in the office about Joost's mysterious past—that he was connected to the underworld. It gave rise to her own suspicions in the wake of some of her deliveries, but she'd always dismissed them. She was seeing the world, writing about it, making incredible money and having fun.

Until a recent trip to Turkey.

She was writing about Istanbul where she delivered a watch to Yuri, a former reporter with Interfax, the Russian wire service.

"And how is Joost, my old spy friend?"

After reading the shock on Aleena's face, Yuri, who had obviously been drinking but was not that drunk, took her to a quiet café and, while hitting on her, confidentially told her, "reporter to reporter," that Joost had once worked for Russian intelligence. All of Joost's spy world friends knew that his magazine was a front for several global smuggling networks, specializing in small, critical items.

"For all you know—" Yuri tapped the watch Aleena had given him before laughing "—you may have just delivered the key to unleashing a biological weapon, or nuclear device."

Yuri's laughter haunted Aleena.

Later, when she confronted Joost, he let a long disturbing silence pass.

"Yuri's weakness will get him killed one day," Joost said before he confirmed everything: he was a smuggler.

Then, very pleasantly, he asked about Aleena's mother, her father, her older sister and her three little nephews, stating specific addresses and personal information that chilled Aleena.

Joost then subtly suggested how Aleena was implicated and it would be better for her to keep secret things secret. He knew about her bank account in Luxembourg, where she'd been hiding the large payments he'd given her for making deliveries.

The truth was sickening, overwhelming.

She wanted to get out of this business, get away from Joost.

But how?

Now, somewhere over the Irish Sea, Aleena confronted her guilt.

All those items I delivered...what were they? Who was at the other end of the emergency contact numbers? Did anyone ever die because of me? I can't keep doing this...I just can't....

She took the ballerina music box from her bag, looked at it. There was nothing unusual about it. What could it be? She opened it and played the most beautiful version of Tchaikovsky's *Swan Lake*.

Tears streamed down Aleena's face.

Will I have blood on my hands?

39

Cole forced himself not to cry.

That bearded guy just killed the man who wanted to kill me. Just shot him in the head.

Tiny prickles of sensation kept running up and down Cole's body as he stared at three fat rats across the factory floor. They were licking the fresh blood streaks where the dead guy had been dragged away.

It got all quiet after they got rid of his body.

And the awful burning smell, whatever it was, was nearly gone now, but Cole was afraid, not knowing what the kidnappers were going to do next.

He didn't want to cry.

His mom held him, rubbing her cheek against his.

"We have to brave, sweetie," she whispered. "Think of all the fun things we'll do with Daddy when we get out of here. Okay?"

She kissed the top of his head where they had jabbed him with their guns.

"Okay?"

Cole nodded, keeping his face pressed to his mother.

Cole wouldn't cry. Not with one of the killers sitting

in the chair about ten feet away. The guy kept scratching himself and yawning. Looking at him with disdain, Cole kept twisting the links of his chain; running his fingers along it was calming.

He just wanted this to be over.

When it all started he thought it was a movie or TV show, like some kind of joke. It happened so fast with these strange men showing them guns, shoving them into the car and sliding hoods over their heads.

This can't be real, Cole had thought.

But it *was* real.

They drove and drove, bringing them to this scary place that stunk like a broken toilet, and handcuffing them with chains and sticking that goof over there to watch them. Cole had trouble understanding their accents as they demanded a backpack with a toy plane. Mom kept telling them they'd made a mistake, that his bag got mixed up at the airport with a bag that belonged to that weird guy, Hans Beck. She kept telling them that they traded bags back with him.

After that they went crazy.

They took Mom away.

Cole was terrified he would never see her again. But when they came back with her, they were even madder and Mom was really, really scared. Then when they saw Dad on TV with all those cops, and those pictures, the creeps freaked out and one of them was going to shoot him.

Feeling that gun on his head, he was never so scared in his life.

Then the leader with the beard killed the guy and told them that *sooner or later we all die.*

Cole understood that.

He knew that everyone died one day. He was there

when his baby sister died. He knew that Lee Ann had gone to heaven first because God needed her there to help get things ready for him and Mom and Dad.

Cole also knew that it was wrong to kill people.

Good people don't kill people.

His mom and dad didn't kill people. They helped people. His dad ran into burning buildings when people were running out. His dad was a hero who saved lives. His dad fixed things and Cole knew in his heart from what he saw on the TV news that his dad was working hard trying to fix this.

Cole shot a vengeful glance beyond the guard who was half-asleep and beyond the blood-licking rats to the tables where the creeps were working. Gritting his teeth, he kept twisting his chain.

My dad's going to kick your freakin' butts.

Cole wanted to kick their butts, too, because what they were doing wasn't right. He hated them for what they did, scaring him, his mom, his dad. Cole sat up, feeling a bit better, while his mom stared off at nothing.

"It's going to be okay, honey. Don't worry."

She said that a lot, like a prayer she was telling herself.

Cole slid his fingers along his chain and looked at his kidnappers. He wished he could fight them, wished he could help, the way he'd sometimes help his dad fix cars.

"Pick up that wrench, son," his dad used to say on days when he worked on the truck. Dad would lift Cole up over the hood. His big strong hands holding him firm, safe. He'd guide him on where to connect the wrench and how to turn it, waiting patiently while Cole made the adjustment.

As Cole moved to reach for the bottle of water, he noticed something for the first time.

On the ground, near the drowsy guard's boot.

At that moment a ray of sun lit upon a small metal object, making it glint. Cole softly nudged his mother, drawing her attention to it.

A small ring with two handcuff keys.

Cole's mom froze, then glanced at Cole.

The keys had fallen from the sleepy guard's pocket.

Cole's mom pressed her lips together, eyed the guard until she was certain he had drifted off. She gathered her chain to silence it and a swift, smooth motion swept the keys into her hand.

She passed them to Cole, nodding to the wall. He quickly hid the keys among the countless cracks.

Then he and his mother looked at each other.

Both had to restrain their excited breathing and pray the guard would not notice.

They would wait for the right time.

40

Brooklyn, New York

"The president of Burundi just canceled the Empire State Building event," Secret Service Agent Tate Eason said through his headset to the agent in midtown heading the detail protecting the dignitary. "Adjust the schedule—go with the flow, Jim, go with the flow."

Under the circumstances, we're all a bit edgy.

Eason took another swallow of his energy drink and continued monitoring his console at "Iron Shield," code name for the Secret Service security command center for United Nations General Assembly.

The center was on the thirtieth floor of an office tower on Adams Street in Brooklyn, home of the Secret Service's New York field office. This field office, more than any other within the Secret Service, was forever and inextricably linked to terrorism because it had been relocated to Brooklyn from Tower 7 of the World Trade Center after September 11.

Eason, the son of a Boston detective, had served six years as an army intelligence officer before joining the Secret Service five years ago. A quick thinker with strong analytical skills—completing puzzles was his hobby—Eason had been posted to the UNGA command center, along with several other agents. He liked this assignment but things had grown a little more tense than usual.

We've got to take down this plot.

He took another drink and shoved a fresh stick of gum in his mouth.

Gotta stay sharp.

The discovery of the microdetonator arising from the abduction had cranked up anxiety levels.

What was—or is—the operation? Who is the target?

The Secret Service was in charge of protecting more than one hundred and sixty world leaders and their delegations while they attended the United Nations gathering. That meant nearly three hundred security details involving the Secret Service and other federal security agencies. The NYPD also played on-the-ground supporting roles at events with crowd control, dog teams, mounted patrols and barricades. They also oversaw traffic routes, helped with motorcades and secured buildings and event sites throughout New York.

Eason concentrated on the task before him and the other agents at the command center. They were responsible for live-time monitoring of every dignitary's delegation, their Secret Service security detail and the dignitary's foreign security detail. Eason and the other agents had to stay on top of every move a delegation made through encrypted radio contact, secure cell phones, texting and surveillance cameras.

They had to ensure their safety at every moment. They fed into the strategies of directing the placement of sniper teams, plainclothes agents, SWAT teams, biological and chemical response teams and medical teams. They also consulted on strategic use of electronic countermeasures that could jam remote or cell phone activation of an explosive device. If there was an incident of any sort, they could activate and direct the evacuation of a leader and, depending on the scale of an attack, they could immediately remove every world leader from Manhattan.

Eason's job at Iron Shield had begun months earlier in Washington, D.C., where he'd worked with the Secret Service's intelligence division to prepare and update the profile of every dignitary to be protected.

Eason and the other agents were expected to be experts on every dignitary, but more important, they were expected to be experts on who might want to kill the leader and how they might do it.

The Secret Service received intelligence from every branch of U.S. national security, including the CIA, the FBI, the NSA, the State Department and the Pentagon. It also had access to data from foreign intelligence agencies. Nearly every country whose leaders were attending the UNGA supplied information to Washington, to help ensure their leader's protection while in the U.S.

In most cases foreign intelligence detailed known threats and assassination attempts, plots, terrorist attacks, alliances and conspiracies. They were constantly alerting the Secret Service to any updates.

With an eye to the unnerving discovery of the micro-detonator, Eason and his fellow agents continued studying the intelligence which outlined major incidents that had taken place over the past five years.

In Pakistan, an extremist group had attempted to kill Pakistan's president with a remote-controlled bomb placed under a bridge over which his motorcade was about to pass. The plot had failed when the bomb malfunctioned.

In India, national security agents, acting on a tip, had foiled a sniper minutes before he'd planned to shoot India's prime minister during an official function at a holy site. The sniper had been contracted by an anti-government network.

In Russia, a rebel suicide bomber was shot before he reached the office of the president of Mykrekistan, a small Russian republic that had endured years of civil strife, which had played out in a number of attacks on schools, hospitals, stadiums, various buildings, and train, airport and subway stations across Russia.

In France, a runway truck loaded with explosives blew up at Charles de Gaulle Airport ten minutes prematurely as the French president's plane was about to land in Paris. An Algerian radical group with ties to international terror networks claimed responsibility.

Antigovernment insurgents in the Ivory Coast had concealed remote-controlled explosives under the clothing of children in advance of the leader making a ceremonial school visit. Sharp-eyed members of the protection detail noticed an exposed wire under a little girl's shirt and the plot was foiled.

In Peru, Shining Path guerillas succeeded in cutting all power to runway lights just as the president's plane was making a night landing in a remote mountain city of Peru. Pilots managed to control the aircraft.

Eason shook his head.

Virtually every leader was a target. In every case there was political or religious motivation from extreme factions. He scrolled through event agendas and scenarios, looking at those most likely at risk.

The president of the United States and the British prime minister were doing a joint open-air event in Columbus Circle.

China's president would face protests when he attended the World Gymnastics Championships at Madison Square Garden.

Protests were expected when the Russian president and president of Mykrekistan visited Ground Zero.

Japan's prime minister would be attending a baseball game at Yankee Stadium in the Bronx, which was a security nightmare. Two Tokyo-based apocalyptic extremist groups with supporters around the world had been issuing death threats and making claims to having access to weapons of mass destruction.

Over the past year, in New York City, investigators had uncovered six plots by domestic terror cells working with help from global networks. One included a conspiracy to bomb Penn Station; one intended to blow up the Brooklyn Bridge; another was to seize JFK. The NYPD had also discovered suitcases filled with N8PTT, a highly explosive compound, abandoned in Grand Central Terminal.

"What do you think, Tate?" Matt Brewbaker, the agent next to him, asked. "The detonator thing with the murders and the kidnappings is freaking everyone out."

"I know. Check out some of the events for lower-level protectees," Eason said.

They browsed the files.

Spain's first lady would be at the Metropolitan Museum of Art to open a new exhibit of Picasso paintings. In Bryant Park behind the New York Public Library, Russia's first lady and the wife of the president of Mykrekistan would be attending a ceremony honoring the discovery of literary papers from Russian and Mykrekistani writers. And Brazil's first lady, a world-famous mezzo, would sing in a special performance of *La Traviata* at the Metropolitan Opera.

"Remember," Eason said, "Chechen insurgents seized a Moscow theater in 2002. About one hundred and forty hostages died."

"I know, I know. We never rule out anything."

This list of potential targets was never ending. Eason entered another database, one that monitored live foreign intelligence, and searched for data that might point to threat of credible plot.

China had nothing. India, nothing. Japan, nothing. Peru, nothing. *What about Russia?* Eason thought. They always had something. Here we go—just the standard update. Various terrorist and insurgent groups with chatter that indicated that they will take action in the United States.

Eason took a slow breath.

It was routine.

Every group threatened to use a world event as a stage for their cause.

But that detonator, the brazen abduction of the mother and her son from Montana, the murders.

It all gnawed at Eason as he stared up at the enlarged backlit map of Manhattan. With blinking lights pinpointing every dignitary and their detail, it was a galaxy of possibilities.

Who is the target?

41

Images of the past few hours, the past days, fueled Jeff's anger.

Sarah's heart beating against me, almost free.

He held on to that moment as he and Ortiz stepped into the hotel elevator after returning from Central Park to resume working with Detective Lucy Chu, the forensic artist. Cordelli was still there, along with another man Jeff didn't recognize. Another desk with more equipment, including a laptop and TV, had been set up. A trolley with sandwiches, sliced vegetables, coffee and soft drinks stood in one corner.

"Any word?" Jeff asked Cordelli.

"Nothing yet."

"Nothing? What about the toy, what's that all about?"

"We don't know enough about it yet. It's being analyzed at the FBI lab."

"Bull. I think you guys know a lot about it." Jeff shot his chin toward the TV. An all-news channel was running a report on the case and the United Nations meeting. "It's tied to this UN thing and plot, isn't it?"

"That's a concern, yes."

"A concern? I told you what the asshole in the van said—that he was going to show the world what it means to suffer. I think you guys know way more than you're telling me. My wife's and son's lives are hanging by a thread. I deserve the truth."

"Jeff, about twenty law enforcement agencies are doing everything humanly possible to return Sarah and Cole safely and arrest the people responsible."

Cordelli told him how the FBI and TSA were analyzing Cole's backpack, how the NYPD were following every tip called in since the press conference. He told him that the Secret Service, which oversees security for the UN event, was helping investigate.

"We're pursuing every possible angle," Cordelli said. "Now, Detective Ron Cassidy, here, is from IDENT." Cassidy rose from his desk and laptop to shake Jeff's hand. "Ron's going to work with you and Lucy to get a package of material together for us to distribute to precincts so we can begin a canvass."

"What sort of package?"

"I've finished the images of all the items you noted in the van," Chu said while typing on her laptop keyboard, "the boots, the take-out bag, the walkie-talkies, the sweatshirt—the ones we worked on. We're setting up an array and slide show that can also be converted to hard-copy stills."

"Officers will canvass key areas with the images—" Cordelli nodded to Cassidy "—and Ron's going to help us sharpen the material. Hang on, you'll see."

Chu entered a few commands and a new presentation appeared showing the items Jeff had described in the van. They were vivid images: take-out food wrappers and a take-out bag, take-out coffee cups, a black boot with a fine line of bright red trim, a duffel bag, walkie-talkies, folded maps, bullet tips in magazines, figures in sweatshirts, hoods up, dark pants.

"Hold it," Cassidy said.

Chu froze the image of the take-out cups. They each had a logo starting with a cursive stylized *L* that capitalized the partial word *Lasa* or *Laksa* in dark lettering on a light-colored cup. Each cup had a black lid.

Cassidy began working on his computer.

"I have access to all of New York City's licenses for restaurants, cafés, etcetera. I'll get a list of every one starting with this description and narrow our search to those establishments. To expedite it, we'll exclude fast-food chains."

Jeff nodded his satisfaction, then Chu resumed the slide show, coming to other items with Cassidy again, explaining how they would attempt to narrow the canvass, as they did with the take-out containers, by directing police based on the details Jeff had provided.

When they arrived at the image of the boots, they stopped. They were dark boots that covered the ankle. They had rounded toes and they had a thin bright red line where the top was stitched to the sole.

Cassidy analyzed the sharpest one and entered notes into his computer. Then his computer screen split into two. One half held Chu's image, while the other blurred as if searching.

"I'm using a program to seek a piece of footwear consistent with the sketch. We're looking at databases of brands, and manufacturers' designs and outsole producers, importers and exporters who might have something consistent with this impression."

Minutes went by without any results.

"I was afraid of that," Cassidy said. "The description is too broad, too vague. I'll keep trying a few things."

Cassidy and Chu continued searching, making calls, consulting with colleagues while refining and adjusting their work. By the time they'd finished, night had fallen. Before everyone left, Chu and Cassidy gave Jeff his own hard-copy package and an electronic version of the images to review.

Unable to sleep, Jeff stayed up for hours, examining them with fervor as one by one they flowed before him.

It's here, he told himself, *the key is here.*

42

"Here we go." Brewer grunted to Klaver.

The bar was at the fringe of the park, not all that far from where Omarr Aimes had lived with his grandmother and daughter.

Brewer and Klaver had used the flimsy lead they'd gotten from Sheri Dalfini on her husband's last movements with Aimes to mine the NYPD databases. Then they hit the street and worked their confidential informants until they got a name.

Florence Payne.

When they ran her name, they learned that she was also known as Mary Ballard, and, according to their sources, was one of the last people to see Omarr Aimes alive.

Looking deeper into her files they learned about her troubles and that Florence was also known as "Miss Tangiers," an exotic dancer at the Cold Room, the bar with a strip club in the basement.

Word was that Florence was performing tonight.

It was 1:35 a.m. when the detectives entered the bar. The joint had vinyl seats patched with duct tape, scarred hardwood floors and chipped brick walls. The basement smelled of beer, drain cleaner and cheap cologne. A bony naked girl twirled around a pole while Tom Jones sang "What's New, Pussycat?"

This is where dreams come to die, Brewer thought.

"We're looking for 'Miss Tangiers,'" Klaver said to a waiter, a man with no neck who was built like a fridge. His droopy eyes rolled to Klaver's badge, then he nodded to the hall and the dressing rooms.

"Number three," the waiter said.

The door for number three bore many fractures.

Brewer knocked twice.

"Next show's in fifteen minutes." A woman's voice was muffled.

"NYPD, Florence, open up!" Brewer said.

A silence, then a curse before a toilet flushed.

"I don't have to talk to you."

"You obstructing us, Florence? Want to dance in a cell tonight?"

Another curse before the lock clicked. The door cracked as wide as six inches of chain would allow. A pair of almond eyes stared up at Brewer.

"We need to talk to you about Omarr Aimes."

"Who?"

Brewer had cued up a photo of Aimes and held up his cell phone.

"Oh, Sweet Time."

"Yeah, Sweet Time. Open up."

"I don't know anything about him."

"Listen up. We can take you downtown right now!"

"That's a lie!"

"It seems your ex says you violated his visitation rights to see your daughter, Trinity. Something about not showing up, disrespecting the terms of what was ordered by the family court judge."

"That is so much bull-fucking-shit."

"Seems he filed a petition with the court and you failed to show at the hearing."

"He's a drunk and a deadbeat who hasn't paid a damn penny in child support. What is the court doing about *my* violation petition? Are you going to help me with that? Jesus, why're you getting in my face like this? It's because of him I gotta work here. All my money goes to lawyers. I'm just trying to make a better life for me and my baby girl."

"Get some clothes on," Brewer said. "We'll talk outside in the fresh air."

"But I got a show in ten minutes."

"Let's go now, Florence," Brewer said.

She closed the door, bustled about the room before emerging in a full-length leather coat with her bag, leading them out the back to the alley. She rummaged through her bag, produced a cigarette and lighter. A flame flickered. She inhaled deeply, leaned against the stone wall, hugged herself and blew a stream of smoke skyward.

"When was the last time you were with Omarr?" Brewer asked her.

"I have the right to remain silent."

"You're not under arrest."

"Then we're done."

"I'll tell you when we're done," Brewer said. "You know about Omarr."

"That he's dead, yeah. Bummer."

"When was the last time you saw him?"

"I didn't kill him, unless dancing on his crotch is a crime."

A bright light suddenly stung her eyes.

"Hey! What the fuck!"

Klaver had a flashlight aimed at her.

"You stoned, Florence? That could be a violation," Brewer said. "You want us to take you downtown, jam you up?"

She was shaking her head to avert the light.

"No, fuck you."

"How about a little cooperation?"

"Shut that thing off."

The light went out.

"Now, when was the last time you were with Omarr?"

"The night before they found him dead."

"Where? What did you do?"

"He came to the bar. He's a regular. I danced for him. He hired me for overtime. We went to my girlfriend's place. I did him all night for five hundred and he left in the morning. There, we're done." She dropped her cigarette and stubbed it. "I have to go."

"Not so fast," Brewer said. "When he came to the bar, was he alone or with anyone else?"

"He was alone."

Klaver glanced over at Brewer. They knew Aimes had a prepaid cell phone. They couldn't trace any of his calling history, nor could they find it.

"When you were with him, did he make or receive any calls on his cell phone?"

She said nothing.

"Think, Florence. Think."

"One. He took one call when he was with me."

"What did he say, who was he talking to?"

"How the hell should I know? Some shit about a job for some guy."

Brewer exhaled slowly, struggling to hang on to his patience.

"We see from your file with the court that you're studying to be a court reporter."

"I told you I was trying to get out of the life, any law against it?"

"You have to have a good memory for that line of work. Prove to us that you have a good memory, Florence, and maybe we can help you."

Florence looked at Brewer, considered his offer and blew smoke out the side of her mouth.

"Think about the conversation Omarr had—it was hours before he was killed. Can you remember anything about his end of it?"

The back door to the bar opened, a man's silhouette filled the doorway.

"Get your ass on the stage, Miss Tangiers!"

Brewer flashed his badge, Klaver revealed his holstered gun. "Police business, back off!" Brewer said.

The man retreated, muttering.

"Think about that call, Florence."

"He was talking to some guy. It maybe had something to do with making a movie, picking something up for him. I don't know. He sounded like he was talking about what they were going to do near Times Square. Then after he hung up he called somebody else and says that some guy named Zeta, or Rama, some crazy Albanian or Russian, got a job for them. Big easy money."

As Klaver wrote it down, Brewer pressed further.

"This Zeta, or Rama, you hear him say anything else about him?"

"No, nothing. I swear that's all I heard. Look, Omarr wasn't there to talk, you know."

Brewer and Klaver let a moment pass.

"We're going to need you to come downtown and make a statement."

"But I have one more show."

"We'll talk to your boss."

"And you'll help me, right?"

"If your information checks out."

43

Most of the travel magazine's staff had gone out for lunch.

Alone at his desk, Joost Smit twisted the cap from a bottle of pink stomach remedy and swallowed a mouthful. Grimacing, he resumed rereading the disturbing email on his computer. Joost had received it ten minutes ago from a friend in Turkey who'd noticed a small news story.

Yuri Kripovanosk, corporate security consultant and former reporter with Interfax, the Russian wire service, was dead at fifty-two. He'd been found in an alley near a busy market in Istanbul.

Foul play was not suspected, according to police.

Joost never trusted police statements when it came to the deaths of people he knew. He reached into his valise for his secure cell phone and called a friend in Vienna to see if he had more information. As the line rang, worry swirled in Joost's mind over Yuri's death. Yes, Yuri drank too much and when he drank he talked too much. He was the one who'd revealed Joost's past to Aleena. But he was Joost's most important associate in his global courier operation. Together they'd amassed sizable fortunes and talked of retiring to Aruba.

Yuri's network was far more extensive and lucrative than Joost's and far more dangerous, given that many of his clients were terrorists.

It was Yuri who'd arranged the music box delivery, through his people who'd brought it to Joost yesterday, near-frantic with instructions that it be delivered in New York within twenty-four hours. Yuri provided the emergency contact number to be memorized. For this job, Joost's share was two hundred thousand euros. Cash. In the standard split. Half now, the remainder upon delivery. Joost did not know who the customer was or what the music box contained, only that it would pass easily through any security checkpoints.

Or so he was told.

And so he'd hoped.

In her last text Aleena had indicated that she'd changed planes in London without a problem and was en route to Newark. That gave Joost a measure of comfort on one front. But the unanswered phone in Vienna deepened his anxiety over Yuri's death.

Joost hung up and swallowed another mouthful of stomach medicine.

His office phone rang.

The number for the receptionist downstairs displayed. Joost answered.

"Two gentlemen to see you, Mr. Smit."

"I'm not expecting anyone. Tell them I am in meetings all afternoon."

Joost hung up, removed his glasses and massaged his tired eyes. He needed to send a wire transfer to his bank in the Cayman Islands.

His line rang. The receptionist again.

"They're from the KLPD."

KLPD? That's the national criminal investigations branch. Joost absorbed the update. "Did they say what it was about?"

"They wouldn't say. They're on their way to see you."

Joost hung up. He had little time to think before two men entered the editorial department, scanned the empty desks, then filled the doorway to his office. One nodded to his nameplate.

"You are Joost Smit?"

"Yes."

"I'm Sergeant Peter Linden and my partner is Sergeant Jan de Groot. We're with the criminal intelligence division."

A ping of uneasiness sounded in the back of Joost's mind. *Their accents were off.*

De Groot shut his office door and proceeded to close all the window shades. At this point Joost thought it wise to cooperate. He stood to greet them.

"Yes, how can I help you?" He extended his hand.

Linden shook it, the glint of a gold filling flashed when he attempted a smile that seemed more like the scowl of a man void of human qualities.

"We have some routine inquiries."

Then de Groot, the larger of the two men, shook Joost's hand. Pain shot through it as if he'd been pricked as de Groot nearly crushed it in his.

Blood oozed from a small, deep puncture in the palm of Joost's hand. Horror blossomed on his face. Gripping his wounded hand he sank into his chair, watching de Groot casually collapse the tiny needlepoint on his large ring.

Joost was aware that he'd been injected with poison.

"Comrade Smit," Linden mocked him. "You're aware who we are and why we're here."

Linden set a small vial with clear liquid and a packaged hypodermic needle on Joost's desk out of Joost's reach.

"Without this antidote," Linden said, "you will die in twenty-five to thirty-five minutes, a heart attack at the desk, so common with men your age."

Joost's right hand was getting numb, sweat formed on his upper lip.

"The FSB in Moscow has been working very hard and that hard work led us to Yuri Kripovanosk in Istanbul," Linden said. "Let me show you the excellent work of our team there."

Linden reached into his pocket for his cell phone and played a short video recording. Yuri was in a darkened room, naked, bound to a table. A man with bolt cutters was amputating his toes. Linden adjusted the volume so Joost could hear Yuri's screams.

"The toes, the fingers, then his cock. You know the drill. Old school but effective, right, Smit?" Linden's gold crown flashed when he grinned. "He cooperated, which brings us to you."

Joost swallowed.

"We have learned of a plot to assassinate our president in New York during the General Assembly of the United Nations. You will tell us about this plot and Russian security will defeat it our way, hopefully avoiding the complication or the embarrassment of involving the Americans."

The numbness in Joost's hand was shooting along his arm.

"I know nothing of any plot."

"This is not the time to lie," Linden said. "Yuri arranged for you to deliver an item containing something critical to this plot. What is it and where is it?"

Joost's shoulder began throbbing.

He glanced at the antidote, then searched around his office, coming to a snapshot of a staff Christmas party, finding Aleena, smiling, innocent. If he gave her up, they would find her and kill her.

"Yuri was mis-mis-mistaken."

Linden said nothing as de Groot began rummaging through files, the schedules, staff lists. Minutes passed as Linden tapped the antidote vial with the frequency of a ticking clock.

Painful spears of lightning shot through Joost's brain.

His body had turned to stone. He saw de Groot drawing his face to a corkboard of upcoming editions and the small harmless note Joost had written on the look-ahead list: "Aleena in NYC for feature."

Aleena's full name was in the magazine. Her desk was a few feet away.

The room began spinning for Joost and he smelled bread.

Warm and fresh.

He was a boy again in his father's bakery in Saint Petersburg. The happiest time of his life, helping box the pies, the tarts, and bag the bread. His Dutch father had big hands and he kneaded the dough like a master. His Russian mother smelled of sugar and cream when she hugged him against her apron.

Before he died Joost embraced the memory of how the ovens kept him so warm through the coldest winters.

44

Cole woke in darkness.

His heart was beating fast because today they were going to get away.

But he didn't move a muscle.

Ever since they'd found the handcuff keys he prayed that the guard wouldn't realize that he'd dropped them. Chances were good they would not be missed, because ever since Cole and his mom were taken, the guards had only used the keys once to release Cole's mom when they took her away.

Cole and his mother had held off acting on their discovery.

"We have to wait for the right time," she had whispered.

Buoyed by the hope of escape Sarah decided they must make their move when their captors were at their weakest.

In the predawn.

"We'll do it before sunrise," Sarah had told Cole last night before urging him to get some sleep.

Now he was wide-awake, his heart racing as he checked on his mother lying on her mattress near him.

Sarah was awake, too, keeping vigil of the men far across the old factory floor where the scene was akin to a military encampment.

Snoring and coughing echoed in the still air.

Most of them were asleep in cots, or in sleeping bags on air mattresses. In the ambient light she saw a couple of them at the tables working at computers, talking softly on cell phones or to each other. The various tiny lights of their equipment winked and light reflected off the metal of equipment peeking from tarps.

Sarah studied their guard.

He was wearing a holstered gun.

He was in a padded high-back office chair some ten feet away where he'd spent much of last night in a lip-smacking feast of spicy-smelling food from a plate on his lap.

Now, his chin was on his chest and he was snoring.

Sarah gathered her chain and inched closer to the guard.

The luminescent digits of his watch showed 3:39 a.m.

The guard was out cold.

Sarah glanced toward the others in the distant darkness.

Now, she thought, *we have to do this now*.

Sarah moved to Cole, who retrieved the keys from their hiding spot.

When he tried the first one in his mother's cuffs, it didn't work. Neither did the second key. He glanced fearfully at her. She bit her lip, checked to make sure the guard was still sleeping, then tried the key in Cole's cuff.

It clicked open.

She gasped, clasped her hands over his cuffs, then freed Cole from the chain. She closed his open dangling handcuff around his wrist so it would not make a sound. He now had two cuffs closed on one wrist.

"Heavy," Cole said, testing the weight.

The metal against metal made a little noise but not too much.

"Okay, honey, are you ready?"

Fear flooded Sarah's voice as she fought to stay calm for Cole.

"I think so."

"Remember what we talked about?"

"Yes."

"Each time I went to the bathroom I loosened the cover of the air shaft," she said. "I'm pretty sure it leads to the next room."

Cole nodded.

"Pull it off and find your way out of here. Just get out and tell the first person you see who you are and to call 9-1-1 and send police."

"I'm scared to leave you, Mom."

"I know but you have to be brave. I want you to get out and be safe."

Sarah took Cole's face into her trembling hands.

She couldn't believe any of this, couldn't believe all that had happened, that she was now pulling her son so tight to her that he nearly cried out.

Am I making a mistake to send him off like this? What if something happens? What if I never see him again? I've already lost Lee Ann. I could not bear to lose him. But it's his only chance to get free, to be safe.

Cole stood; she kissed him frantically, squeezed his hands, tight.

So tight.

"I love you so much, honey!"

"I love you, too, Mom!"

Cole hugged her and she heard him gasp for air.

Then he moved soundlessly, crouching and gathering his chain, pulling it into the bathroom and carefully closing the door. If the guard woke it would appear Cole was using the toilet.

Their guards didn't pay much attention to Sarah and Cole when they used the toilet because they were chained.

She watched as his tiny figure vanished in a blurring stream of thick, salty tears.

Inside, Cole flushed, using the loud splashing to mask the sound of him removing the air-shaft cover. He lowered himself, then entered the hole, glad there was enough ambient light for him to quietly squirm and crawl along the tin shaft until he exited through an uncovered end that opened into another large room that flowed into the rest of the factory.

Cole stood, then hurried from the room and across the edge of the factory floor.

He was nearly blinded by the dark.

Fear tightened his chest. He had to take baby steps.

I gotta get out of here.

As his eyes adjusted, Cole distinguished a dark minefield of shattered glass, pieces of twisted metal, broken boards with exposed nails and drums filled with unknown liquids. The scratching sounds and squeaks of small living things scurrying near him made his skin crawl. *This place stinks.* Holes in the floor opened to the lower level, like portals to an abyss. *If I fall in one of those, I'm dead.* And everywhere, bird droppings and the flap and coo of pigeons.

He tried to get a sense of the layout, a sense of direction.

I don't know where to go. How do I get out?

The factory windows were at least ten feet from the floor, so trying a window wouldn't work. Cole decided to stay close to a wall and follow it, hoping he would come to a door. Taking a moment to get his bearings, straining to see in the darkness, he slowly began navigating his way around stacks of pallets, crates, abandoned lathes and heavy motors smelling of oil, rubber and hydraulic fluid.

As he got closer to the wall, he was certain he'd glimpsed a metal railing for stairs. It looked like a landing and a door. Cole inched his way toward the stairway. He grew more certain it was a door out. His hope rising, he tried to hurry when the air exploded with the metal rattle of a steel bucket crashing a great distance.

He'd stumbled and kicked it.

Cole froze.

They must've heard the noise.

Cole headed for the landing and the door.

Please be the door out of here! He seized the handle and pulled but nothing happened. The door was sealed. Cole's heart pounded with ferocity.

Should I go back and help Mom? Should I keep running?

Before he could answer he was moving fast along the wall until he spotted a set of metal stairs leading to a darker, lower level. There was a handrail; he seized it and as quickly as he could descended the stairs.

He nearly gagged at the smells of feces and sewer.

Holes in the floor above allowed for dim, diffused light.

Cole recognized the shapes of drums, a network of pipes and the outlines of massive generators.

Help me, please help me find a door, a window, something!

His pulse pounding, Cole spotted the shape of a door on the other side of the section. Hurrying toward it, he felt the odd sensation that he was flying, *no, falling,* into blackness…falling, falling—his stomach lifted to his mouth…*oh, God, Mommy, Daddy*—falling, then he was wet because… *Water*—he was completely submerged and sinking. His ears rang and he felt his body lifting. Breaking the surface, gasping; swinging his arms wildly, Cole seized a steel beam and felt a stone wall.

Brushing water from his eyes, Cole lifted his head to the gloom above, realizing he had fallen into a deep pit.

45

New Jersey

Aleena woke stiff, sore and a little disoriented.

The two sleeping pills she'd taken earlier, to adjust to New York time, had put her out. Her body was bouncing gently in her window seat as her Boeing 747 encountered turbulence a few hundred miles out of Newark.

She yawned, snuggled under her blanket and gazed at the clouds.

As wisps of memory assembled in her brain, a chime sounded.

The captain announced that they would soon begin their descent into Liberty International Airport. He estimated an early arrival at the gate at 10:15 a.m. local time.

"As for the local weather, it's a clear morning and seventy-four degrees."

Aleena had to pee.

She contorted her way around the two other passengers in her row, inhaling the locker-room reek of the cabin air. The flight was full. The smell of the tiny lavatory was overpowering with industrial-strength freshener. While washing her face, Aleena returned to her dilemma.

I don't know if I can do this.

She met her fearful reflection in the mirror.

But I have no choice. If I fail to make the delivery, Joost will harm my family. I've been around the world, I've seen the people he knows.

She brushed her teeth, changed into fresh clothes, returned to her seat and fished out the music box again, wondering and worrying about its significance. *What makes this so important?* As she examined it, the woman in the seat beside her smiled.

"It's very pretty," she said.

Aleena nodded and closed the box.

She put it away and glanced down the cabin, forcing herself to think of something, anything, else. But her stomach slowly knotted when she spotted the raised portion of a broadsheet newspaper. As a former reporter, she identified it as the *Telegraph,* a leading British paper.

Murder-Kidnap Case Stirs Terror Fears at UN Meeting in New York.

What's that all about? She'd missed that story in Amsterdam.

Could the music box be connected to it? No, not if the other case has already happened. Maybe what I'm delivering is actually just a music box, some valuable item someone's paid for. What if it is related to the terror story? I should throw the box away.

Aleena bit her bottom lip.

Stop this. You're driving yourself crazy.

She grappled with her problem until the landing gear lowered with a hydraulic groan into the air rush and locked with a thump.

The ground blurred and the runway gently met the jumbo in a smooth landing. After it came to a full stop, Aleena gathered her bags and waited her turn to file off of the plane.

She used the mundane process to mentally repeat her memorized emergency contact number, starting with the area code 718. If anything went wrong with the delivery she was to call the number for instructions.

As the plane cleared, she fell in with other passengers making their way through the terminal toward U.S. immigration where she joined the enormous line for non–U.S. citizens.

There would be a long wait.

Six other international flights had arrived, four of them 747s, one from Singapore, a flight from Tokyo and four from Europe.

Joost had once told her that whenever possible he strategically booked flights for her that were scheduled to land during an airport's busiest hours. That's when agents were usually overwhelmed. It increased the chance of less scrutiny entering a country.

She could not know that today, at Newark, scrutiny was intensified.

The delay arose because the Office of Enforcement at U.S. Customs and Border Protection headquarters in Washington, D.C., was acting on intelligence from the FBI through Homeland Security to tighten inspections, especially at all entry points for New York City. Alert status was already high because of the UN gathering. The abductions, the murders and the discovery of evidence tied to a potential terror plot had pushed security even higher.

Lines moved with glacial speed.

Finally, the U.S. immigration inspector waved Aleena

to his desk and received her passport. Coming from the Netherlands she did not require a visitor's visa or any other documentation. She was photographed and fingerprinted on a scanner, then the inspector studied her passport and then her face, ensuring it matched her photograph.

"Where were you born?"

"Amsterdam."

"And what do you do there?"

"I work for a travel magazine."

"As what?"

"A travel writer."

"I see you've been to many places, the last one you visited was Yemen."

Aleena had forgotten how that might not sit well with U.S. authorities for a foreigner about to enter America.

"What did you write about in Yemen?"

"The city of Shibam."

"Shibam?"

"It's about two thousand years old and has skyscrapers made of mud. And I went to Socotra Island to see the strange vegetation and snow-white sand dunes."

"What's the purpose of your visit to the U.S.?"

"I'm writing features on New York City."

"What sort of features?"

"About Times Square, Ground Zero."

The inspector's eyebrow arched and he looked again through Aleena's passport. It had been a long time since he'd seen one where an individual had been to so many countries. Yemen. Yemen was a red flag.

"All right, we're going to need to have a look in your bags." He raised his arm to summon another agent. "Go with this guy coming over."

The U.S. customs officer was grim-faced.

"May I see your passport and ticket, please?" he said, then inspected Aleena's papers. "You have no checked bags to claim?"

"No." She pushed her hair back.

Aleena swallowed hard.

She'd traveled the world. She'd encountered security hassles in Libya, Syria, Colombia, Mexico, Hong Kong and Kuwait City, but her instincts were screaming that today, of all days, something was wrong.

This is bad.

At that moment, she heard the yelp of a dog as the officer led her to an inspection zone with body scanners, X-ray machines, sniffer dogs. At an array of tables people were being searched, wanded, patted down, their belongings emptied from their luggage, sifted, scrutinized, swabbed.

"Put your bags on the table, please," the officer said.

An inspector, an older man with blue latex gloves, sent Aleena's bags through an X-ray machine while she endured a full-body scan. Then a female inspector patted her down and swabbed her hands for any trace of explosives.

With her belongings exposed the older officer examined every item—Aleena's toiletries, her underwear. They opened her laptop, turned it on, swabbed it. Then the man held up the music box.

"Is this yours?"

"A gift for my girlfriend in New York. I plan to wrap it here."

He opened it and it played. He closed it, then sent it through the X-ray machine again.

All the saliva in Aleena's mouth evaporated.

God, what's in that music box? What did Joost give me?

When it came through, he opened it and carefully began to take it apart, examining the cylinder and gear mechanism. The officer called into his shoulder microphone.

"Art, bring your partner over here, would ya?"

A dog yelped, a chain jingled and an officer with a German shepherd on a leash arrived, sniffing everything belonging to Aleena. The dog's wet snout sniffed and snorted the music box's mechanism.

Aleena's stomach twisted at the fear her life could stop right here. If they found something, she'd be arrested, charged and end up in a U.S. prison.

Please. She blinked. *Please.*

"It's good," the dog handler said.

The inspector then swabbed it and submitted the sample to the machine for analysis.

"Okay, thank you." The older officer returned all Aleena's papers. "Get your things together, fill out an entry card and have a nice day."

Aleena's pulse was pounding as she repacked, shoving the music box deep into her bag as if it were an unwanted companion who'd misbehaved.

Exiting the airport she got a cab.

"The Grand Hyatt in Manhattan, near Grand Central Terminal," she told the driver.

As they pulled away from the curb her heart was racing. It would be a long time before relief began to seep into Aleena's veins. The first thing she would do at her hotel was take a long hot shower. Again she tested her memory on the emergency contact number: 718-555... As they glided along the freeway the flames of doubt began burning again. As the span of the magnificent George Washington Bridge rose in the distance Aleena struggled. She gazed across the Hudson at Manhattan's glorious skyline.

She looked in her lap.

She was clutching the music box.

She pushed the button to lower her window and New Jersey's industrial air rushed in tugging at her hair as she turned the music box over and over.

Maybe I should just throw it out the window?

Will I have blood on my hands?

46

Jeff was rising, surfacing from a sleep too deep for dreams.

Despairing cries clanged in the darkest reaches of his mind.

Lee Ann, Sarah, Cole.

Images whirled.

Grotesque ghost masks, Sarah's face, Cole's smile. Shoes. Take-out cups. News cameras. Motorcades. Toy airplanes. Planes hitting the towers. Lee Ann's grave.

We fear the things we can't control and grapple with the things we can.

Jeff woke, unable to move. His body ached. The aftereffects of stress had fused his bones to the bed.

Where am I? What's happening?

As he struggled through his dazed numbness, his synapses fired and hurtled him with crystalline force back to his living nightmare.

He hefted himself and sat up at the side of his bed.

He was alone.

He inventoried the room. Morning after an intense battle: the two desks, chairs, were askew. Cordelli,

Ortiz, Cassidy and Chu had taken away the crumpled notepaper, cables and other equipment. All that was left in the aftermath were empty soda cans, coffee cups, napkins, wrappers and the food trolley. Jeff was haunted by mental pictures of Cole, Sarah, and felt overcome with waves of helplessness.

Don't wallow, do something, Griffin, haul ass!

He shaved and showered, making the water as cold as he could stand it, letting icy needles prick him until he was alert. He dressed, gulped cold coffee, then picked the most decent-looking food: a wrapped ham-and-cheese sandwich, an apple and a bottle of water.

That was breakfast.

He switched on the TV, keeping the volume low. It didn't take long before he found a local New York news channel.

"...yes, and sources say that fears of a terrorist attack during the UN General Assembly have been heightened in the wake of two murders connected with the abductions of..."

Sarah and Cole stared back at him from the screen. Then Jeff saw himself at the podium, making his plea at the press conference. The faces of Donald Dalfini and Omarr Aimes surfaced before the news story cut to the UN building, motorcades, footage of world leaders coming and going in New York.

I'm wasting time. Come on. Do something.

There was a soft knock on the door to the adjoining room.

"Let us know when you're ready, Mr. Griffin."

Ready for what? To twiddle my thumbs while you babysit?

The FBI had placed two agents in the adjoining room "to assist you and for your protection, sir."

Right.

Truth was, the investigators—Brewer, Cordelli, the FBI, all of them—did not want him left alone. They expected him to sit here in this room and do nothing.

"As hard as it is for you," Cordelli had warned him last night, "you have to sit tight and let everyone do their job."

To hell with that.

"I need a few minutes, please," Jeff called back.

He glanced at his nightstand, which held his personal laptop and his hard copy of all the images Chu and Cassidy had worked on.

But there was more.

He started his laptop. Last night, Cassidy had finally come up with a list of restaurants licensed by the city that began with *L* and prioritized those remotely resembling *Lasa* or *Laksa*.

The stylized image had stemmed from the logos Jeff had recalled from the discarded wrappers and cups in the van. Precincts would use the list for the canvass. But this was not the only lead investigators were chasing. Late last night, Cordelli and Ortiz had reiterated how upward of twenty agencies were going all out on every aspect of the case he could imagine.

That was good, but Jeff was not going to sit in this room and watch soap operas and game shows while time ran out on his family, not after he'd been so close—*so goddamned heartbreakingly close*—to rescuing Sarah.

I slept, did absolutely nothing, while Lee Ann died alone in the next room. Nothing is going to stop me from finding my family.

More knocking at the door.

"Not dressed yet!"

During last night's session, Jeff had glanced over

Cassidy's shoulder at his laptop screen and made mental notes on the list of restaurants, cafés and coffee shops Cassidy was preparing.

Later that night when he was alone, Jeff used that information and his own laptop to go online and develop his own list. He was confident that his list was similar to Cassidy's. It was tricky and challenging but Jeff had succeeded in downloading the list to his cell phone.

He was set.

He checked the battery strength of his phone. It was good. He collected his paper map, wallet, ball cap, glasses, then left his room for the elevator.

47

Manhattan, New York City

Getting a feature film, TV show, commercial or anything like that shot in New York City required permits.

And depending on what was involved, those permits required forms to be completed, fees to be paid and supporting documents to be provided to the mayor's office of Film, Theater and Broadcasting.

That's plenty of red tape, Brewer thought as Klaver parked their Crown Victoria on Fifty-third Street. The mayor's redbrick office of film was not far from Broadway and where they did *Late Show with David Letterman.*

"This could be like searching for a needle in a haystack," Klaver said.

"Humor me, right now it's our best long shot," Brewer said as they took the elevator to the sixth floor, then walked down the hall to the office of Betty Bonner, permit coordinator.

"Larry, you old flatfoot! Give me a hug," Bonner, a woman in her late fifties wearing a loud print dress, orange-framed cat eyeglasses and hoop earrings, greeted them. Her bangle bracelets jingled when she hugged Brewer. "Is this your partner, the one who never talks?"

"Detective Klaver." Klaver extended his hand. "Larry tells me that you two go way back."

"We worked traffic together in another life, before I retired to the movie business and the job turned Larry into the crackerjack crime fighter and the bastard he is today."

"Are we good to talk here, Betty?" Brewer asked.

"Follow me. I've got things set up."

Bonner led them into a small meeting room and a table with file folders arranged in neat stacks.

"So you're looking for someone involved as crew named 'Rama' or 'Zeta' who may be Russian, or Albanian?"

"Let's say Eastern European."

"But you're not sure if it's a feature, TV movie, TV episode, commercial, music video?"

"No."

"Domestic, or international production?"

"Not sure."

"That's a tall order, so let's get going. Okay, these—" Bonner set her hand on all white files "—are all permits of everything still in production. And these—" she touched yellow folders "—are option permits, while these—" she touched blue folders "—are all ongoing international productions."

Bonner picked one up.

"Now, each of the permit folders and each of the international production folders contain any required visas, for temporary worker visas for non–U.S. citizens."

"That's a lot of folders," Klaver said.

"Domestic and international productions commonly

employ non–U.S. citizens, depending on their profession or skill."

"Isn't this computerized?" Klaver asked. "Can't we just run a few keyword searches?"

"No, because most of our records are original," Bonner said, "this is the best way to do this without a warrant. These are essentially public records. Now, you will find contact numbers of crew chiefs. And I have contacts in immigration and the State Department that can help us further once you nail something down."

The detectives spent the next hours reading quickly through every folder, sorting through every permit, scouring crew lists. They sifted through forms, applications, copying down names and phone numbers.

By the time they'd completed the last file they were frustrated.

Nothing resembling Zeta or Rama with a connection to Albania, Russia or any Eastern European country had surfaced.

"Looks like we lost here," Klaver said.

Brewer massaged his tired eyes.

"No. No. We haven't exhausted this lead yet. We'll keep going," he said, consulting the names and numbers he'd copied. "Let's start calling a few of these location managers. Somebody knows something about this guy on a set or location somewhere in this city."

48

Somewhere in New York City

Bulat Tatayev bent over the worktable.

He studied a map of New York City, took a pencil and made a small neat *X* on a Manhattan street, then marked a second *X* on the map several blocks from the first one.

Reflecting on all the new and careful changes, adjustments and recalibrations he'd made to calculations that he'd labored on over the past few weeks, Bulat sipped the take-out coffee one of the men had picked up from the Slavic place nearby.

It was good, for coffee made in America.

Swallowing the last of it, Bulat pushed aside any trailing bittersweet thoughts of Zama. The fool had to be removed. At this stage of the operation all liabilities had to be eliminated. Nothing could jeopardize their work.

Nothing could be permitted to stop them.

He needed the woman and boy alive to make the new recalibrated operation work.

Bulat crushed his cup and glanced at Alhazur, the man to his right, talking softly on a cell phone. The backup plan to obtain the component was in play and everything hinged on it. When Alhazur ended his call he hesitated to speak.

"Well?" Bulat asked. "What is the status of the device?"

"It has arrived here from Europe safely and the courier has just departed Newark for Manhattan."

"Good, you lead the pickup team. We've salvaged the operation. A few more steps and we'll launch."

Alhazur lit a cigarette and drew on it hard.

"There's a problem," Alhazur said. "Our sources tell us the contact in Amsterdam has just been killed. They suspect Russian security agents. We don't know how close they are to us, or if they've alerted American intelligence. What if they put surveillance on the courier?"

Bulat held up his hand to stem Alhazur's suppositions as he absorbed the complication and analyzed it.

"We proceed," Bulat said.

"But it's dangerous."

"Everything we do is dangerous. We've come too far to turn back. Send your team now to meet the courier." Bulat shot a finger at him. "No mistakes. We must have the device, at any cost."

After Alhazur's small team left, Bulat sat before one of the laptops, searched an encrypted file to obtain a telephone number. He then selected one of the prepaid, untraceable cell phones from the two dozen on the table and placed a call to a number with a 646 area code.

The line rang. He turned to look in the direction of the woman and the boy. Yes, they were now Bulat's assets. They would play a vital role in the operation. He squinted. In the distance he saw some sort of commotion among a few of his men near the hostage area.

Bulat's concern shifted when the line was answered. "Hello."

It was the voice of an older woman Bulat had known from his days of traveling the world, establishing a network of support cells.

"This is the prodigal son," he said in their mother tongue. "We met when I visited at your home the last time I was in New York."

"Yes, I remember."

"Are you willing to help us?"

"I am willing to do whatever is needed."

"Good. I will contact you with further instructions. Goodbye."

"Wait!"

"Yes?"

"You are a hero to our people."

Bulat allowed himself the beginnings of a smile. It died when he ended the call and took notice of the commotion by the hostages.

As he strode across the vast factory floor the situation came into focus. Several men were shouting, smacking the young guard's head, holding up the end of a chain.

Where was the boy? Did he get away?

"Sir!" One of the men stiffened. "This moron fell asleep and let the boy escape."

Bulat examined the chain while the guard dropped to his knees.

"Commander, the chain was faulty. Forgive me!"

Bulat looked at the woman, took quick inventory of the area as his blood began pulsating.

"How long has he been free?"

"Sometime before the dawn, a few hours?" one of the men said.

Volcanic rage rose in Bulat's gut. He stepped up to the frightened guard and slapped his face.

"You insult the blood of the revolution!"

"I'm sorry, Commander."

"You," Bulat ordered his men, "secure the woman. You three! Take this sorry excuse for a life below to the furnace!"

Bulat's breathing quickened.

"The rest of you find that fucking boy and bring him to me!"

Bulat's nostrils flared and his eyes widened with wrath as he squatted down in front of Sarah and softened his voice.

"You'd better pray to your God that your son got away."

Sarah battled the panic rising around her.

Cole is free.

She said this to herself over and over after Bulat had walked away and his men started scouring every part of the old structure. They overturned steel drums, smashed wooden crates and toppled old equipment. The menace was almost palpable.

Pop!

Sarah convulsed—the air had split with the firecracker bang.

A gunshot. In the lower level.

Cole? No! They didn't shoot Cole!

Sarah cried out for him.

Then she looked at the two new guards a few feet away, assessing their low-toned mutterings and body language for any hint of what had happened below.

They wouldn't shoot an innocent boy? They couldn't shoot an innocent boy? What have I done? Was I wrong to send him off alone? I should've kept him with me. Oh, God, please let him be safe.

The shot echoed like an accusation until she could not longer bear it.

"What was that?" Sarah asked.

The guards glared at her, saying nothing, then she realized that the gunfire was for the young, terrified guard they'd led away. He paid for his mistake with his life, like the creep before him, who was going to kill Cole.

Then it hit Sarah, hit her the same way reality hits an ill-fated climber in the instant before the plunge.

I'm going to die.

There was a sense of finality in the air, a sense that their plot may be a massive suicide mission. They'd killed four people so far, surely they'd kill Sarah and Cole.

We've seen their faces.

For one terrifying moment she fell into a comalike stupor.

But Cole's not here. Cole is free.

She had to believe that he got away, that he'd make it back to Jeff and back to Montana and a life without her.

Sarah fought her tears and tried to think clearly through her exhaustion, through her fear, taking comfort in her one hope, her prayer.

Cole's not here. Cole is free.

She let her anguished mind take her back home, back to where she was standing on a gentle hill that offered her the great sweeping plain and the eternal sky.

God, please let Cole be safe.

49

Dawn.

The first light of day made its way into the old factory, spilling down forty feet to the bottom of the pit where Cole Griffin was shivering in stinking water.

He struggled to be brave.

Don't cry.

Then he heard the *swish-splash* again. Something else was in the water—*something alive.* Cole was unsure what it was but images and shapes were slowly emerging in the faint light. *Keep away from me!*

The pit was as big and round as his friend Tim's aboveground pool. You could maybe fit a car in there. And the water—*I hope it's water*—was deep.

Cole stretched. He couldn't reach bottom with his feet.

His fingers and arms were sore from holding on to the metal bar so that he could keep his head and shoulders above water. Broken metal filing cabinets and twisted sections of tin ductwork were clustered near him. He was so cold his teeth were knocking together. He had to find a way to get out of here.

Swish-splash.

There it is again.

It came from the opposite side of the pit. Cole searched around for something, anything, to defend himself against the *thing,* or *things*.

He found nothing.

The dark circular brick walls rose to the world above. It was impossible to climb out of here. He clawed and pounded at them, banging his handcuffs against them.

It was futile.

Cole was overcome, on the verge of tears, ready to cry out for help, when the increasing light slowly revealed hope in the form of rusted metal rungs embedded into the stone, ascending to the surface.

I'll climb up. I'll get out and get help.

But as fast as Cole's heart soared, it sank again.

His escape ladder was on the other side of the pit, where the *thing* was. Cole would not only have to swim across the murky water but he would have to confront whatever was splashing in it.

I can't do this. Not with that thing over there.

At that moment he heard shouting, men arguing far off.

Searching.

Now they know I got away. They're looking for me.

He stared at the ladder. He had to reach it, had to get out of there but that option vanished when he heard a loud bang, like a gunshot. Then the building reverberated with the nearing clamor of the searchers.

They're closer now, much closer.

Keeping his grip on the bar, Cole moved and maneuvered to the heaped file cabinets and misshapen ductwork, hiding among them just as spears of light pierced the pit.

They're right above me looking down with flash-lights.

Their voices dropped into the pit along with small stones, nails and bits of debris that cascaded to the water.

Swish-splash.

Cole froze. He felt weight on his left shoulder, tiny claws suddenly dug through his shirt as a rat rose from the water. Cole stifled a scream. He couldn't make a sound because flashlight beams lit the water, probing the junk around him. If he yelled they would hear him.

The rat moved closer to Cole's head, poking its nose in his ear.

Cole couldn't bear it. He swatted the rat away, the splash triggered voices of reaction above. The flashlight beams raked wildly over the water until they locked on to a furry back moving on the surface away from Cole.

The water plinked as bolts *whizzed-splashed* near the rat.

The men were trying to hit it.

Laughter from above and the light beams vanished as the men left the pit to resume searching other areas of the factory.

They didn't see me.

Embracing a measure of relief, Cole took a few breaths.

He had to get to the ladder on the other side.

But I can't, the big rat is there waiting to eat my face. He wanted to give up, cry out to the creeps. *Take me back to my mom—I can't do this!*

But his mother's words, telling him to get help, still echoed in his head, driving him to be brave, to face his fear. Yes, but the rat was fearless, big and getting bigger.

A monster.

I can't, I can't go over there, oh, help me....

"Cole, stop this now! You have to listen to me, son, and you'll be fine!"

His dad's voice suddenly came back to him from so many years ago when they were at his dad's friend's cabin at the lake in North Dakota. They'd gone up for a weekend of fishing. Cole was about six or seven and had gone off alone, stepping into a little rowboat tied to the dock. He was looking at the fish swimming around it, not knowing that the rowboat had come untied and he'd drifted. He didn't know how to use the oars, panicked and cried for help.

"Listen to me, Cole!"

His dad's voice boomed from the dock, over the quiet laughter of the other men urging him to go get him in another boat. But Cole's dad had decided to use that terrifying moment in Cole's life to teach Cole how to survive on his own.

"Push down on the oar handles... Now, push the oars away from you... Now, lower them into the water! Now, pull them hard to you!"

Cole's first efforts failed. The coordination was hard; his dad and the men at the dock were getting smaller as Cole drifted farther away.

"I can't do this! I can't."

"Yes, you can! Listen to me! Stay calm, think this through and you'll be fine, son!"

Cole struggled, sobbed, but his dad would not let him quit and eventually Cole made it back, stronger than when he'd left, for he'd mastered the skill of rowing a boat and in the process had defeated a fear. Cole loved and respected his dad for teaching him how to survive.

His father's words guided him now.

Stay calm, think this through and you'll be fine.

Cole reached deep into himself for every molecule of strength and courage he had left.

All right, I'm going to do this—one, two, three.

Cole let go of the metal bar and began swimming toward the ladder. *If you come at me, rat, I'll punch the crap out of you.* Cole used breaststrokes, traveling without splashing. His heart skipped when his leg brushed against something alive. Then his hand touched something furry, telling him instantly: *there's more than one rat in here.*

He felt a tugging at his sneaker, a gnawing. He retaliated with a kick, and swam faster until he grabbed the rungs. His feet found the rungs under the water and felt lighter as he hefted himself from the water.

Rung, handgrip, footstep lift—his rhythm was swift, sure and steady.

Cole thought of nothing but his immediate goal.

Get to the top.

Rung, handgrip, footstep lift.

When he lifted his head to check his progress, one side of the rung he'd grasped broke free from the wall. The other side remained precariously anchored with Cole dangling on it as it swung like a hinged door, carrying Cole out from the wall.

Cole's breathing stopped.

In the strong light he saw the bottom of the pit and dozens of rats swirling in the water. Cole kicked against the wall and swung back toward the ladder just as his damaged rung gave way and fell into the water below, making a splash.

He managed to secure himself on the rungs, and after a minute to catch his breath he hurried to the surface.

I did it. I did it, Dad. I climbed out. Okay, okay, I have to get help.

Adrenaline pumping, Cole moved faster now. In the daylight he found the stairs to the main floor and threaded his way through pallets stacked with old machinery, motors and abandoned equipment. He could hear men throughout the factory as they searched. He found the wall, stayed close to it, looking for a door, a window, any way to escape.

As he neared a corner he found a sheet of aged plywood partially bolted to small section of the wall that had decayed. The plywood was loosened by time and Cole pulled it out to see how the wall had cracked, crumbled to the point of creating a jagged gap about a foot wide.

Cole glimpsed a grassless patch of earth, gravel, a chain-link fence.

He wedged himself behind the plywood, then twisted and angled himself through the gap and…

Freedom.

He was standing in the sun at the side of the building, a few feet from a ten-foot fence topped with coiled razor wire. Cole moved along the building, his heart racing, knowing he was seconds from finding a way to the street and help.

As he rounded the corner he ran directly into the arms of a man waiting by the loading bay of the rear shipping entrance.

"Please call police! My mom and me were—*mfph!*"

Cole stopped when pain shot through him and he'd recognized that the man, Bulat Tatayev, had seized his wrist and moved quickly to take him back inside. Bulat yelled out to his men before lowering himself to Cole.

He stared into his eyes, saying nothing until the men arrived.

50

Jeff had slipped away from the FBI.

Outside, he hurried along Forty-fifth Street until he was a safe distance from his hotel and stepped into the lobby of the Roosevelt where he used his phone to open Cassidy's list of restaurants, cafés and coffee shops.

His knees nearly buckled and he sat in a wingback chair.

There had to be more than a thousand, no, two, no, more. It went on and on as the listings of every restaurant and coffee shop blossomed on his phone's tiny screen.

He could scroll for an eternity.

Then he realized he could manipulate the list to display only those that started with *L* and resembled *Lasa* or *Laksa*. He exhaled. That brought the number way down to under a dozen for the five boroughs. After a few tries he was able to map the list on his phone, in order to make the most effective search of the listings.

As he started off his cell phone rang.

"Mr. Griffin, this is Agent Miller at the hotel. Sir, what is your location?"

"I'm outside at the moment. I needed some air."

"Sir, we request that you return to your room, now."

"I can't do that, Agent Miller. I have some things to take care of."

"Mr. Griffin, we respectfully request—"

Jeff ended the call and picked up his pace. The TV news report echoed in his mind. His fears were mounting; he sensed that he was running out of time as he arrived at the first candidate. The Café Lastanya was in the low twenties on East Forty-first Street. It had a small front with four tinted-glass panels. It was crowded. He made his way past the sandwich and pastry cases to the coffee area and studied the take-out cups. The logo bore no resemblance to the discarded cups he'd seen in the van.

He moved on.

Jeff went back to the street, checked his phone and started walking to the second possibility, the Lassoed Pony Diner, near Grand Central and Forty-second Street. It specialized in cheesecake and was a favorite of commuters catching trains at Grand Central. He examined the logo of the take-out bags and coffee cups— a distinctive horse's head with the red-and-white stripe logo—and crossed the diner from his list.

Not even close.

Back in the street he flagged a cab for the next one but before he got one his cell phone rang again.

"Jeff, it's Cordelli. We need you back in the hotel room."

"Is there a break in the case? If there is, tell me over the phone."

"Jeff, were you contacted again?"

"No. I'm just looking for my family."

"Do you have information we should be aware of?"

"No."

"Because you shouldn't keep information from us. It leads to problems."

"Am I under arrest, Cordelli?"

"No."

"Am I a suspect?"

"No."

"Am I in custody?"

"No, but for your safety we want you to—"

"*My safety?* The bastards who took my wife and son may be planning to kill them."

"Jeff, we're on your side, you have to let us do our jobs."

"I came within a heartbeat of rescuing Sarah and if you think I'm going to sit on my ass and do nothing, you are wrong. Dead wrong! I'm going to find the people who took my family and I'm going to kill them!"

"Jeff, I know this is difficult—"

Jeff hung up and waved until he succeeded in getting a cab.

As his taxi navigated through traffic he accepted that there was no logic to what he was doing. How could he possibly find the *exact same* diner or restaurant where the killers bought their coffee, simply from his memory of the vague image of a take-out cup's logo? Was he not just going on the blind hope that somehow, someway, he'd find his family again?

All he knew was that he had to keep searching.

The next possibility on his list was Lake of Dreams Café on Seventh Avenue.

Plain white take-out cups, no luck there.

Looking at his map Jeff saw how the other locations on his list webbed across New York City. Before resuming, he went to an ATM for more cash, then flagged a taxi and negotiated a flat rate to hire the driver to take him to every location.

They crossed the Brooklyn Bridge and went to the Lasagne Table in Brooklyn. Take-out cups bore no logo. It was the same at Laserinta Café. Then they moved on to Queens and Uncle Lassiter's Bar and Grill. Nothing. Then on to Lasha's Ukrainian Roadhouse without success before going to the Bronx and Lakeshi's Gourmet Diner. Nothing there. Then to uptown Manhattan, striking out there before working their way to the Village and down to Battery Park where Jeff paid the driver, then queued up for the Staten Island Ferry.

He had two final places to check on his list, the Last Drop Coffee Den and Lakasta's Eatery. He got a cab at the dock, headed to the locations, struck out in both cases and returned to the ferry.

During the twenty-five-minute ride across New York Harbor back to Manhattan, he looked at the Statue of Liberty and thought of how badly Cole had wanted to visit the landmark.

Jeff took in the view of Lower Manhattan's bridges and the skyscrapers. The enormity of the metropolis overwhelmed him. But fear was driving him, fear and the unshakable faith he could not, would not, ever give up looking for Sarah and Cole.

He searched the majestic skyline for hope.

51

Grand Central Terminal.

From her balcony table in Michael Jordan's restaurant Aleena Visser looked out over the Grand Central's main concourse and took in its cathedral splendor while finishing her tea.

She set her cup in the saucer with a nervous rattle as the knot in her stomach tightened.

The time was drawing near. She could still pull out, toss the music box and walk away. *But I would pay a heavy price.* She could go to police. *But there's no guarantee I won't be charged and sent to prison.* Aleena had no options.

She'd go through with it.

But this would be the last time. When she returned to Amsterdam, she'd go into Joost's office and she would tell him that it was over, she was done. She'd quit the magazine and go back to newspaper reporting in Rotterdam, back to a normal life.

After today's job, her life as a smuggler was over.

It was nearly 11:00 a.m.

Time to go.

In keeping with Joost's instructions, she took an orange scarf from her bag, tied it to her shoulder strap so it hung prominently, making it easy to identify her in a crowd.

She went to the information booth in the main concourse and waited for her contact. They were to arrive precisely at 11:00 a.m. according to the big brass clock above the booth.

At 11:00 a.m. no one had approached her.

By 11:15 a.m. no one had shown.

Aleena grew anxious.

She started to walk slowly around the booth area amid the gentle rush and hum of thousands of people going about their business.

I want to be done with this.

Maybe she had confused her instructions from Joost? She reviewed them again.

"Go to the Grand Central Terminal the morning you arrive, tie an orange scarf to your bag and at precisely 11:00 a.m., New York time, stand near the information booth with the brass clock in the main concourse. Your contact will approach you and say something about your flight and ask about a gift."

Aleena had followed Joost's instructions to the letter.

She glanced at faces in the crowd to determine who among them might be her contact, even though she had no idea what her contact looked like. She knew she was being watched on Grand Central's closed-circuit security camera system. She'd seen the radiation detectors and motion sensors placed throughout the terminal. And there was no shortage of police officers. Everyone knew that Grand Central was considered a terror target, but how could you tell by looking at the thousands of travelers who passed through it every day what their intentions were, Aleena thought.

She searched the sea of faces again.

Maybe my contact is out there watching me?

It was now 11:32 a.m.

Or maybe the contact was not coming at all? Maybe the delivery had been canceled, called off, abandoned? The possibility gave rise to hope. Before considering it further Aleena was interrupted. Her phone vibrated in her pocket with a text message from Alice, her co-worker at the magazine in Amsterdam.

I'm sorry to tell you that Joost has died.

Aleena caught her breath and responded.

No! What happened?

We don't know. Police are asking questions. They think it was a heart attack at his desk.

This is terrible. What are police asking?

About the two men who visited him before he died.

Who were the two men?

Marta in reception said they were KLPD.

What did the KLPD want with Joost?

It's a mystery.

This is horrible. Prayers to everyone. Will call later.

Joost was dead.

Why had the KLPD visited him? Could this be connected to her delivery? Aleena covered her mouth with her hand and thought of the emergency contact number: 718-555-76—

"Excuse me, miss, you look lost. Can we help?"

Two uniformed NYPD officers had approached Aleena. Both men looked to be her age. They surveyed her jeans, short-sleeved top, tattoos and blond hair.

"Oh, no, thank you." Aleena flashed her beautiful smile. "I'm waiting to meet a friend, who is a little late."

"That's a nice accent you got there, is it German?"

"Dutch."

"What brings you to New York?"

"I'm a travel writer for a magazine in Amsterdam."

"That so?" The cops gave her another subtle head-to-toe look. "Well, enjoy your visit. Hope you write nice things about the town."

The officers strolled away and about a minute later she bit her bottom lip and thought of leaving.

"Aleena?"

She turned to a tall man in his early thirties with a medium build. He wore a navy T-shirt, faded jeans, a ball cap and sunglasses. His face was dark from several days' growth. He carried a construction worker's lunch box and looked like any other tradesman in the city.

"Yes," she said.

"How was your flight?"

"It was good."

"And you have brought a gift?"

"Yes."

"What did you tell the police officers?"

"They asked if I was lost. I said I was waiting for a friend who was late."

"Is that all?"

"They asked about my accent. I told them I was a travel writer from Amsterdam. That's all."

After considering her answers, he glanced around. "Walk this way." He nodded across the concourse.

At that time, two men, who had been provided security camera footage of Aleena in the preboarding area of Schiphol Airport, arrived out of breath and started searching the terminal for her.

Scanning the crowd, one glimpsed a bright orange scarf—the telltale identifier from central intelligence in Moscow. The two men began making their way through the forest of commuters to catch up to their target.

When Aleena and her contact cleared the concourse area, the man said, "May I have the gift, please?"

Aleena reached into her bag and handed him the music box. He stopped and immediately examined specific points. He was meticulous until he'd confirmed the item as being the one he needed. He placed it in his lunch box, then, as quickly as he'd emerged, he disappeared, leaving Aleena alone.

The delivery took less than thirty seconds.

Aleena decided to return to the concourse and leave from that level. As she walked, she took stock of the thousands of innocent people going about their lives in Grand Central, then thought of the millions busy with their lives across New York City, and recalled the headline in the newspaper on the plane about murders, abductions, fears of terror attacks at the UN meeting.

Is any of this connected to me?

Tears stung her eyes.

Struggling to comprehend, she put her hand to her face.

Joost was dead.

Why were the KLPD talking to him? What did they know? Nothing made sense.

Icy threads of fear webbed up her back.

I am done with smuggling. I need to get home as quickly as possible. I'll call my friend Harm Bergen at the newspaper in Rotterdam and ask about a job. First things first—I'll get back to the hotel. I'll change my ticket to get on the next flight to Amsterdam.

Her mind was racing.

Which way out of Grand Central will take me to the hotel?

She searched the main concourse for a landmark, a sign. Was it west, or east? She'd go back to the information booth and get directions to the hotel there. She headed toward the booth when suddenly two men materialized, walking on either side of her. They were big men in sport jackets.

"Aleena Visser?"

"Yes."

One flashed an official police ID.

"FBI, come with us, you're under arrest."

"Arrest? For what? May I see your ID again?"

One of the men gripped her upper left arm. The other man had her right.

"Don't resist."

They escorted her through the terminal, to the nearest ramp down to the trains. Something about the look of the men, the cut of their hair, their facial features, told her that they were not Americans.

They were Eastern European, Russian.

Aleena's pulse quickened—her thoughts swirled.

Joost was rumored to have many enemies in Russian security. *Who are these men? What will they do to me?*

Amid the throngs of commuters, the men practically

lifted Aleena as they hurried her down the stairway, closer to the trains. A rush of hot air thundered toward them, the grind of steel on steel.

Oh, God, they're going to kill me!

Aleena's primal instinct to survive took over.

She had taken self-defense courses and with cobra speed succeeded in breaking free and gripping the groin of one of the men, squeezing, crushing with every iota of strength until he doubled over, stopping them dead on the stairs. At the same time commuters bumped and shoved them, enabling her to shake herself loose from the second man, rush down the stairs and up another flight to the main concourse.

Aleena moved fast.

The men pursued her, frightening her with their speed.

On the main concourse she ran for the first door, fearing there might be others with the two strangers. She shifted around people on Manhattan's busy streets with one thought propelling her.

Run. Run. Run.

Glancing over her shoulder, she saw the men were gaining. *Oh, God, they're fast, too fast.* Aleena had to get away, far enough ahead to jump in a cab. She'd try around the next two blocks to get out of sight.

Aleena darted through traffic as fast as her feet could go.

Two blocks away, the dual stacks of a Peterbilt triaxle dump truck belched black smoke as Tony Grabeltinni grinded the gears of his eighteen-speed transmission. Tony, the owner-operator from Newark, was pissed off. Traffic was costing him money.

The lights were right; he had the chance to advance

three blocks if he could cut around the idiot double-parked Mercedes. Tony upshifted and pushed the big Cat engine, getting his rig up to forty, fifty, fifty-five when—*Jesus Christ*—something blazed directly in front of him.

Tony knew his reflex to brake was too late—the blur of a hand, a foot, a bag was hurled and an orange scarf landed on his windshield flapping like the flag of surrender.

Aleena Visser had been bounced some thirty feet.

A crowd gathered. A halo of blood grew around her head.

"I never saw her! Christ, she ran into me!" Tony said as people called for help on cell phones. A woman was holding Aleena's hand, touching her neck for a pulse.

Among the bystanders were the two men in sport jackets.

They gazed down at the scene until they heard the approaching sirens, then they walked away.

One of them reached for his cell phone and spoke quietly in Russian.

"Yes, we're certain that she was never out of our sight," he lied, preferring not to mention they'd lost sight of her for nearly a minute because he was confident she'd had no contact during that time.

"Yes, we maintained surveillance and confirm that she never made contact. Yes, she's been removed. The threat has been removed, struck by a truck. It is clear that she may not survive her injuries."

52

Battery Park, Manhattan, New York City

Jeff was running out of time.

He fell in with the passengers disembarking at the ferry terminal, feeling that every minute was working against him. His search across five boroughs for any lead to where the killers had bought coffee and take-out food had yielded nothing.

But he was not defeated.

Cutting through Battery Park near Ground Zero he found a bench and unfolded the color printouts Detective Lucy Chu had made for him. Shuffling through the sharp images, he examined the black boot with a fine line of bright red trim, the duffel bag, walkie-talkies, folded maps, bullet tips in magazines, figures in sweatshirts. He continued with the take-out food wrappers, a take-out bag, take-out coffee cups.

He'd been fixated on the logo.

Was it the key?

Again, he had to accept that his obsession was not founded on any real, logical belief. Besides, the NYPD was going to canvass all the restaurants and coffee shops on Cassidy's list.

Maybe they already did that? So why am I doing this?
Jeff continued searching the pictures. *Because I can't give up, there has to be something I've missed, overlooked or haven't tried.*

Sitting there, in the shadow of the new One World Trade Center soaring over the site of the twin towers, his heart was racing. He was not afraid, not in the physical sense. He would stand up to any fight. He'd charged into fire to save people and he would do it again. He was prepared to lay down his life for Sarah and Cole.

What he feared was loss and the things he couldn't control: *Lee Ann's lifeless body in his arms... Her tiny casket sinking into the earth under the eternal sky... His utter sense of weakness, guilt and helplessness. I can't understand how a person can suffer a wound like this and live.*

Jeff looked up at the tower, then toward the water at the Statue of Liberty, knowing he faced impossible odds but refusing to give up hope that he'd find some way to rescue his family.

I can't lose them. I can't lose Sarah and Cole.

A rush of wind rolled in from New York Harbor and tugged the pages from Jeff's hands, sending them skipping into the park. He rushed after them, collecting them one by one as they bounced deep in the northwest section. He found the last page pressed against a tree; it was the picture of the take-out coffee cups with a stylized *L* logo. As he reached for it, he froze with sudden understanding. The page was angled and for an instant he saw the *L* as a *V* and it hit him.

That's it!

It was a V. *The logo was a* V! *Yes!*

Gripping the page in his hand, his breathing quickened.

The memory, the image from the van, came to him like a crystalline photo. *The logo did not represent Laka, or Laska.* The logo started with a *V* and the first letters were *V-A-K-H*. He was certain. He needed to get online fast. He wasn't that good at using the phone for internet searches. He kept walking until he was out of the park and on West Street where he came to the Ritz-Carlton. He hurried into its soft lit, spacious lobby and went to the desk.

A man in a gray jacket and tie lifted his head from a keyboard and smiled. "May I be of assistance, sir?"

"Yes, I'm very late and don't have time to go up to my room, could you please look up a couple of addresses for me?"

"Certainly, sir."

"I only have a partial name, I need the proper name and address of a restaurant or coffee shop somewhere in New York, but I only have the start."

"Shouldn't be too difficult, what do you have?"

"It starts with a *V* for *Vak* or *Vakh,* something European similar to that."

The keyboard clicked as the clerk launched a search.

"Hmm, I have some Russian places?"

"What are they?"

"They are all excellent, by the way. I have Veselka over in the East Village, and two others. Let's see, Uncle Vanya is in midtown and the Russian Vodka Room is in Times Square, but technically these don't start with a *V-A.*"

"Is that all you have showing? Nothing with *V-A-K-H?*"

"Hmm, I'm not having much luck. I'm afraid there's not much showing that fits your information." The clerk's brow furrowed and he tapped a few more keys. "Is it in Manhattan, sir?"

"Not necessarily."

"Because— Oh. Wait. I have something in the Bronx called Vak—not sure if I am saying it right—Vakhiyta's Kitchen, spelled *V-A-K-H-I-Y-T-A,* specializing in Eastern European food."

"Starts with *V-A-K?* That could be it. Can you give me the address please?"

"Printing for you now."

"Great, I'll need a taxi."

"The doorman out front will arrange for one. Here's your address."

Jeff thanked the clerk with a five-dollar bill and rushed for the door.

53

Bulat Tatayev gazed into the jaws of disaster.

A troubled warlord on his throne, he sat in a swivel high-back executive chair, left elbow propped, fist supporting his chin as he watched one minute melt into the next on the digital clock of the worktable.

Still no word from Alhazur on whether they'd received the component.

We need the microdetonator.

Alhazur was one of his best men.

Without the component we fail.

At every step, circumstance had conspired to thwart his mission. Zama, the passionate fighter, proved himself a fool by losing the critical detonator, then drawing attention with the murders and kidnappings. And now Russian agents were closing in on their backup plan.

Then the boy escaped. Only by luck was he recaptured.

We cannot fail. Our blood cries out.

Bulat drew upon the horror of the tanks mashing his mother's and father's corpses in the blood-soaked snow and mud and pulling the bodies of his wife, Leyla, their son, Lecha, and Polla, their little girl, from the rubble after the bombings. He remembered all the innocents who'd been murdered, the brave fighters who'd sacrificed their lives for freedom. Everything Bulat did, he did for those martyred before him.

I will not fail them.

Throughout his life Bulat had learned to turn adversity to advantage. Instead of killing the woman and the boy, as he'd planned, he would incorporate them into his new plan, which had a new fail-safe element.

Yes, it's a much better plan.

One of the cell phones on the table vibrated. It was Alhazur.

"Yes," Bulat answered.

"Success."

Bulat stood, cupped his hands to his face, letting relief wash over him until it gave way to concentration and he summoned some of his men to the table. Again, they studied computer and paper maps, calculating distances, travel times. They scrutinized scores of photographs taken by the advance teams. A good number of his men were U.S.-born and had come from New York, Philadelphia, Boston and Chicago cells. They examined aerial maps and reviewed range, structures and crowd size.

Bulat produced a classified agenda obtained through threats made on the family of a member of a VIP security agent. The agenda provided invaluable security details, locations, dates and times.

Less than forty-five minutes after Alhazur called, he'd returned with his team and presented Bulat with the ballerina music box. Bulat stared at it, then opened it to hear Tchaikovsky's *Swan Lake*. The tiny dancer pirouetted.

"Like Pandora's box," Alhazur said, "opened by the

first woman, unleashing all the evils to plague humanity."

"Leaving only one thing inside," Bulat said. "Hope."

Bulat placed the box on a clear section of the worktable where his engineering expert, trained at MIT, was poised to dissect the item with only Bulat and Alhazur watching.

The engineer adjusted his magnifying lamp and set to work. With the precision of a surgeon he meticulously disassembled the box, piece by piece, examining each one until he found the tiny wafer detonator. Holding it between the tongs of his tweezers, he placed in on a slide and set it under his microscope.

He took his time inspecting it.

He admired its construction—similar to a ceramic element glazed with polyimide but reconstituted with near-invisible radio static chips the diameter of a human hair. It was designed to use a dedicated current pulse, activated by a preset or dialed-in frequency.

Nothing could jam it or stop it.

That was why it was critical for this time. Across New York City, security for the United Nations General Assembly was at the highest levels. National security agencies would be using state-of-the-art detection and jamming technology, but this rare microdetonator would defeat any detection or jamming effort.

It was unstoppable.

The rumors held that the device had been created in a North Korean lab by perverting technology stolen from Japan. In other circles, the story was that the device was born in a secret military installation hidden in Syria.

"Well?" Bulat asked.

"It's in perfect condition."

"How long to install it?" Bulat checked the time.

"We need to make final preparations. We're down to a few hours at best."

"It will be close," the engineer said.

"Get going."

Bulat needed more coffee and something to eat. He dispatched one of the men to get an order of food. Then Bulat walked across the factory floor.

Sarah and Cole were bound with extra chains and under the watch of three guards. Bulat stood over them, staring down at them for nearly a full minute before lowering himself.

"Soon your names, our names, will be used to re-write history."

Sarah and Cole said nothing.

"In Montana you have lived a quiet and free life. It is what we want for our people, too."

"You're murderers! Terrorists!" Sarah said.

"As were your American forefathers. How does it go on the license plate? 'Give me liberty or give me death'?"

Bulat waited for an answer that never came.

"We are all freedom fighters, we are all terrorists. And sooner or later, we will all die," he said before returning to the table to review the time and the agenda as his men continued their preparations.

54

New York City

Ken Forsyth stared somberly out the window at the Brooklyn Bridge.

The FBI supervisory agent with the NYPD–FBI Joint Terrorism Task Force was alone in the boardroom of the FBI's New York headquarters getting ready to lead the latest case-status meeting.

Glancing to his files, Forsyth's jaw muscles bunched, as they often did under stress. In his brief solitary moment he assessed the monumental challenge they faced.

Who's the target? What's the plot? Who's behind it?

Forsyth realized they had nothing more than a few disparate pieces and little time to put them together. The president was due to arrive in Manhattan in three hours for an event later in the day.

Give us something.

Anything.

Investigators from the NYPD, the FBI, the Secret Service, Homeland, Port Authority, State Police, ATF, Customs and several other agencies soon took their places and Forsyth started the meeting. He raised his voice to take a roll of those on the teleconference call from Washington, D.C., before going around the table.

"We have no significant developments to report. Every thread of the investigation that can be pursued is being pursued," Forsyth said. "We'll go to everyone for updates, then we'll look at next steps. Adam?"

Adam James, senior agent with the Secret Service, which headed security for all world leaders attending the United Nations General Assembly, led off.

"I am circulating detailed agendas, these are highly classified. Those on the line should be receiving password-encrypted copies. I'll go through today's events. As you know the president arrives in three hours, two hours in advance of his joint open-air event with the British prime minister near Columbus Circle."

"We're adding another one hundred officers to security there," NYPD Lieutenant Ted Stroud said.

"Right," James said. "I'll go over our list of events taking place now and those carrying on through the evening. China's president will attend the World Gymnastics Championships at Madison Square Garden. We expect protests there. We also expect protests that could get ugly when the Russian president and president of Mykrekistan visit Battery Park today. There have been threats for that event that arise from the unrest in the Russian republic.

"Japan's prime minister will attend a baseball game at Yankee Stadium in the Bronx. As noted, two Tokyo-based apocalyptic extremist groups with supporters around the world have been issuing death threats and making claims to having access to weapons of mass destruction. We have special teams assigned there.

"This afternoon, Spain's first lady will be at the Metropolitan Museum of Art to open a new exhibit of Picasso paintings. In Bryant Park behind the New York Public Library, Russia's first lady and the wife of the president of Mykrekistan will be attending a ceremony honoring the discovery of literary papers from Russian and Mykrekistani writers.

"Malaysia's prime minister will be at a luncheon at the Waldorf. The American Sports Academy hosts the Australian prime minister for a fundraiser at the Saint Regis Hotel. Vietnam's prime minister will be at an outdoor cultural event in Queens in Rego Park—protests are expected.

"A number of threats have been issued against Iran's president, who will be attending an exhibition soccer game between Iran and the U.S. national team in Flushing Meadows this afternoon. Germany's chancellor will be opening a new Manhattan office for Lufthansa. And later tonight, Brazil's first lady, a noted mezzo, is going to sing in a special performance of *La Traviata* at the Metropolitan Opera.

"Let's go back to the president's event with the British P.M.," Forsyth said. "Have the White House and British security considered canceling?"

"We broached the subject and were told that neither office would cancel."

"What is the likelihood of canceling any of the other events?"

"The answer is no. In fact, we've been advised via State that none of today's events will be canceled because we have, and I quote, 'not verified the validity or target of the threat.'"

Forsyth tapped his pen on his files.

"What are we hearing from the foreign security teams?"

"Not much. Japan's security detail is passing us all

new intel picked up by Tokyo. British intel is keeping us updated. The Russians said they are aware of threats but offered little more."

"Are we getting the whole story from foreign security?"

"We're never certain. The Russians were reluctant to provide details, only to say they would not cancel any planned events for their president while in the U.S."

"Anything further, Adam?"

"We are going full bore on intel and investigating. Iron Shield, our command center in Brooklyn, is monitoring on all fronts."

"Thank you, Adam." Forsyth leaned into the speaker. "Our folks on the line, can you add to that?"

The officials with the CIA and the NSA confirmed they were monitoring all chatter and that, to date, nothing "of consequence" had emerged.

"What about the task force on the explosives aspects?" Forsyth asked an FBI agent three chairs from him.

"We've put out classified alerts and we've got agents canvassing suppliers on any recent, large or irregular purchases."

"And?"

"Nothing to note, the canvass is ongoing."

"All right," Forsyth said. "Let's update the evidentiary aspects of this investigation."

Forsyth went around the table for status reports on the tips called in since the press conference with Jeff Griffin.

"Ninety-one tips so far. All are being processed," said NYPD Lieutenant Fred Ryan.

Forsyth then moved on for summaries of the status of the arson, the crime scene investigation, the FBI's lab work on processing the detonator and the backpack. He got updates on video analysis by the NYPD's Real Time Crime Center. Then he went to the airports.

"Glen, where are your people at with the origin of the backpack?"

Glen Healy, a security director with the Transportation Security Administration who oversaw airport screening and checkpoint operations for the New York area, loosened his tie.

"In working with the airlines, this is the best we have at this time. As we know, the Griffins flew from Billings, Montana, connected in Minneapolis–Saint Paul to LaGuardia. The bag mix-up was just an erroneous grab from the carousel. We've also learned that other airline tickets may have been purchased for a passenger Hans Beck. At first we believed he'd arrived at LaGuardia, via Montreal and Paris."

"Was that wrong?" Forsyth said.

"No, but here's the complication. It turns out there may be more than one person traveling as Hans Beck. Our updated investigation shows he may have also entered through JFK, linked to one of several flights originating from four potential locations and airlines served by Kennedy—an Aeroflot flight from Moscow to terminal one, one from Pakistan International Airlines out of Lahore to terminal four, a Turkish Airlines flight out of Istanbul to terminal one and one with Uzbekistan Airways, to terminal four. It is unclear how it happened."

"Maybe they used decoys as part of the scenario?" Forsyth asked.

"We can't rule it out," Healy said. "We are working with the airlines, scrutinizing all passenger manifests, records and surveillance of airport baggage check-in, drop-off and handling."

Forsyth went to NYPD Lieutenant Ted Stroud and his team for the status of leads arising from the SUV used in the abduction and its ties to the investigation of a global auto theft ring by the D.A.'s Organized Crime and Rackets Bureau, the NYPD Auto Crime Division and the Insurance Frauds Bureau.

"I'll turn that over to Detective Brewer, who is leading that aspect," Stroud said.

"With respect to our investigation on the two deceased—Donald Dalfini and Omarr Aimes—confidential sources arising from inquiries on Omarr Aimes led to Florence Payne, aka Mary Ballard, aka Miss Tangiers, an exotic dancer, thought to be the last to see Aimes.

"We interviewed Payne, who indicated that on the night before his death, Aimes took a cell phone call from a man she referred to as—" Brewer read from his notebook "—'Zeta' or 'Rama.' She said, 'It maybe had something to do with making a movie, that some guy named Zeta or Rama, some crazy Albanian or Russian, had a job for them that was big easy money.'

"We've investigated records through the mayor's office of Film, Theater and Broadcasting. Subsequently, we've contacted location managers and we're waiting to hear back for leads in this direction."

"Thank you, Detective Brewer."

Forsyth then turned to Cordelli.

"Detective Cordelli, you're working with Jeff Griffin on any subsequent leads based on his contact with the suspects. What do you have?"

"Working with Detective Lucy Chu, one of our forensic artists, we compiled a series of images based on what Griffin saw in the van. Using that material we're in the process of canvassing targeted locations for leads."

Forsyth glanced at his files, spotted a note and frowned.

"Excuse me, I've received this from our agents with you, but am I to understand Griffin left his hotel unescorted and we've lost track of him?"

Cordelli cleared his throat.

"That's correct. But I remind everyone he is not in custody."

"Has he been contacted again by the suspects?"

"All indications are that he has not had any further contact."

"But we don't know what he's up to or where he is?"

"No, but it was the FBI who were assigned to him this morning."

"I don't care," Forsyth said. "Lieutenant Stroud, were you aware that we'd lost Jeff Griffin?"

"No, I was not." Stroud glared at Cordelli. "Triangulate his phone. Track him down. He should not be out of our sight."

"We're done for now." Forsyth recapped his pen, closed his folders.

As the meeting broke up, investigators checked their phones while standing to leave.

Detective Brewer was the last to remain seated. His full attention was on his phone and the message he'd just received from Chuck Pennick, a location manager from Los Angeles in New York working on a film. Betty Bonner, Brewer's ex-partner in the film office, had said, "If anyone knows what's going on here, it's Chuck." Betty said Pennick was plugged into all foreign productions and crews.

Brewer read Pennick's message.

Detective: I heard a foreign crew was working without permits in a warehouse in the Bronx maybe making porn, or horror, or thriller. It's all rumor but I can try to find out more, if you like.

55

Purgatory Point, the Bronx, New York City

"You're sure it's in here?"

Minutes after Jeff's cab had left the Major Deegan Expressway, it rolled into a wasteland, making him doubt this was the location of the restaurant's address on the printout.

"Yeah, man, relax," the driver said. "I told you, my ex grew up here. I sent the bitch four years of support payments to this freakin' zip code. It's cool."

But what Jeff saw was an industrial graveyard of abandoned factories and decaying warehouses built in the late-nineteenth and early-twentieth centuries. They passed a crumbling tool factory, then a shirt factory that had been established in 1889, according to its massive decaying sign.

On the way out of Manhattan, the driver had explained how "the Point" used to be a grim section of the southwest Bronx, with the Harlem River to the west, and the East River to the southeast. You could see Rikers Island out there, and across the river you could see the planes lifting off and landing way out at LaGuardia. The cab now weaved through along hulking public housing projects, dingy apartment buildings and squat houses on deserted streets.

"A lot of people are on welfare and there's a lot of crime," the driver said. "I guess it's getting better. People have fixed up big chunks and stuff. Most people here, like me, are Puerto Rican, but in the past few years a lot of art pothead student types and a lot of Eastern Europeans, Albanians, Turks, Chechens, Bulgarians, Russians, people like that, have moved into the neighborhoods and it's been good, or so friends tell me. I live in Yonkers now."

Jeff saw the architectural and esthetic changes emerging as they came to the revitalized business district. There were blocks of tree-lined sidewalks with inviting benches, neo-Victorian streetlamps adorned with hanging planters bursting with flowers. Older buildings had been converted to condos and lofts above new galleries, specialty shops, boutiques and offices.

"Here you go." The driver nodded to a sign that read Vakhiyta's Kitchen.

"Go another block and drop me there."

"Okay."

Before Jeff got out, he paid the driver and gave him another twenty.

"Can you stay here and wait for me? I'll need a ride back."

"Sure." The driver handed him a card with his cell phone number.

Jeff adjusted his ball cap and dark glasses and headed for the restaurant. Since his face and identity had been published after the press conference he couldn't risk being recognized.

Come on, this is crazy. I'm out of my mind to think

this will amount to anything except pissing off Cordelli, Brewer and the FBI.

So what? I refuse to do nothing.

Vakhiyta's Kitchen was old-world plain. The name was painted on a wooden sideboard over a weatherworn brick storefront. It had dirty windows with half-drawn shades. A yellowed menu was taped to the glass-front door under the Open sign.

Jeff went in and was greeted with the smells of boiled cabbage, cooked meat and spices. High-backed red vinyl booths lined the sides; about a dozen wooden tables and chairs filled the dining room floor that led to a dark wooden front counter and the kitchen.

Jeff took a booth on the left. The place was about a third full with a dozen customers. Old travel posters of the Caucasus Mountains had been taped to the wall. Soft, mournful violin music flowed from ancient speakers. The atmosphere was sleepy, akin to an outdoor café or gathering spot, where people passed time with idle talk. The pieces of conversation he picked up were not English. Given the restaurant's specialty, he figured them for Eastern European.

The staff: a couple of women and men were deep in conversation behind the counter. No one came to take Jeff's order. He noticed a spread of newspapers near the counter. It gave him reason to get closer to search for the take-out logo. He went to the counter and sifted through the papers—most were foreign, Russian, he guessed—before glancing around for a stack of take-out coffee cups.

"You would like something to eat?" asked one of the women, a heavyset babushka with an apron and head scarf.

"Yes—" Jeff had to buy time "—coffee to go and something to eat here."

"Sit, sit. I bring you menu."

Moments later she came to his table with a cracked laminated menu that listed a few dishes, none of which he understood.

"Maybe you like to try our soup? We make very good." She smiled.

"Yes."

"I bring you today special cream of potato, the best in New York."

"Yes and coffee to go in a take-out cup, please?"

She nodded and returned with the coffee, creamers and sugar. Jeff's attention flew to the logo and his heart skipped.

It bore a stylized *V* with blue letters spelling *Vakhiyta's Kitchen.*

"Excuse me." Jeff tried to stay calm. "Is this the only Vakhiyta's Kitchen in New York? Do you have more at other locations anywhere?"

The woman held up a single, thick finger.

"Only one in the world," she said.

When she left, Jeff took a few slow breaths. *I should call Cordelli and Brewer, alert them.* He struggled to understand what he had. He carefully withdrew one of Detective Chu's pictures from his pocket, unfolded and turned it so the *L* resembled a *V.* He compared it with the logo on his take-out cup.

This is it. This is definitely it!

Jeff was convinced the killers had been in this restaurant, had bought coffee and food here, because he'd seen the containers in the van.

Okay, what now?

Think.

Were the killers just passing by? Or were they near?

He took slow inventory, assessing the customers, searching for anything to help him. He saw a young well-dressed couple he'd figured for Russian tourists. He took note of some old men playing chess. A group of other men were talking about matters they pointed out in the newspapers. *Issues in the old country?* Before Jeff could continue, a bowl of soup and slab of home-made bread with butter were set before him.

"You will like," the babushka said.

In the time the soup came, Jeff ate it, liked it and continued eyeing the customers. After the woman took his bowl away, he continued his vigil. He declined more food and eventually feared that his investigation had stalled. He felt the futility, the weight of all his failures, come crashing down on him.

He called Cordelli, got his voice mail but hesitated. He didn't leave a message. He couldn't risk being over-heard.

It can't all end here.

Jeff glanced at the well-thumbed copies of the New York papers and reports of the investigation, the head-line Murder-Abduction Trigger Terror Plot Fears, at his photo and those of Sarah and Cole. He touched his fin-gertips to their faces.

I can't give up.

What if I am close?

Jeff was so lost in the faces of his wife and son he hadn't noticed the man who'd entered the restaurant. His age was difficult to determine but from his body and posture, he had to be in his early thirties. He was about six feet tall, medium build. He wore a dark sweatshirt with the hood up, dark pants and work boots.

The man was standing at the counter near the cash,

waiting as the babushka lady packed up a take-out order of coffee and food. He was solemn, engrossed in the newspaper reports on the "terror plot." The chime of the register pulled Jeff from his thoughts in time to notice the man walking by his booth with his take-out order.

Jeff glanced down at the man's boots. They were dark boots that covered the ankle. They had rounded toes and a thin bright red line where the top was stitched to the sole.

Jesus.

Jeff swallowed, fumbled for cash and tossed a few bills on the table.

He left his booth and, keeping a safe distance back, followed the man along the street, his heart hammering.

That fucker is one of them.

56

Darmstadt, Germany

"The game is going ahead as scheduled. Our team is favored to win."

The American intelligence officer sat up in his chair at his computer monitor and used both hands to press his headset to his ears.

He quickly reread the notes the traffic operator, the linguist and the cryptologist had provided, then he replayed the recording.

"The game is going ahead as scheduled...."

The officer worked in a corner of a listening station that was part of a U.S. military complex hidden in the forests of the Rhine region, less than an hour's drive south of Frankfurt. It was an ultrasecret tentacle of the National Security Agency's foreign intelligence surveillance operations that few people knew existed.

Code name: HUSH.

The system had grown from ECHELON, a Cold War communications network operated by Australia, Canada, New Zealand, the United Kingdom and the United States, to eavesdrop on the Soviet Union and the Eastern Bloc. Since then it had emerged to monitor activities of pariah countries, insurgency, organized crime and terrorist plots.

HUSH went beyond monitoring satellite telecommunications traffic. It also used an advanced network of secret listening stations around the world that were strategically placed near major switching bases for fiber-optic communications.

In this sector, the path of much of Europe's internet communications traveled through a critical exchange point near Frankfurt International Airport. Here, through its Darmstadt station, HUSH had been running a long-standing operation of tracking, capturing, decrypting and analyzing the phone and web traffic of scores of terror groups.

In most cases the targets used untraceable disposable phones, or encrypted satellite phones, or coded internet communication. HUSH's experts drew upon information harvested from captured suspects and equipment. They also relied on the work of intelligence officers in the field whose sources and informants provided key but ever-changing numbers, codes, positions and data.

Intelligence operators and traffic analysts had to contend with some seventy languages and dialects. Linguists where often challenged understanding everything they'd heard. So much could be lost if one didn't understand the cultural contexts. All intelligence operators, despite listening in on targets for months, feared they could miss something. They used technology and human resources to sort through millions of intercepted calls, decode keywords for further analysis.

The intelligence officer continued concentrating and replayed the fragment of captured communications several more times.

"The game is going ahead as scheduled. Our team is favored to win."

These calls were very recent and had pinballed from Istanbul to Athens, from Grozny to Makhach-kala, Dagestan, from Amsterdam to Mykrekistan, from Munich to Queens, New York.

The languages on this file had been a mix of Azeri, Chechen, Dargwa, Greek, Kumyk, Lezgian, Mykrekistani, Tabasaran, Turkish and Russian.

The officer checked his notes.

The targets had been European cells supporting a dangerous group of insurgents in the Caucasuses. CIA informants had indicated the insurgents had boasted of an attack planned for the UN meeting in New York City and that when the target's plans moved closer to activation, the targets would encrypt their conversations to sound like they were talking about a specific football match—the game between the U.S. and Iranian national soccer teams to be played today in New York City.

The officer signaled to a supervisor.

"Sir, take a look at the notes, and listen," the officer said. "I think we have something."

The supervisor listened on his headset.

"The game is going ahead..."

He listened twice, consulted the notes and drew upon all the alerts he'd been privy to from the past forty-eight hours.

"Okay, get this to Langley and Iron Shield in New York."

57

Don't lose him.

Jeff's breathing quickened. Keeping a safe distance back, he followed the man from the restaurant, watching him turn a corner.

Two blocks later the man vanished into an alley and Jeff rushed to the entry. The narrow passage darkened between two buildings. Jeff saw the man's silhouette at the opposite end and tried calling Cordelli.

This time the detective answered.

"Cordelli?"

Jeff kept his voice low. "It's me, Griffin. I found them!"

He stayed on the phone, never removing his eyes from his subject, and started down the alley keeping a distance.

"What's going on? Where are you, Jeff?"

"The Bronx in— Wait."

The man suddenly vanished at an angle to cut across the next street. *I lost him. Damn.* Jeff trotted down the alley, phone pressed to his ear.

"You're breaking up," Cordelli said. "Where in the Bronx? Give me an address!"

At the end of the alley Jeff scanned the street, his heart rising to his throat. No trace of the guy.

Damn. Damn. Damn.

"Jeff! Can you hear me? Give me a location. Brewer and I are in the Bronx following a lead. Where are you?"

"I'm in a warehouse in Purgatory Point a few blocks from Vakhiyta's Kitchen!"

"Say again, I didn't get all of that! Repeat your location!"

At that instant Jeff's focus went across the street and straight through an empty office building. Behind it he glimpsed the man making his way over a large vacant lot toward a larger building.

Reflex kicked in.

Jeff shot across the street, triggering a horn blast as he just missed being hit by a car. He lost his balance and his cell phone, which fell to the pavement. He was not hurt but the phone looked broken. The impact had knocked the battery free. Jeff collected the two pieces in time to see the man pass through a gate to a huge old building in the distance.

Jeff shoved the two pieces into his pocket and jogged along the edge of the vacant lot, using the line of small trees and brush for cover as he neared the building, an imposing four-story stone structure.

The immediate area was desolate, the dirt and gravel surrounding it a graveyard of abandoned hulks of rusting machinery. The property was protected with a ten-foot chain-link fence topped with barbed wire. The gate the man had entered through was padlocked.

Jeff moved fast along the perimeter, coming to an isolated section with a stand of trees and overgrowth. Judging from the empty beer cans, the smashed liquor bottles and fire pit, this was a drinking party spot. Someone had positioned wooden shipping pallets ladder-style against the fence. Jeff climbed it, moving with care over the razor wire, then lowered himself inside the property.

He moved quickly along the length of the aging building, searching for an entry point. Doors he came upon were locked. Windows were sealed. He traveled an entire length, moved on to the next, then the next, before he'd reached a corner where a section of wall had crumbled. It had been patched with sheets of plywood that had grayed, rotted and frayed.

Jeff pulled back on the plywood, and wedged himself through the jagged gap to the inside.

Inhaling air that was a rank mix of a chicken coop and neglected machinery, he took immediate inventory of his surroundings.

Be careful where you step.

The floor was covered with metal shards, broken glass and wood with exposed nails. Near him were pallets of lathes, crates and motors stacked haphazardly and reeking of hydraulic fluid, oil and bird shit.

He heard the hum of voices and the static-squawk of emergency scanners in the near-distance. But saw nothing. He hid among the pallets and began reassembling his phone. With his hands shaking, he replaced the battery and tried to power up.

Come on. Come on.

The phone flickered to life. *Good.* Battery power showed fifty percent. He silenced the ringer and vibrating features, then called Cordelli. His trembling sweating fingers caused him to misdial and he was about to try again when he heard a shout and footfalls.

Someone was approaching his area.

He shoved the phone into his pocket and moved along the pallets navigating around rotting lumber, drums of trash, some leaking with fluid, eroding concrete columns and vines of wiring flowing from the great ceiling with its aging, broken windows.

As Jeff made his way through the labyrinth of chaos, his ability to hear the voices improved. Men were speaking English and something Slavic, he guessed. Amid the double- and triple-deck rows of neglected and rusted junk, he glimpsed flashes of movement near tables with electronic equipment, yet he was not sure what he saw.

It was difficult to get closer without risking being discovered.

He kept moving along a stretch of tarpaulins draped over vehicles; a long row of them pointed to an interior driveway clear to a ramp and secured garage door. *What kind of vehicles?* Jeff saw the tires, but little more. He couldn't risk looking, or making a sound. He moved beyond the vehicles until he came to a narrow wooden hallway that was open to the ceiling.

It looked makeshift.

Jeff moved along the passage quickly.

"Here!"

Jeff flinched, then froze.

The voice on the other side of the paper-thin wall startled him. He stopped and sat with his back to the wall and tried to control his breathing.

"Put the flag here, now!"

Jeff felt the thud of a hammer driving small nails, saw the nails puncture the wall.

They're on the other side!

The only thing separating me from the killers is a quarter inch of wood!

Table and chair legs scraped on the floor.

"The camera's set up, we're ready."

Feet shuffled. Jeff noticed the wall did not touch the floor. There was a four-inch gap. He swallowed and lay flat on the floor and saw movement, boots, but nothing to indicate Sarah and Cole.

"I want to do one rehearsal read first."

Tables and chair legs scraped again.

"Ready?"

"Yes. In five—four—three—two—go."

A throat cleared, paper rustled.

"'Greetings from God's slave to the United Nations. You did not start this tragic war but if you are people with courage, determination and humanity, you will acknowledge our action today as the final call to end it....' No, stop. I want to change something before we start again."

Jeff's heart stood still.

They're making a video—a demand or ultimatum for maybe an attack on the UN!

Realizing what was unfolding, he had to do something fast.

He dragged the back of his hand across his mouth, knowing that he was exhausted, not thinking clearly. He couldn't leave until he found Sarah and Cole.

He grabbed his phone and in several quick texts to Cordelli, Jeff alerted him that he couldn't talk. He'd found the killers in a factory in Purgatory Point in the Bronx. It was extremely urgent that Cordelli give him a number by which he could relay live critical one-way information.

Jeff's last text ended with:

It's life and death. Time is running out!

58

Tremont, the Bronx, New York City

"He's in a warehouse in Purgatory Point," Cordelli told Brewer.

Brewer was driving.

"That's five miles from here, we'll take Major Deegan." Brewer checked his mirrors, then rolled his unmarked Crown Victoria west out of Tremont, a section of the Bronx once known as a neighborhood of lost causes.

Brewer and Cordelli had come to Tremont to follow Brewer's lead that a foreign crew was making a film without permits in the Bronx. Brewer's source, the film location manager, was able to narrow his information to a factory in Tremont but the detectives had found nothing, even after a call to the Forty-sixth Precinct for help. Nothing had surfaced.

Their frustration underscored Brewer's simmering resentment.

As he knifed through traffic on the expressway, he could not stop considering it punishment that he had been ordered to partner with Cordelli for the rest of this investigation.

Klaver had been assigned to work with Ortiz to help teams completing the canvass of restaurants and various outlets based on Jeff's recalled details from the van.

Nothing had come out of that aspect of the investigation, either.

Until now, with Jeff's call, no major breaks had surfaced for anyone, not the Joint Terrorism Task Force, NYPD, Homeland, FBI, Secret Service and the thirty agencies that were going full tilt on the case.

With a threat looming, the fear of being powerless to stop it intensified.

Brewer had to get his anger off of his chest.

"I don't understand how you could just lose Griffin," he said. "The last time that happened he made contact with the suspects."

"The FBI had him. Nobody 'lost' him, Larry. He was never in custody."

"Did they triangulate his phone?"

"They had him leaving Battery Park, then northbound near the Queensborough Bridge. Then they lost his roaming signal."

"I would have never let him out of my sight."

"No one can hold a candle to your police work, Larry. Look, we've got him again so why don't you push this 'my way' crap aside so we can take Griffin's lead and work this thing through."

Brewer swallowed the remnants of his bitterness.

"Call the Fortieth," Brewer said. "Request some help to meet us at this Vaketa Kitchen, or whatever it's called, so we can find the warehouse. Better get ESU on standby."

Cordelli was staring at his phone. Something had come in.

"It's a text from Griffin," Cordelli said. "Give me your phone, I've got to make a call."

"What's he saying?" Brewer passed Cordelli his cell phone and, while reading Jeff's message, Cordelli called the NYPD's Real Time Crime Center. His call was answered on the second ring.

"This is Detective Cordelli with an urgent request. Is this Renee?"

"That's right, Renee Abbott, Detective. How can I help?"

"You're going to get a call from Jeff Griffin. He will leave his phone on for a one-way transmission of critical information, originating from the suspects. Do not respond. Mute your line and patch it through to the task force for processing. Alert them now. Are you ready for Griffin's number?"

"Ten-four."

"Okay, it's 646-555…"

59

Purgatory Point, the Bronx, New York City

Jeff called the number Cordelli had texted him.

No one spoke at the other end but the display window showed that his call had connected.

Good.

Jeff activated his cell phone's speaker and set the phone on the floor on his side of the wall. Then with the utmost care to be quiet he slid the phone under the gap. It picked up the sound just as the man on the other side resumed making his statement.

"'Greetings from God's slave to the United Nations. You did not start this tragic war but if you are people with courage, determination and humanity, you will acknowledge our action today as the final call…'"

Jeff's heart hammered against his chest with such force he feared the men would surely hear it. He worked on controlling his breathing while praying that Sarah and Cole were near.

God, please let them be alive.

Jeff drew back when the statement suddenly ended with a burst of activity.

"Let's go! This is it! You know your jobs!"

From that point on, orders were shouted in a foreign language over the movements of people rushing, equipment cases being loaded and snapped shut, zippers being closed, computers shutting down, tables and chairs shoved.

Jeff grabbed his phone, then lay flat on the floor, pressing his face to the gap to see what was happening. His view was restricted to the boots of men hurrying, moving out. *How many were there—twenty, two dozen?* Then he heard the *ring-clink* of chains and held his breath.

Then he saw small white sneakers contrasted against the large military boots.

Those are Sarah's shoes!

She was wearing them when they'd left the hotel to visit Times Square.

Jeff then saw a set of smaller khaki canvas sneakers.

Those belong to Cole!

His wife and son were right there, so close. Jeff's stomach twisted. He wanted to bust through the wall but was helpless. There were too many opponents. He'd be overpowered, captured, killed. He drew his fingers into fists; his agony turned to rage.

Vehicle doors opened and closed, engines started, revved, and within seconds they were gone.

60

Manhattan, New York City

Underwater.

Aleena Visser was below the surface.

She could not open her eyes. The roar of the pressure throbbing in her brain and her ears was deafening.

I'm awake. I'm not awake. I'm dreaming.

Remembering and not remembering.

A story in New York.

"We need a special edition on New York.... Would you to please deliver this for me...?" A gift, a pretty music box. *"Would you please deliver this for me in Manhattan?"*

Joost insisted.

Joost was dead. No! No, it's not true! It can't be true!

"Would you please deliver this for me in Manhattan?"

The newspaper headline on the plane: Murder-Kidnap Case Stirs Terror Fears at UN Meeting in New York.

She delivered the music box.

The strangers. My contact. It's true. All true. Being chased by two strangers. I am guilty.

What's in the music box?
The strangers. They're chasing me. They'll kill me. No!

Aleena was swimming, swimming hard underwater. The forces chasing her were faster. *Open your eyes! No! Open your eyes, you must see! The water is dark. I can't see!*

Swimming up with powerful save-your-life strokes, kicking up.

Breaking the surface to see, she gasped at the horror enveloping her.

Blood!

Aleena was swimming in blood and the screams pierced her ears.

No!

Thrashing, she felt the tubes on her face, the IV fastened to her arm, and she smelled the antiseptic tape, the disinfectant in the air, the starch of laundered sheets, her hospital bed.

"Noooooooooo!"

Nurses flew into the room to hold her, comfort her—one called for the on-duty resident, another soothed her.

"The number, call the number...718-555-768—"

"Easy, sweetheart, you've been in an accident. Easy."

"She's still in shock, delirious. Incoherent," one of the nurses said.

But through her tears Aleena knew.

"Call the police! I need to tell them the number! Oh, please call the police! I need to tell them the emergency number...."

"Shh-shh, the police know about your accident, dear."

"Everyone's going to die if you don't call the fucking police now!"

61

Jeff held his breath and waited.

Long after the vehicles had left, he remained fused to the wall, cursing himself for not knowing how many vehicles there were, or the makes, or the destination.

Where did they take Sarah and Cole? Their manifesto vowed imminent pain and suffering—but where, what are they planning to do? Oh, Jesus!

The questions tormented him as the building fell silent.

Was it safe to move now?

He swallowed, uncertain exactly how much time had passed, but he couldn't wait any longer. He needed to investigate for anything to lead him to his family. Jeff stood and hurried quietly along the wall until he came to its end and peered around it to the vast factory floor divided by decayed half walls, heaps of rotting lumber, wiring, piping and drums of trash.

It appeared deserted.

He made his way to a corner with two mattresses, chains, junk-food wrappers and a toilet.

This must be where they held them.

Battling his anger, he turned.

In the distance he saw the remains of offices, tables, workbenches, and headed toward them. The area had been cleared, little left but trash. He sifted through it until his cell phone's red light started blinking with a text from Cordelli.

Safe to call you now?

Yes.

Jeff's phone rang.

"What's the situation in there?" Cordelli asked.

"They're gone. They've taken Sarah and Cole!"

"We're out here with ESU. Come out to the large open door to the west with your hands up palms out so they can clear the building and we can pursue them."

Jeff trotted to the door and raised his hands as instructed.

Within minutes heavily armed ESU members wrapped in body armor swept into the building and scoured it. Cordelli and Brewer arrived after them, wearing Kevlar vests, weapons drawn. They took Jeff aside.

"Are you hurt?" Cordelli asked.

"No. What did you get from their demands on the call?"

"The task force is processing it with national security," Cordelli said.

More investigators arrived from the NYPD, FBI, Homeland and other agencies. As they began processing the scene, radios crackled and the air thudded with an approaching helicopter. Brewer was sober-faced and anxious.

"How many people were there?" he asked Jeff.

"Maybe two dozen."

"And they had vehicles?"

"Yes."

"How many were there? What were the makes, colors? Did you get plates?"

"No, I got nothing. I only heard them rolling out."

"You really didn't see much."

"No."

"How did you get here?" Brewer asked.

"Luck." Jeff found an empty take-out cup and held it up. "See, it was a *V,* not an *L.* It led me to the restaurant and I followed a guy here."

"If you'd worked with us we could've set up on this place," Brewer said.

"None of that matters now!" Jeff said. "They've got my wife and son. You heard their message. They want a lot of people to suffer. We have to find them before it's too late!"

62

Manhattan, New York City

After crossing the Robert F. Kennedy Bridge, the white EMS ambulance moved southbound on FDR Drive.

A marked NYPD patrol car and a marked NYPD van followed a few car lengths away but close by.

All three vehicles maintained the posted limit. None were using sirens, or emergency lights. There was nothing out of the ordinary as they traveled deeper into Manhattan along the parkway that paralleled the East River.

Traffic was moderate to medium.

Inside the ambulance, the radio's volume had been turned low as it chattered with dispatches. The two paramedics were clean shaven. Their uniforms were new, crisp blue with the six-pointed Star of Life patches. The coiled cord of the medical radio's microphone knocked gently against its base. The shelf of trauma supplies holding the IV bags, gloves and defibrillator rattled softly as the vehicle swayed. The stretcher was secured to the antiskid floor and emitted low *squeak-creaks* from time to time.

The "patient," Sarah Griffin, had been strapped firmly to the stretcher.

An oxygen mask, covering her face and mouth, was affixed tightly to her head. Tears rolled from her eyes, leaving tracks.

Sensing a terrible end was upon her, she prayed for Cole and Jeff.

If any authority needed to check the ambulance, something highly unlikely, they'd find nothing unusual with this patient transfer, unless they looked closely.

Unable to move, Sarah stared at the ceiling.

Expertly taped at strategic points, she saw rivers of braided colored wiring that flowed throughout the interior of the entire ambulance.

63

New York City

Across Manhattan at the NYPD's Real Time Crime Center, Renee Abbott typed with incredible speed as she processed Jeff Griffin's eavesdropped call.

He'd captured the suspect's manifesto, which was clearly meant to be delivered after an attack. Renee alerted the Joint Terrorism Task Force, then sent them the message, which was shared instantly with national security agencies.

The Secret Service, Homeland, the CIA, NSA, Defense, FBI and other security experts moved quickly to study it. Taken with the known facts of the abductions, murders and microdetonator, deeper examination of the information was needed to reveal the target and the people behind the plot. The full message stated:

"Greetings from God's slave to the United Nations. You did not start this tragic war but if you are people with courage, determination and humanity, you will acknowledge our action today as the final call to peacefully end our struggle for a free nation.

"To date, twenty thousand of our children have been murdered by the occupational forces, and the UN does

nothing. You force us to avenge the atrocities committed by these criminals—everyone must be made to understand our pain.

"We offer a solution for peace. Withdraw the troops, dissolve the puppet regime and acknowledge a free and truly independent Mykrekistan. We will end our armed struggle and any further nation-liberating acts of self-protection. We offer peace. The choice to accept it is yours."

In Washington, FBI counterintelligence examined the statement's text, as did the Secret Service's domestic and foreign intelligence branches.

In Langley, the CIA saw a link to the message and the most recent chatter captured by the NSA's listening station in Darmstadt, Germany. *"The game is going ahead as scheduled. Our team is favored to win."*

According to CIA intelligence, there were six different insurgent groups in the Caucasuses confirmed to have committed various acts of terrorism in support of the violent nationalist movement in Mykrekistan. The agency needed to do more analysis to determine which terror group had the money and ability to carry out an attack in the U.S.

Investigators had less than two hours before the president touched down in New York for his event with the British prime minister later in the day. Other world leaders continued to proceed with their scheduled engagements related to the United Nations General Assembly.

In Brooklyn, Iron Shield, the Secret Service's security command center for the UN gathering of world leaders, issued a top-secret threat alert. The center then double-checked the real-time whereabouts of every dignitary through encrypted radio contact with protective details.

Within minutes of the preliminary analysis, security chiefs ordered immediate protective action.

"Start evacuating the Security Council and General Assembly, the entire UN complex. We have a credible and potentially active threat," said Adam James, a senior agent with the Secret Service. He then called in to Iron Shield for a status report on the Russian delegation.

"Right now the Russian president and the president of Mykrekistan are at Ground Zero for a memorial ceremony," said Tate Eason.

"Get the detail on the line. We need to postpone, or delay."

"Sir, it's already started."

64

Battery Park, New York City

As the president of Russia stepped to the podium, security agent Nikolai Vlasik adjusted his earpiece while standing watch near the dignitaries' platform in Battery Park near the World Trade Center.

Vlasik was counting the hours until he was back in Moscow and finished dealing with Sergei Serov, the arrogant prick.

Vlasik headed the Russian Presidential Security Service team protecting the Russian delegation during its official visit to the United States. Serov was the intelligence boss whose anti-American posturing was a throwback to the Cold War. It blinded him to the point of making him a liability.

"The Americans have just issued a threat alert," Vlasik said into his radio. "We should cut this event short."

"No. Don't be concerned," Serov responded. "Things are in control."

Serov outranked him, had powerful friends and was untouchable.

Vlasik gritted his teeth and shook his head slightly to his American counterpart, Hank Young, a senior agent with the U.S. Secret Service, standing post at the far end of the platform.

Vlasik's gesture signaled that he'd been overruled by Serov.

Young acknowledged Vlasik. Then the American's chiseled face tightened as he received more information from another U.S. agent.

For his part, Vlasik used his anger to concentrate on his job. From behind his dark glasses he scanned the faces of the crowd of several thousand that had gathered for the ceremony.

The Russian government was presenting a gift to New York City, the sculpture of a rising angel by an artist from Mykrekistan. The president of Mykrekistan, New York's mayor, New York's governor and several local officials were participating in the unveiling of the memorial artwork dedicated to the "triumph over terrorism."

In scrutinizing the crowd, Vlasik looked at faces and hands for telltale signs of anything sinister—for someone who was not smiling, or was "off," or someone fidgety, or who was reaching for something. The chance that an explosive or weapon was overlooked during the security check was real, despite the heavy emergency presence of patrol cars, fire trucks and ambulances.

Helicopters passed overhead and the thud gave way to the screams of protestors who the NYPD had contained to one side behind interlocking metal barricades. When the Russian president reached the podium there was the sudden blossom of signs denouncing Russia, alleging human rights abuses, atrocities against those struggling for an independent Mykrekistan.

Sensing a potential eruption, the cameras and news crews turned their attention to the protestors. Such demonstrations were common whenever the Russian president visited other countries. But today Vlasik's unease had been deepened by the increasingly disturbing U.S. intelligence on threats. His preference was to heed the U.S. Secret Service, cut this event short and go to the backup plan, which was to move the presidential delegation to Bryant Park where, in a short time, the Russian first lady and the Mykrekistan president's wife would take part in the presentation of literary works to the New York Public Library.

Hank Young approached Vlasik and spoke directly into his ear.

"The threat is credible, Nick. Prepare to pull your guys out of here, fast."

"I'll inform Serov."

Vlasik went to the intelligence chief and relayed the latest update from the Secret Service.

"Tell him we are aware of the threat and not concerned," Serov sneered. He'd been in contact with top Russian agents with military and foreign intelligence. "Nikolai, we've already removed this threat right here in New York, right under the noses of our American friends. They're just catching up with us."

Vlasik returned to Young and informed him.

"Your boss could soon be overruled," Young said. "We expect an update any second now."

Above them, on the platform, the president began speaking, triggering an instant reaction from the protestors who yelled and howled in an attempt to drown out his words.

"The great city of New York and the great people of America have prevailed..." the president began.

A loud metal clanking rose as the protestors began rattling the barricades and blowing whistles.

"You're a murderer!" a woman shouted. "A war criminal!"

65

"Greetings from God's slave to the United Nations..."

Several miles south of downtown Washington, D.C., in a section of CIA headquarters that overlooked the Potomac River, Lilly Fong, one of the agency's leading experts in behavioral biometrics, worked fast, analyzing the statement.

Who is this guy?

The sound wizards down the hall had already enhanced the recording's quality. Lilly played it repeatedly, noting the speaker's style, voice pitch and other aspects before she processed the recording using several advanced speech recognition programs.

She then ran the sample through a CIA database of recordings and voiceprints of known terrorists and suspects until she found a match for the voice.

Bulat Tatayev.

"Good job," Lilly's deputy director said.

The CIA immediately set out to track and hunt Tatayev.

The deputy began digesting the agency's file on Tatayev, his nerves straining as he read. Bulat Tatayev was a warlord based in Mykrekistan, an ex-soldier, an engineer expert in explosives who became a leader of Mykrekistan's violent struggle against Russia for independence. After his parents, wife, daughter and son were killed in the bloodshed arising from years of unrest, he became one of the world's most dangerous men.

Bulat Tatayev or his followers were tied to or claimed responsibility for killing more than three hundred people.

The deputy director flipped through the summary: one hundred and twenty-one people died in an attack on a resort hotel on the Black Sea after a four-day siege; forty-six people were killed in the Christmas bombing of a shopping center in Saint Petersburg; twenty-two people died in an attack of a restaurant in Mykrekistan's capital; thirty-one people were killed in the seizure and gassing of a Moscow theater; forty people died in an attack of a subway station in Moscow; twenty-nine people died in the bombing of a Moscow airport; eighteen killed in an attack of a Russian consulate in Turkey; sixty-two people killed on an attack of a train to Moscow from Grozny.

The deputy scanned the section outlining how the insurgents regarded the president of Mykrekistan as a puppet traitor and the Russian president as a war criminal. Tatayev was known to have financial backing from wealthy corporate interests in the Caucasuses and the support of a global network of highly skilled militant cells.

Tatayev's dark eyes burned from a photo, his hatred intensified by his full unkempt beard.

Tatayev had vowed to take his cause to a world stage by sending a "martyr brigade" to carry out a "historic" attack at an international event.

The deputy pressed a speed dial number on his encrypted phone for security chiefs in New York.

"Alert the detail for the Russian delegation. We have a credible and active threat. The suspect is Bulat Tatayev, leader of a Mykrekistani terror faction. We're sending his photo and file now. The delegation is the target. Evacuate them now!"

66

In Manhattan, the white EMS ambulance and police vehicles stopped in a narrow alley somewhere off of Broadway.

The rear doors opened to several uniformed NYPD officers.

Two of them stepped into the ambulance and approached Sarah, who was still strapped to the stretcher. The one who sat on the bench next to her was the leader. He was clean shaven and unrecognizable from the way he'd looked at the warehouse.

He would bear no resemblance to the photograph the CIA would provide for circulation to national security and NYPD officials within the next twenty-five minutes.

He was a different man.

His face was a study of resolve as he removed her oxygen mask.

"Pay attention," he said.

She was trembling under her bindings.

"It's very important. Do I have your attention?"

Sarah swallowed and nodded.

The officer standing over them turned his cell phone to Sarah, showing her a small video of Cole. She saw his head and shoulders. His face was a mask of fear while offscreen an adult said something inaudible, prompting Cole to look at the camera.

"I'm so scared, Mom. Just listen to them."

Sarah cried out in agony for Cole.

The phone was taken away.

"Listen to me," the leader said. "Are you listening?"

Sarah nodded.

"If you want to see your son again, you will do as we say. If you try to escape or attract attention, your son will die. You will do what we tell you when we tell you. Is that understood?"

Sarah nodded.

The men removed her restraints, gave her a new ID that had been made using her driver's license photo. It said Press and a forgery of the correct media credential for the event. It looked completely authentic. They gave her a ball cap, dark glasses, a notebook.

They led her out of the ambulance through the front passenger door.

The leader and one of the other officers started escorting Sarah through the streets of New York. Behind her she saw the emergency vehicles ease from the alley.

Sarah could not believe what was happening.

"Today is a day of glory," the leader said as he looked to the crowd in the near-distance.

67

Purgatory Point, the Bronx, New York City

The old factory was filling with investigators and controlled chaos.

Cordelli and Brewer had huddled at one of the unused worktables with the brass from the task force, Homeland, FBI, NYPD and Secret Service.

Jeff was left straining to make sense of what was unfolding as the rapid radio dispatches and cell phone conversations exchanged among the investigators grew ominous. He moved closer to hear and determine what he needed to do next when suddenly Cordelli and Brewer broke from the huddle and started to leave.

"You need to stay here, Jeff," Cordelli said. "Ortiz and Klaver are on their way to this building. We have to go."

"Go where? Where're you going, Cordelli?"

The detective shot a glance toward Brewer, who had his cell phone to his ear and was several paces ahead, then back to Jeff.

"I deserve to know what's going on, Cordelli!"

"Jeff, it's better for you to stay here. Let us handle things."

Jeff grabbed the detective.

"I deserve to know, Vic."

Cordelli scratched his chin, glanced around and lowered his voice.

"They think the target is the Russian delegation in Battery Park, the Russian president and the president of Mykrekistan. They're trying to evacuate them now."

"What about Sarah and Cole? Is there any trace of them?"

Cordelli shook his head.

"We're looking. Everyone's looking. Stay here with Ortiz, Jeff."

At that moment, a Secret Service agent arrived and passed them while talking on his radio. "The wives? No, no, the target is the Russian president at Battery Park. The Russian first lady and the Mykrekistani president's wife are at Bryant Park for an event with the library. We're beefing up things there now…preparing to evacuate right…sending more people…"

Jeff turned back.

Cordelli was gone.

As Jeff walked toward the factory's large open door he fought to absorb what he'd just heard, tried to figure it all out. It could've been instinct based upon what he'd experienced, he wasn't certain where it came from, but a powerful gut feeling gnawed at him.

Jeff's focus went back to his battle with the killers in the van, back to the words: *Very soon we will show the world what it is to suffer—to lose what you love.*

Jeff walked to the door and yard, which was guarded by several uniformed officers from the Fortieth Precinct keeping unauthorized people out. Every investigator and emergency officer at the scene was doing their job. No one noticed as Jeff pulled on his ball cap and dark glasses and walked out of the building. In the factory yard he saw the tangle of emergency vehicles and the plastic tape of a police line at the fence gate keeping news crews and rubberneckers back.

Jeff searched his pocket for the number for his cab-driver, hoping that he was still waiting. He found the card but before he called, his spirits lifted. Beyond the news trucks he spotted his driver, leaning on his parked taxi. The press people had encircled a police official and Jeff edged around them and a fire truck to the cab.

"Hey, man," the driver said. "What are you doing here? I was gonna leave when I saw all this commotion. What the hell is going on in there?"

"I need to get back to Manhattan as fast as possible."

"Let's go."

The driver and traffic were good. Within twenty minutes they were on the other side of the river rolling smoothly southbound on FDR Drive.

"So what's going on back there? One of the press guys said something about terrorists?"

"I don't know exactly." Jeff shrugged.

Only half listening, Jeff was still processing what he'd heard with what he knew as the driver fiddled with his radio, searching for an all-news station.

"Manhattan is jumpy. Something's up," the driver said. "I heard they're evacuating the UN building and my dispatcher said something's going on down at Battery Park. They're closing streets for a big show with the Russian president. But I think there's more to it." The driver checked his dash-mounted GPS. "We may need to find a different way in. That's where we're going, right? Back to Battery Park where I picked you up?"

The driver checked his rearview mirror for an answer.

Jeff was thinking.

No, he thought. *No, it's not Battery Park.*

Again Jeff concentrated on his moments in the van and the killer's words: *"Very soon we will show the world what it is to suffer—to lose what you love."*

That's it. That has to be it. "To lose what you love."

It's not Battery Park.

"Hello?" the driver said. "Battery Park?"

"No, no, I need to get to Bryant Park as fast as possible!"

"Bryant Park? All right, Bryant Park, it is."

At that point, the driver turned up the cab's radio. *"—breaking news again, this is just in. We have unconfirmed word of an incident—we repeat, unconfirmed— of a possible attack in the park... We have few details... Emily Tucker is there, we'll go to her, live now. Emily?"*

68

Battery Park, New York City

As the Russian president neared the end of his speech, the catcalls from the protestors increased.

Nikolai Vlasik's jaw muscles throbbed as Sergei Serov took him aside. Hank Young, hand cupped over his ear as information was relayed to him, had again urged the Russian delegation to evacuate.

Again, Serov had refused, saying the delegation would depart only after the event was finished, only after the other dignitaries had spoken.

Irritated, Young left to seek authority to overrule Serov. When Young was out of earshot, Serov smirked to Vlasik.

"We have the situation under control," Serov said. "Never forget, Nikolai, Mother Russia has the best intelligence-gathering apparatus the world has ever known. We do not frighten easily and have no intention to leave until the dedication ends."

Vlasik ignored Serov and performed another radio check with his team, scanning the crowd. The protestors wailed as the president said, "I wish to express my respect for the courage of the people of—"

The president stopped.

His head snapped up as if he'd been shocked. Bright red droplets suddenly appeared on his face and red streaked across the Mykrekistani president's face and neck as he'd risen to rush to the podium.

By reflex, Vlasik and the Secret Service detail's training kicked in. Within a heartbeat agents covered the Russian president, shielding him amid screams as other agents yanked dignitaries from the stage.

Chairs were toppled and the crowd erupted as terrified people ran, crouched and crawled in every direction as security teams drew weapons.

A wave of uniformed NYPD officers charged at the protestors.

News crews swung into action covering all angles of the turmoil.

Frantic calls were made to news desks to go live with coverage as one seasoned network crew, already live, issued a report within seconds.

"...yes, it appears the Russian president has been wounded in some sort of attack! Other dignitaries have also been injured...."

69

Bryant Park, Manhattan, New York City

Jeff's mind was racing when he got to Bryant Park.

The property sat in the heart of midtown on ten treed acres of beautiful green lawn behind the New York Public Library's main branch.

The urban oasis was surrounded by glass-and-steel skyscrapers, including the Bank of America Tower, whose height rivaled the Empire State Building.

A crowd of nearly fifteen hundred people had gathered for an event to take place on a platform raised at the rear of the library overlooking the great lawn.

Russia's first lady and the wife of Mykrekistan's president were leading an outdoor cultural presentation of newly discovered archived manuscripts by Russian masters such as Tolstoy, Dostoevsky, Chekhov and Mykrekistan's literary greats.

The dignitaries who would accept the donation were the wives of New York's mayor, New York's governor, the head of the New York Public Library and several other officials. The public would be allowed an exclusive viewing of the documents immediately after the event.

However, the ceremony was late getting started. A man in a suit approached the podium. His face was grim.

At that point, Jeff had arrived on the Fortieth Street side of the park, which was ringed with barricades, uniformed officers and security agents wearing earpieces and dark glasses. Emergency vehicles were positioned everywhere at Fortieth and Forty-second Streets, Fifth and Sixth Avenues.

At the periphery there were pockets of protestors displaying placards that were anti-Russian and called for an independent Mykrekistan. Jeff walked by them just as the air split with an announcement over the public-address speakers from the lone man on the stage.

"Our apologies, ladies and gentlemen," he said. "We have to delay just a bit longer. We ask for your understanding, but we may be forced to postpone today's event. We'll get back to you shortly. Thank you for your patience."

Groans rose from the crowd with ripples of questions.

"Postpone? Why? What for? What's going on?"

Jeff noticed a cluster of news vehicles a distance away just inside the barricades not far from the platform. Crews were on cell phones or radios, some were anxious, yelling questions into their phones, while others were packing up.

Maybe they know something?

Jeff hurried toward them.

Behind the stage, out of public view, the Russian first lady, her face taut with concern, was talking on a cell phone to Nikolai Vlasik.

"He's all right, ma'am," Vlasik shouted over sirens and uproar. "We've got everyone out!"

"Put him on the phone, Nikolai!"

There was commotion.

"Hello, my love, I am fine. We are all fine! Carry on! I'm going to change out of my ruined suit. You carry on!"

The first lady was encircled by Russian and U.S. security agents. She smiled at the good news, nodded big nods to the Mykrekistan president's wife and the two women hugged each other in tearful relief.

Word was immediately passed to the officials that the Bryant Park event was to continue as planned.

The metal police barricades separated Jeff from the news crews but from his side he'd gotten near enough to see a woman in an intense cell phone conversation.

"Do we go to Battery Park, or stay here, Gilroy? Wait! Len's got something."

A man stepped out of their news van, the words and logo for *99 NewsLine* blared across the panels.

"NBC's reporting that the Battery Park protestors tossed balloons filled with stage blood at the Russians to represent the bloodshed of the unrest in Mykrekistan. They're shaken up but no injuries, nothing more."

"Okay, Gilroy?" the woman said into the phone. "Did you get that? What's Len got from NBC? We're going to stay at Bryant and cover. Okay."

The woman hung up.

"Excuse me!" Jeff said, removing his ball cap and glasses. "I need some help fast."

After a moment, recognition dawned on the faces of the seasoned newspeople.

"Hey, you're…"

On the opposite side of Bryant Park on Forty-second Street, two uniformed NYPD officers approached other officers posted at the barricade. They nodded to the woman with them with the press tag, notebook and worried look on her face under her sunglasses and ball cap.

"She's late for this thing," Bulat Tatayev told the young officers. "We're taking her in."

The two cops looked the woman over.

"She's with you, then?" one of the cops said to Tatayev.

"Unfortunately."

"Who're you guys with? We got a lot of new faces down here."

"The Forty-sixth."

"The Forty-sixth in the Bronx? You have our sympathies. Be our guest."

The officers stepped aside and Tatayev and the other "cop" escorted Sarah through the crowd, positioning her in center front of the platform just as the event resumed, with the dignitaries taking their designated seats near the podium.

At a Fortieth Street entrance to Bryant Park, two NYPD uniform officers were instructing police to open the barricade so the idling white EMS ambulance they were escorting could enter.

"Whoa, whoa, hey, what is this?" one of the officers guarding the entrance asked the newcomers.

"We got orders to get this vehicle inside and close to the platform?"

"Who authorized that?"

"Our Lieu. We're beefing up after Battery Park. This event is getting started. Come on, buddy, open up!"

The ambulance was edging forward to emphasize the point.

After a few seconds the officer and his partners relented and opened the barricades, allowing the ambulance entry into the park not far from the platform.

* * *

Upon recognizing Jeff Griffin, Joyce King and Len Lustig, producers with *99 NewsLine,* took him into their large van.

It was filled with equipment and an array of small monitors. While Jeff talked with King and Lustig, another crew member was working remotely, communicating through a headset to their cameraman, who was providing images of the Bryant Park ceremony as it got under way.

"Let me get this straight," Lustig said to Jeff. "You think your wife and son are here somewhere with the terrorists?"

"Yes."

"And you're part of that thing going on in the Bronx right now, in Purgatory? We've got a crew there, right, Joyce?" King was on a cell phone to their desk, and nodded to Lustig. "Christ, this is a helluva thing," Lustig said. "Okay, tell us what we need to do to help you?"

"Can you search the crowd with your camera? I know it's a long shot but everything tells me they're here."

Lustig tapped the shoulder of the technician.

"Tell Sonny to take a lot of long cutaways and pan the crowd, get faces and anything unusual." Then to Jeff, Lustig said, "You'll see what the camera sees on the monitors. If we need to zero in on something, tell me."

Sarah was terrified.

Standing in front of the platform, gripping her notepad, she wanted to scream out to the real police who were nearby.

She didn't. She couldn't because of Cole.

The threat they'd made against Cole prevented her

from doing anything that would put her son's life in further danger.

God, please help us get through this. Please, I'm begging You.

The event commenced with a few opening words, then a performance by a Russian dance group. As it ended with applause, Tatayev spoke into Sarah's ear.

"We want you to faint and not move!"

Sarah didn't respond.

"You will go down in five seconds if you want to see your son!"

Sarah took a deep breath and started counting. When she reached five she collapsed. Tatayev and his partner feigned an attempt to catch her as she fell on her back.

People near her gasped.

A woman knelt down and took Sarah's hand.

"I'm calling 9-1-1…." A man reached for his phone.

"We've got it." Tatayev stepped into their view, raised his radio and called for medical help. "We're right here."

Two paramedics from the white EMS ambulance responded quickly, bringing a stretcher and bag to the front of the platform where they began working on Sarah. The TV cameras in front of the platform turned to the medical emergency. The incident caused some confusion among the other emergency crews at the event.

They radioed to each other.

"Who are those guys? What's going on? Did we miss something? Somebody should check this out."

After tending to Sarah, the paramedics lifted her onto a stretcher, then one made a radio call for his ambulance.

"We're going to need our rig in here," he said.

"Wave it in!" Tatayev nodded.

People shuffled aside as the white EMS ambulance

began inching through the crowd to where Sarah was in front of the platform.

Medical crews and security officials were puzzled as to why the paramedics were disrupting the event. Why not transport their patient to their ambulance, why waste time moving it to the platform? As the vehicle crept forward, a befuddled official knocked on the driver's window.

"Hey, hotshot, what're you doing?"

The driver ignored him and continued inching the ambulance forward. Inside, the driver checked a cell phone keypad. It was secured on the overhead console in a motherboard that was linked to a detonation system and a nest of wires, duct-taped to the ceiling, as they flowed throughout the interior.

The ambulance was equipped with reinforced suspension because it weighed nearly three times more than a standard EMS ambulance.

The rotating emergency light mounted on the dash of Detective Juanita Ortiz's unmarked Impala painted her face red.

The car's siren died when she braked on the Fortieth Street side of Bryant Park and got out with Detective Klaver.

They'd been ordered to locate Jeff Griffin, who was not answering their calls. Upon discovering that he'd left the scene at the factory in the Bronx, Ortiz got the name of the cab company Jeff had used from a cop at the scene. Klaver had reached the driver through his dispatcher for the location where he'd dropped Jeff.

Investigators were concerned that Jeff may again have had contact with the suspects, or come upon new information.

"This guy." Klaver held up his phone showing Jeff's photo to several uniformed officers at one of the entrances.

"That's the Montana guy whose wife and kid were abducted," said one of the young cops.

"That's correct," Klaver said. "We've got to blast this photo to everyone working the park now. He's here somewhere. We need to find him now!"

"Hold on," said one of the officers, checking his phone. "We just got an arrest-on-sight alert for this guy, Bulat Tatayev."

Officers had been provided color front and profile photos of a bald white man with a wild black beard that emphasized the fierce intensity of his dark eyes.

Inside the *99 NewsLine* van, Jeff studied the TV monitors and the images of the crowds before the camera cut to the woman on the stretcher who was being treated by paramedics.

He didn't recognize her.

Then the camera pulled back and Jeff's breathing stopped.

"Hold it!"

"What is it?" Lustig asked.

"Tell your cameraman to zoom in on the woman on the stretcher, her shoes."

"Tell Sonny to get tight on her feet," Lustig said.

The woman's sneakers filled the monitors.

"How's that? Is there something there?" Lustig turned to Jeff but saw only his ball cap and sunglasses on the chair.

Jeff had left the van to charge into the crowd toward the stretcher.

As the dance group took bows on the platform, the

library official hosting the event was mindful of the apparent medical incident a few feet below them.

The VIPs seated on stage behind her were still whispering small talk about the Battery Park incident. The Russian delegation was anxious, something underscored by the ambulance inching forward.

The library official was about to announce a pause in the program but became distracted by a disruption at the periphery of the terrace.

"Sarah!"

Jeff called for her, consumed with one thought.

I can't lose her again!

"Sarah!"

Pushing through the crowd Jeff's entire being had become a driving force bent on saving his family. He didn't think of getting help or alerting police, not even when he slammed into the back of the NYPD officer who was talking to Ortiz and Klaver.

The detectives turned.

"Hey, Jeff!" Klaver yelled. "That's our guy!"

Ortiz and Klaver pursued him as the uniformed officer shouted alerts into his radio.

Jeff advanced far ahead of them and fought his way to the stretcher.

"Sarah!"

Hearing her husband's voice, Sarah opened her eyes.

"Jeff! Oh, God! Jeff!" Sarah's voice broke. "They still have Cole!" She pointed to Tatayev, dressed as an NYPD officer. "Stop him!" Then she pointed at the two paramedics. "Them, too, they're the killers! There's a bomb in the ambulance!"

In an instant Tatayev reached into his breast pocket for a cell phone and began entering the call code to activate the detonator. Before he could complete the call,

Jeff tackled him, knocking his cell phone from his hand. Tatayev, Jeff and the paramedics struggled for it as onlookers, thinking Jeff was dangerously disturbed, debated intervening while yelling for more police to back up the cop and paramedics.

Others screamed about a bomb. Terror, panic and confusion spread through the park. Jeff was overpowered and Tatayev recovered the phone. Without getting up he resumed entering the code.

Sarah smashed her foot on his hand before he could complete the call.

Ortiz, Klaver and several other NYPD officers arrived. They subdued and arrested Tatayev and the paramedics.

Jeff and Klaver rushed to the ambulance, coming first to the rear and opening its doors. There was no trace of Cole. Instead, Jeff and Klaver saw the wires and the driver begin to press numbers on the mounted cell phone keypad.

Klaver drew his weapon.

"NYPD! Freeze!"

The driver continued pressing keys and Klaver fired two bullets into his head, killing him instantly. More people screamed at the sound of gunfire as police battled to take control and clear the park.

"Everyone get the hell away from the ambulance! Get out of the park!" officers yelled as people ran in all directions. Security details moved instantly to evacuate the delegation.

As Tatayev, his hands cuffed behind his back, was taken by police from the park, Jeff and Sarah confronted him.

In the mayhem in front of news cameras, they implored the warlord to tell them where Cole was.

"We will exchange his life for the lives of the Russian criminals."

Sarah slapped his face.

"Where's my son, you bastard?"

"On his way to heaven."

70

Ozone Park, Queens, New York City

About ninety minutes after the Bryant Park plot was thwarted, police had followed a tip that led them to a home in a blue-collar section of Queens, a three-bedroom stucco bungalow south of Liberty Avenue on Eighty-sixth Street near the Bayside Cemetery.

Through binoculars, Cordelli, Brewer and several other investigators watched the house from down the street.

The people inside had no inkling of what was coming for them.

Patrol units from the One Hundred and Sixth Precinct had taken the outer perimeter. They'd stopped all traffic for several blocks around the hot zone while officers had swiftly and quietly escorted residents from homes that were in the line of fire. They'd moved them to safety near the cemetery while members of the NYPD's Emergency Service Unit took the inner perimeter and were setting up on the house.

The shades were pulled on all the main floor windows; sun-faded orange curtains covered those in the basement. The neighbors had told police that a man and woman lived in the home and "kept to themselves." An older neighbor, a woman holding a cat, said that earlier that morning the couple had been visited by strangers who'd backed a panel van into their driveway. A small Nissan, registered to the address, was parked out front. None of the neighbors could confirm if there were guns in the house. None were registered to the address.

The unit was braced for any outcome.

"Stand by," the ESU squad commander said to his team through his throat microphone. Given the magnitude of what had happened in Bryant Park, its ties to the murders and abduction, the squad, one of the NYPD's best, was preparing to make a no-knock forced rapid entry.

The team was positioned and ready.

The area fell silent.

After one last round of radio checks, the commander said, "Go!"

Glass in the main floor windows shattered as stun grenades were fired into the house with a series of deafening bangs and blinding flashes. Heavily armed ESU members wearing body armor smashed through the back and front doors to find a man and a woman in the living room watching TV news.

"New York Police Department! Get on the floor now!"

Disoriented and confused, the couple offered no resistance as they were handcuffed. While ESU members continued searching the house, others took the suspects to the command-post bus. Inside, FBI and NYPD investigators from the Joint Terrorism Task Force read them their rights and, after separating them, began questioning them independently.

"Is there anyone else inside?" Brewer asked.

The property owner was Natasha Barlinsky, a thirty-six-year-old American teacher of Mykrekistani descent. Five years earlier she'd taught English in Mykrekistan where she'd met Andrei Propov, a thirty-three-year-old ex-Russian soldier, who was sympathetic to the independence movement.

They married and Propov moved with Barlinsky to the U.S.

Barlinsky's name surfaced while Cordelli and Brewer were at the factory in the Bronx. It arose from a detective investigating the case of Aleena Visser.

The detective had informed Cordelli and Brewer that Visser, a Dutch national, had been critically injured after she'd been struck by a dump truck near Grand Central. From her hospital bed, Visser had told the detective that the number 718-555-7685 was connected to a terror plot, that she believed she'd smuggled a key item into New York. She'd delivered it to a Russian-looking stranger for Joost Smit of Amsterdam, a former Russian security agent, who'd died the previous day.

Through an immediate and combined effort of the Joint Terrorism Task Force, the CIA and the NSA, investigators confirmed much of Aleena Visser's information. They'd managed to track the 718-555-7685 number to a cell phone, a prepaid model. It was purchased several weeks earlier at a drugstore along with toothpaste, shampoo, vitamins and several other items. It was a cash purchase. However, a customer points card was also used; the card was traced to Barlinsky. Barlinsky's husband, the CIA had learned from sources in Europe, was said to be part of a U.S.-based support cell for Mykrekistani insurgents.

Propov refused to utter a word to investigators after he was arrested.

Barlinsky requested a lawyer.

Inside the house, ESU officers scoured every room, checking furniture, the shower, closets, walls and ceilings for signs of other people. One member moved through the basement, careful to inspect the washer and dryer. On another assignment he'd found a female suspect curled up in a dryer. He looked under a workbench. *Nothing.* Then he checked large storage bins, unrolled a carpet. *Again nothing.*

All clear here.

Turning to go, he noticed that a section of the room's wall paneling seemed ever-so-slightly out of line. He tapped the wall. The board was loose. He used his knife to pry it a little and the entire section gave way, revealing a large hidden room.

In his time on the job, the officer had come upon many heart-stopping moments, but this one took his breath away.

"Jesus Christ!"

Across New York City, in midtown, police had diverted traffic around the incident, and then launched the evacuation of the surrounding streets exposed to Bryant Park while they worked on the ambulance.

The vehicle had been implanted with enough explosive material to make it one of the largest bombs the NYPD had ever faced.

At a command post two blocks away, Jeff watched paramedics assess Sarah as she agonized over Cole.

"Where is he, Jeff?" she pleaded from the back of ambulance. "Why won't they tell us anything?"

He looked to Ortiz and Klaver nearby, among the group of NYPD and FBI investigators talking at a cluster of emergency vehicles. The two detectives nodded to the supervisors while shooting glances at Sarah and Jeff before approaching them. Their grim faces and body language deepened Jeff and Sarah's fears and she squeezed his arm so tight it hurt.

"We found Cole," Ortiz said.

"Oh, God, is he hurt?" Sarah asked.

Ortiz exchanged a subtle glance with Klaver.

"Is he alive?" Jeff said.

"Yes."

"Where is he? We want to see him," Sarah said.

"He's in a house in Queens," Klaver said.

"Take us there now," Jeff said.

"It's better if you wait here," Klaver said.

Jeff glared at both detectives.

"Tell us what's going on—is he hurt? Tell us."

Ortiz swallowed. Her eyes softened and in that instant she was more mother than detective when she touched Sarah's shoulder.

"He's wired to explosives."

"Oh, God!" Sarah screamed. Jeff cupped his hands to his face as Ortiz and Klaver tried to console them.

"We've got people working on it, good people," Ortiz said.

"Where in Queens? We want to go there now!" Jeff said.

"We need to be there," Sarah said. "No matter what happens, Cole has to know we're there with him, near him. Please."

Ortiz absorbed Sarah's anguish before taking the request to Gabe Kreston, one of the task force commanders. Kreston listened as Ortiz explained. When one of Kreston's FBI counterparts saw that he was considering the request, he said, "You don't want the parents at the scene if this thing goes bad, Gabe."

Knowing she was out of line, Ortiz said, "Sir, I think
they deserve to be there. We can keep them back." Ortiz
nodded to some news trucks. "Those guys already have
cameras on the house. One way or another they'll see
the outcome."

Kreston rubbed his chin, then nodded.

"Take them to the command post in Queens. Let
Cordelli and Brewer know."

In Ozone Park, in the basement of the house, Cole
sat on a swivel office chair, crying softly under the tape
sealing his mouth.

Four white bricks of C-4 were duct-taped to his chest,
as if he were wearing a bizarre vest made of butter
sticks. His arms and legs were taped to the chair. Tears
and sweat dampened Cole's face, but the lone ESU officer sitting with him was instructed not to touch him.

All he could do was try to keep Cole calm.

"It's gonna be okay, son. Our best guy will be down
here."

After the officer had flagged the situation to his
squad members, all radio and cell phone communication in the area had been cut, in case the bomb was remotely triggered by a wireless device. A shadow, then
a small tap on a basement window, signaled that help
had arrived.

The floor above creaked from a colossal weight as an
alien being in a hulking green canvas suit, resembling a
mix between an astronaut and deep-sea diver, descended
the stairs with the speed of Frankenstein's monster.

Detective Bill Grant was inside the suit and he was
pissed off. Upon arriving, he'd lost an argument with his
boss. Grant did not want to wear the suit for this case.

"The boy has no protection and when he sees that

I do, it tells him that I'm prepared to fail and he could die."

Grant's boss had to think about policy, liability and potentially losing Grant. It sickened him, because he agreed with Grant, but he could not allow his man to be unprotected.

In the end, it wouldn't help anybody.

Once he made his way to Cole, Grant gave him a thumbs-up.

"Hey, there, Cole. My name's Bill and I'll get you out of this thing just as soon as I can, okay?"

Cole nodded.

The ESU officer smiled at Cole. He wanted to stay but had been ordered to leave.

Grant knelt before Cole and in the quiet began surveying the setup. He made no assumptions. The best bomb builders could be deceptive, lead you to think that the architecture was basic, simple, a walk in the park to defuse—then it was over. Grant estimated that this bomb had enough velocity to take out most of the house.

He set to work.

Half a block away at the command post, Jeff and Sarah waited next to Cordelli and Brewer. With power, communication, traffic and all activity halted, the street had fallen eerily quiet.

Like the church after Lee Ann's funeral, Jeff thought as the minutes passed.

In Manhattan, Aleena Visser was floating in and out of consciousness in her bed in the hospital's intensive care unit. Through her morphine-induced fog she woke, urging the nurse to let her know, needing to know.

"…help, did the number help police…did I help them?"

The nurse keeping vigil turned to the detective in the room who nodded. The nurse soothed Aleena's brow and spoke softly into her ear.

"They said you helped them save lives."

It took a few seconds before it registered with Aleena. Then she let go.

The machines monitoring her began sounding alarms and although the medical team tried to resuscitate her, Aleena Visser, the former newspaper reporter from Rotterdam, died.

At that moment, in Ozone Park, NYPD bomb technician Bill Grant was taking meticulous care with the explosives attached to Cole. Again and again he examined the detonation system, the wiring to a cell phone and the insertion points of the blasting caps.

The heat in the suit was unbearable, making Grant sweat profusely. He continued studying everything, scrutinizing the arrangement, double-checking and triple-checking for any decoys until he was satisfied the device was built to be triggered by a call to the cell phone. It could be detonated by one call from any phone anywhere in the world.

With all the care and precision of a surgeon, Grant deactivated the detonation system.

He swallowed, allowing relief to wash over him.

He had defused the bomb.

"That does it." Grant winked at Cole. "Now hold still while I take care of a few little things."

Grant cautiously detached the explosives from Cole, then helped free him from his bindings and told him to get out and go to the police vehicles.

Cole raced up the stairs, ran out of the house to the street, looking to the left and to the right before he'd spotted the police line. He cut a small, vulnerable figure in the empty street, then heard his parents' call.

"Cole!"

He ran toward them, faster than he'd ever run in his life.

Jeff and Sarah had broken through the line. Cole flung himself into his mother's arms. Jeff took both of them into his, engulfing them as it all burst open inside him—all of his anger, guilt, confusion and fear, giving way to the flood of love and thanks for the gift he had been given.

Epilogue

Laurel, Montana

Late Friday afternoon. Sunlight streamed through the open bay doors at Clay Platt's Auto Service where Jeff finished repairing a clutch on a Chev.

He went to his bench and reviewed the sheets of all the work he'd completed today. It included two brake jobs, a timing chain, a leaky radiator and three oil changes. *Not bad. Everything's in order.*

Time to clock out.

Jeff changed out of his coveralls, washed up, then stuck his head into the small office. Old Man Platt looked up at him from the books.

"Heading out?"

"Yeah."

"Give any more thought to my offer to sell the shop?"

"I did."

"Could work out nice for you, what with a new baby on the way."

"I know. I've been talking it over with Sarah. We'll give you an answer Monday."

"All right, you have a good weekend, Jeff."

It was now nearly four months since they'd returned from New York City. Guiding his pickup through Laurel's quiet streets, Jeff reflected on its small-town heritage, from the days of the settlers to its evolution as a railway hub and a God-fearing community outside of Billings. To the west he glimpsed the Beartooth Mountains, never tiring of the view and what it meant. Life out here, where the earth meets the sky on even terms, where your sense of self-importance is either exaggerated or diminished, suited him.

Now more than ever.

He was not as shaky as he first was on everything that had happened in New York. On some nights, during the first month, Sarah woke in tears and he'd hold her until she stopped trembling. Other nights they'd hear Cole crying out in his sleep and they'd both go to him.

And there were times early in those first weeks when Jeff was jarred awake, adrenaline pumping, heart hammering with overwhelming terror, forcing him to check on Sarah and Cole to prove that they were still there.

Since then, parts of it remained crystalline. Others were a blur, like the days of the immediate aftermath. The questioning by the NYPD and the FBI, the press conference that was carried live around the globe and later the endless network interviews.

"Joining us now in our Manhattan studio, Jeff, Sarah and Cole Griffin. They're going to recount their terrifying experience, which has captured the world's attention...."

In those early stages, talking about it seemed to help. It meant they were alive, that they'd survived. They told their story over and over, then again when they returned to Laurel.

Friends embraced them, supported them.

"That's a hell of a thing to face," Old Man Platt had

said. "Especially after all you've been through, Jeff, a hell of thing."

In the time that followed, Jeff grappled with questions.

Why did these things happen to my family? Why us?

There were no answers.

The way to surmount it all was to feel whatever they were feeling, hang on and help one another.

"Take every day as it comes, and as an act of faith believe that it will get better," Kransky told them in their counseling sessions.

And it worked.

Little by little they'd regained control of their lives. Sarah resumed teaching, drawing strength from her work. While Cole was resilient, Jeff noticed steadfastness in his eyes, but he'd endured.

Hell, we all endured.

Jeff smiled to himself as he rolled through his town. There was a silver lining. It had obliterated all of his doubts about Sarah, about holding his family together.

That, and the private trips he made to the children's section of the cemetery at the edge of Laurel.

Jeff realized his place in the world was to take care of his family, to help others every chance he could. Being a good husband, a good dad, fixing cars and volunteering for emergencies seemed just about right, for him.

He turned his truck's radio to his favorite country station, glad to catch "I Walk the Line." Listening, he thought the song suited his state of mind as he came upon his home on Coyote Ridge Road.

They had a ranch-style bungalow on half an acre, but they started dreaming again of getting a bigger place at Pheasant Brook. There were some nice properties out there.

He eased his Ford into the driveway, killed the engine and radio. He hesitated before he got out. Through the front window he caught the scene: Sarah, standing behind Cole, who was working at the computer. Sarah was pointing at something on the screen, likely Cole's geography project.

Cole had chosen to do it on New York City.

They'd promised him they would go back one day for a real vacation.

Jeff smiled to himself.

As the truck's engine ticked down he continued looking into the window. This was a portrait of a perfect life.

My life.

They were not the same family anymore.

They never would be.

They were stronger, and no matter what they faced, nothing could ever, or would ever, defeat them.

* * * * *

REQUEST YOUR FREE BOOKS!

2 FREE NOVELS
FROM THE SUSPENSE COLLECTION
PLUS 2 FREE GIFTS!

YES! Please send me 2 FREE novels from the Suspense Collection and my 2 FREE gifts (gifts are worth about $10). After receiving them, if I don't wish to receive any more books, I can return the shipping statement marked "cancel." If I don't cancel, I will receive 4 brand-new novels every month and be billed just $5.99 per book in the U.S. or $6.49 per book in Canada. That's a saving of at least 25% off the cover price. It's quite a bargain! Shipping and handling is just 50¢ per book in the U.S. and 75¢ per book in Canada.* I understand that accepting the 2 free books and gifts places me under no obligation to buy anything. I can always return a shipment and cancel at any time. Even if I never buy another book, the two free books and gifts are mine to keep forever.

191/391 MDN FEME

Name	(PLEASE PRINT)

Address	Apt. #

City	State/Prov.	Zip/Postal Code

Signature (if under 18, a parent or guardian must sign)

Mail to the **Reader Service:**
IN U.S.A.: P.O. Box 1867, Buffalo, NY 14240-1867
IN CANADA: P.O. Box 609, Fort Erie, Ontario L2A 5X3

Not valid for current subscribers to the Suspense Collection or the Romance/Suspense Collection.

Want to try two free books from another line?
Call 1-800-873-8635 or visit www.ReaderService.com.

* Terms and prices subject to change without notice. Prices do not include applicable taxes. Sales tax applicable in N.Y. Canadian residents will be charged applicable taxes. Offer not valid in Quebec. This offer is limited to one order per household. All orders subject to credit approval. Credit or debit balances in a customer's account(s) may be offset by any other outstanding balance owed by or to the customer. Please allow 4 to 6 weeks for delivery. Offer available while quantities last.

Your Privacy—The Reader Service is committed to protecting your privacy. Our Privacy Policy is available online at www.ReaderService.com or upon request from the Reader Service.

We make a portion of our mailing list available to reputable third parties that offer products we believe may interest you. If you prefer that we not exchange your name with third parties, or if you wish to clarify or modify your communication preferences, please visit us at www.ReaderService.com/consumerschoice or write to us at Reader Service Preference Service, P.O. Box 9062, Buffalo, NY 14269. Include your complete name and address.

SUS11

RICK MOFINA

31301	THE BURNING EDGE	___ $7.99 U.S.	___ $9.99 CAN.
32948	IN DESPERATION	___ $9.99 U.S.	___ $11.99 CAN.
32794	THE PANIC ZONE	___ $9.99 U.S.	___ $11.99 CAN.

(limited quantities available)

TOTAL AMOUNT $ _____
POSTAGE & HANDLING $ _____
($1.00 for 1 book, 50¢ for each additional)
APPLICABLE TAXES* $ _____
TOTAL PAYABLE $ _____
(check or money order—please do not send cash)

To order, complete this form and send it, along with a check or money order for the total above, payable to Harlequin MIRA, to: **In the U.S.:** 3010 Walden Avenue, P.O. Box 9077, Buffalo, NY 14269-9077; **In Canada:** P.O. Box 636, Fort Erie, Ontario, L2A 5X3.

Name: _____
Address: _____ City: _____
State/Prov.: _____ Zip/Postal Code: _____
Account Number (if applicable): _____
075 CSAS

*New York residents remit applicable sales taxes.
*Canadian residents remit applicable GST and provincial taxes.

HARLEQUIN® MIRA®
www.Harlequin.com

MRM1012BL